LETHAL CONTROL

A DUPAGE PARISH MYSTERY

GREGORY ASHE

H&B

Published by Hodgkin & Blount
https://www.hodgkinandblount.com/
contact@hodgkinandblount.com

Published 2022
Printed in the United States of America

Cover design by Lyrical Lines

Version 1.04

Trade Paperback ISBN: 978-1-63621-047-6
eBook ISBN: 978-1-63621-046-9

I

Beware the Rougarou in the swamps at night. He'll try to trick you and give you a fright.

- *Rougarou Stew,* Kat Pigott

ELI (1)

"I am going to murder those kids," I said when I stepped up onto our gallery. Shards and splinters of glass pumpkins (the retail world's contribution to the season) slid under my New Balance and crunched against the boards. I studied the disaster zone for a minute, thought about my aching back, my feet sore from a day spent walking tourists around cemeteries. I went around to the shed, got Dag's old baseball bat, and swung it in slow motion like I was hitting a grand slam. I pictured a decapitated head sailing into left field.

It was October, three days before Halloween, and it was late. On our normally quiet street in New Orleans, the streetlights made a low ceiling that papered over the stars. The air was cool enough to make my skin tighten—but big surprise, I was cold all the time lately—and it smelled faintly like spray paint. From down the street came the murmur of voices and a laugh like a slinky going down a flight of stairs.

Bat swinging lazily at my side, I started in the direction of the voices.

The homes here were stolidly lower-middle-class, shotgun-style houses built on narrow lots. Most of the houses had galleries built onto the front. Some of them had the occasional upgrade—a stained-glass window, or Greek-style columns on the gallery, or gingerbread woodwork. The kind of things, back when people had been building these homes, that were meant to show a degree of financial success—or at least good taste. Some of the houses were painted the bright colors people expected from New Orleans, like the peach-and-lime one at the end of the street. Dag called it, "James and the Giant Peach," which I told him was too long and gentle to be a genuine burn. When we'd bought ours, it had been turquoise, with red and yellow trim. It was now powder blue with eggshell trim. I'll let you figure out which one of us—quietly and persistently and with tremendous kindness—won that battle.

I found them on the sagging gallery steps of the Crawford house. It was the kind of place that people looked at, even just driving by, and discovered the latent arsonist in their heart. You couldn't look at the Crawford place, with its mildew and canting frame and junkyard litter, without being inspired by the limitless possibilities of a cleansing fire. There were three of them, white boys, and until they'd reached eighth grade this year, they'd never been a problem: Charlie Crawford, Michael Mince, and Stephen Sanders. Now, the Alliteration Gang had reached the age where biology turned them into a cross between an acne convention and a boner on legs. Dag didn't believe me, but hand to God, I'd seen Mikey humping an old tire once. It kept rolling away, and he kept humping after it.

The war had started with Dag reminding them—politely, because it was Dag—to wear helmets when they skateboarded. That night, there'd been a bag of flaming dog shit on our gallery. Dag hadn't believed me when I'd told him who'd been behind it. The old Eli might have left things alone at that point, with nothing worse than dirty looks for the boys and some thorough bitching-out behind their backs. But over the last year, I'd made some changes. I'd added on muscle—surprisingly easily, in fact, maybe because I'd spent so long trying to avoid bulking up. And I'd made a conscious decision to allow absolutely zero fucks to enter my life. It was a very good life hack. It had even come from a book. *Take No F*cks.* Or maybe *Take No Sh*ts.* Although the latter one sounded more like a medical problem.

In any case, I'd taken matters into my own hands when it came to the Alliteration Gang. The next time one of the little turds left his skateboard outside, I'd wrapped it in plastic wrap. Tight. Charlie, the little twat, had spent most of an afternoon getting it free. They'd egged our house a week later, and Dag had been the one to spend a hot September day cleaning the siding in the stink. I'd waited for my opportunity, and I'd gotten the three of them with a paper bag full of tomato soup and breakfast cereal, which I'd allowed to cook in the sun for a couple of days. They'd screamed for a satisfyingly long time, and later, I'd seen Stephen crying as his dad hosed him off in the backyard.

Now, my pumpkins.

Stephen noticed me first; he was the one who always wore a little smirk, and he was wearing it now—albeit, diluted by the hint of paint around his mouth and nose. It took me a moment to spot the can and the rag on the step between him and Mikey. Mikey had some paint on his face too, and his eyes were glassy. Charlie looked boneless, propped up against the railing. My general sense was that Charlie was a pure follower—he'd been the sweetest kid until the evils of puberty, and I pegged him as one of those kids who just wanted someone to accept him. Not an excuse, as far as I was concerned.

I stood there, bat hanging from my hand.

Stephen gave me more of the smirk. "What?"

Charlie must have thought Stephen was talking to him because he mumbled something. Mikey flinched. The movement made him bump the can of spray paint, and it clacked against the steps before Stephen caught it and righted it.

"What?" Stephen asked again, the smirk growing.

"You know what," I said.

He looked at his buddies. Charlie was comatose, but Mikey was trying to play along, eyes wide and innocent as a shit-eating grin spread across his face. They were stupid at the best of times, and huffing paint hadn't made them any smarter.

"That was seventy-five dollars' worth of pumpkins from At Home, you little bitches."

They just traded looks again.

"Tomorrow, I'm getting new pumpkins. And a camera. And if you come anywhere close to my house, I will ruin your lives, get it? My boyfriend used to be a deputy, and if you keep screwing around, he will end you." I pointed the bat at each of them in turn. Stephen's smirk was practically a grin by now. "Get it?"

He shrugged. Mikey tried to copy him and almost fell off the step. Charlie was moaning and fumbling around, probably trying to get another huff.

"This is where it stops," I told them. "Don't fuck with me."

I waited. They dropped their gazes and shifted on the sagging steps. After another moment, I headed back up the street. I heard movement at the Crawford's door, and I could visualize them slinking inside. I couldn't have gone more than twenty feet, though, when I heard Stephen say, "Next time, send the pussy, and he can suck our dicks."

I spun around, bringing the bat up.

Stephen was smirking and throwing double eagles. Mikey was copying him.

I sprinted toward them, but I hadn't closed half the distance before they were inside the house, and the door slammed shut. Poor Charlie had been left out in the cold. I watched him for a minute, and then I propped him up so he wouldn't fall over and choke on his tongue or anything.

I eyed the Crawford house. I considered using the bat to leave a message, maybe by destroying their antique, uh—well, maybe the plastic kiddie pool that was sticking out from under the gallery. After a few more deep breaths, I gave it up and turned around.

When I got home, Dag was on the sofa, working on school stuff. My boyfriend was almost five years older than me, and at twenty-nine, his hair had already gone this beautiful gray. He was my height, packing a lot more muscle, and sometimes he did things—like hoist a fifty-pound bag of cement without even blinking—that made his biceps pop, and every twink in a five-mile radius died from overexposure to daddy rays. He didn't even know, of course. I just swept up the twinks and prayed he wouldn't figure it out and realize he could do better than me.

As I watched, one of the biceps did very interesting things as he uncapped a highlighter and marked something on a page. Dag was the brains in our couple. He was also the looks, but I tried hard not to let him know that. The cardboard trays from two frozen dinners lay on the floor at his feet, and butter chicken sauce made a trail down his chin, Tulane t-shirt, mesh shorts, and, of all places, his knee. I knew he'd showered and changed that morning, but somehow, he still managed to look like he'd slept in his clothes.

"Hey," I said. "How's the presentation coming?"

"Huh?" His head came up. He had a green highlighter tucked behind one ear, and a yellow one behind the other, and in his mouth, he held a pen. "Wha?" He spat out the pen when I dropped onto the sofa, and he gave me a kiss. "When did you get home?"

"A couple of hours ago."

His eyes got huge.

"Like, two minutes ago."

"Are you hungry?"

"Not really." Which was the truth; somehow, over the last year, I'd gotten my old metabolism back, which was awesome. Subtract love handles. Add abs. And it wasn't like I was starving myself. I honestly wasn't that hungry. Hardly ever, actually. But Dag was still watching me, and I knew the rules, so I said, "But I should eat something."

"Uh huh," he said. "Butter chicken? Sorry, I forgot to cook."

"Sounds great." My smile must have looked tired, because Dag frowned, but he kissed me again and disappeared down the hall.

We lived in an old shotgun-style house—the idea of a shotgun-style house being, in theory, that you could stand at the front door and fire a shotgun down the hall, and you wouldn't hit anything because it would go straight out the back door. The living room was at the front, then the bathroom, then our bedroom, then the kitchen.

Dag was moving around back there. The fridge door shut, and bottles clinked.

Since we'd moved in a couple of years ago, Dag had worked steadily on the house, making all sorts of improvements and upgrades and repairs—little things, you know, like catching the termites before they literally ate every scrap of wood in the place. He'd sanded and re-stained the floorboards a weathered gray. I'd added a leather sofa that still smelled new, as well as the Bluetooth speaker for the built-in shelves Dag had worked so hard to get right. The shelves were important. I needed space—lots of space—for important things like even more (indoor) seasonal pumpkins and seasonal plastic leaves and seasonal words carved out of wood that said things like I LOVE FALL MOST OF ALL and, well, seasonal candles. Seasonal candles, as I had explained to Dag during what had quickly been approaching a fight, were very important to the gays. He had spent the rest of the day in the shed, allegedly working on the shelves.

I sat on the sofa and picked up Dag's notes for his presentation. They were on predators—the whole class was on predators, from what I could understand. Control mechanisms, that was part of it. Lethal control. Non-lethal control. Dag, of course, preferred non-lethal, which made me feel bad about the baseball bat all over again.

Mostly, though, I couldn't make sense of the notes because my eyes kept skipping across the cards, so I set them down again. I thought about how Dag's arm had looked when he'd highlighted those words. I thought about how his ass looked in those shorts. God help me, I thought about the butter chicken stain—and what did that say about me, honestly? I stood up. I tried to sit on the arm of the sofa and told myself it looked casual. Then I imagined how I looked, and I asked myself if I was doing a photo shoot for a fucking cologne ad. I stood up again. I clasped my hands behind my neck. I folded my arms across my chest. I twisted the hem of my Northshore Adventure Tours polo until I thought I heard a seam give.

A knock at the door saved me from myself.

Oh no, I thought. No fucking way. Come back in twelve to twenty-seven minutes.

"Can you get that?" Dag called from the kitchen.

"I didn't hear anything," I said.

The knock came again. It didn't exactly rattle the door in its frame, but whoever was out there probably had a hell of a handshake.

"E?"

I waited for what I thought was a believable amount of time and said, "Wrong house."

A moment later, Dag came into the living room, drying his hands on a dish towel. He frowned at me, and then he said, "No, sir. You're going to bed, and I've got to finish my notecards."

"Excuse me?"

"Not tonight, Eli."

"I literally haven't said anything."

He looked at me. He didn't even raise his eyebrows.

I mustered up, "Somebody's got an inflated ego," but by that point, we both knew I'd lost the battle.

When Dag opened the door, his body language changed: he became still, and he stared out into the night. I barely recognized his voice as he asked, "What do you want?"

I turned, and I stopped too. I recognized the man who stood on our gallery: I'd met him in a juke joint called the Stoplight. He'd tried to cruise me, and he worked for one of the most dangerous people I knew—who also happened to be a witch. His skin was darker than mine, and he had to have been close to Dag's age, and he was built strong under a washed-thin Cowboys tee and stiff Levi's. He kept his hair in a skin fade, and he wore a prosthetic hand. For one dizzying moment, it didn't look like a hand at all—it looked like something twisting and writhing, like shadows crawling across a wall. Then it was nothing but polymer again.

His mouth quirked soundlessly once, and then, in a deep, cracked voice, he said, "I need your help. He's gone."

DAG (2)

"Who's gone?" I asked. Eli took a step forward, and I put a hand back to stop him. I recognized the guy from the juke joint—the bartender—but if I'd known his name, I'd forgotten it. His skin was ashy in places, and his skin fade looked shaggy. If I had to guess, I'd say he'd been wearing those clothes for a couple of days, and he probably hadn't been doing much sleeping. As I watched, he rocked slightly on his feet, like he was fighting to stay upright. I tried to judge his eyes. When I'd been a deputy, I'd seen guys with eyes like that, and they'd never once done the right thing. The best thing to do when you saw eyes like that was move them along and hope whatever they did, they did it to themselves and not to anybody else.

"Reb." He put a hand on the door jamb. "Rebellion. I call him Reb. We all do."

The year before, Lanny—who was, to give you an idea, a hot mess of coon-ass stupidity and pure trouble, and also my ex—had gone to the Stoplight with a woman named Fen, and between the two of them, they'd shot the place to hell. I'd found this guy, the bartender, hiding in a walk-in freezer with a pretty white boy. My guess, although it wasn't much of a guess: the white boy was Reb.

"We haven't seen him—" I began.

"Dag," Eli whispered. In a louder voice, he said, "Do you want to come in?"

For a moment, I thought the bartender would start crying. He nodded.

I put my hand on the door. "He doesn't need to come in. We don't know anything about his boyfriend—"

"Come on," Eli said, shouldering me out of the way. He put a hand on the bartender's shoulder, and the man flinched, but he let Eli urge him inside. Two minutes later, he was sitting in the La-Z-Boy with some of my Sugarfield. You could see he was trembling by the way the bourbon moved in the glass.

Eli sat on the couch, and he looked at me until I sat next to him. Eli kept looking at me. I knew what he was thinking, and I frowned. His eyes got wider. I'd seen this look before—once, when he wanted me to buy him a t-shirt that he liked, but he wanted me to do it without him telling me to do it because, well, something about how I should have known he wanted it. He explained that later. Loudly.

To the bartender, I said, "I don't know your name. Why don't we start there?"

"Posey. Posey Rawlins." He had the tumbler in his prosthesis. The thumb, I saw now—and memory flashed of the stale, sour smell of the juke joint—had been replaced with a bottle cap opener. Someone had drawn an arrow along the polymer hand, pointing to the opener, and then, in huge letters, the words USE ME!

"All right, Posey. What's going on?"

"Reb's gone. He's—I think something's wrong."

"Who's Reb?"

For a moment, Posey didn't seem to understand the question. "You know him. You met him at the Stoplight." When I didn't say anything, Posey flexed his fingers around the glass. "He's...he and I..."

"He's your boyfriend?" Eli asked gently.

Posey barked a laugh and shook his head. But then he shrugged and nodded.

"He's the pretty little white boy," I said. "Blond. Looks all of seventeen."

Turning slowly, Eli gave me a look, but Posey nodded and whispered, "Nineteen."

Because that was so much better.

More details were starting to filter in. I remembered the aluminum trailers behind the juke joint. I remembered Lanny talking about a boy they kept there, a boy with eyes like a husky. You could pay, Lanny had told me.

"Why don't you tell us," I said, "instead of us trying to guess?"

For a moment, Posey looked like he was bracing himself. He dashed off a drink of the Sugarfield, which was wasting it, in my opinion. Then he scooted forward in the seat. He took a breath. "Reb's—Reb and I—" He put back the rest of the Sugarfield, and when he brought his chin down, his face was flushed and he blurted, "I love him."

Eli smiled and nodded.

"It's not the way people think. It's complicated."

"Lots of things are complicated," Eli said after a moment. "Dag's complicated."

"Not really," I said.

"I'm complicated," Eli said. "I'm very complicated. Ask Dag."

"No comment."

A hint of a smile flickered on Posey's face. His death grip on the tumbler relaxed. "Reb's real quiet."

"How'd you meet Reb?"

"The Stoplight. Nelda Pie brought him." His voice sounded tight when he added, "The way she brings all of us."

I opened my mouth to ask about that, but Eli said over me, "I remember seeing you together. You and Reb looked like you care about each other a great deal."

"He can't have a boyfriend." Posey rushed through the next sentence, stepping on his own words: "You're supposed to call it sex work now. He can do it if he wants. It's his body."

I wondered how many times Reb had said that before Posey learned the lines by heart.

"Is that why he can't have a boyfriend?" Eli asked.

Posey gave a miserable shrug.

"I still don't know why you're here," I said. "If your friend ran off, I'm sorry. If you think he's in trouble, that sounds like a matter for the police or the sheriff."

"Dag—" Eli began.

"I'm not trying to be unkind, E, but it doesn't make any sense. I'm sorry, Posey, but I've seen you twice in my whole life, and both times were over a year ago. Heck, buddy, I didn't even know your name. I don't know why you thought we could help—"

"Because you know." The last word burned with intensity, and Posey looked up, his dark eyes fixing on Dag. "You know this—" He gestured around him with the tumbler. "You know there's more."

I did my best not to look at Eli. Over the last two years, we'd bumped into things that were—well, supernatural was a word people used to describe things they didn't understand yet, so maybe that was the right word, because I sure as heck didn't understand much of what had happened. We'd fought creatures with abilities and powers I'd never imagined. We'd met witches and seen magic. We'd run from crazy monster hunters who wanted to kill anything that wasn't human. Posey wasn't wrong; there was so much more.

"No," I said.

"Dag—"

"No, E." To Posey, I said, "I'm sorry."

"I'll pay." Posey set the tumbler on the floor and drew a wad of crumpled bills from the Levi's front pocket. "It's a couple of hundred, but I'm good for more—"

"No."

"Dag—"

"I hope Reb's ok," I said, "and I hope you find him—"

It was his eyes that gave him away. His hand dipped to the small of his back, and then he lunged out of the seat, three inches of steel coming toward Eli.

I was ready for him. It was stupid to try to grab a knife, so I kicked him in the leg. Posey stumbled sideways. Eli let out a shout and scrambled backward. I launched myself at Posey, and I hit him as he was righting himself. I got hold of his wrist with one hand, and with the other, I grabbed his Cowboys tee—I didn't think he could grapple with the prosthesis, so I ignored it for the moment.

It was the wrong move; I was trying to force him to release the blade when he grabbed me with the prosthetic hand. But the thing was, it didn't feel like a hand. It didn't even feel like polymer. It felt soft at first, then densely firm, and a moment too late, I realized he was much stronger than I'd expected. He threw me across the room. Literally.

I flew through the air high enough to clear the couch, and I hit the wall. It was lath and plaster, and I felt it flex under my weight. The whole house shivered. I slid to the floor. And for a moment, it was like I had stopped but the world kept flying. Then I got to one knee.

By the time I was on my feet, he had Eli: the arm with the prosthetic hand wrapped around Eli's waist, trapping Eli against him, and the knife against Eli's throat. I still hadn't gotten my breath back, so I shook my head.

"I won't hurt him," Posey said, the words fraying. "I just need him."

"No," I croaked.

"Stay there." He took a step back, hauling Eli with him. "We're going out the back. Stay there, and I won't hurt him."

"Posey," Eli said. "You don't want to do this."

"Let him go," I said, the words still choppy.

"We want to help you," Eli said. "You're scared. I get it; I'm scared all the time. You're scared for Reb. And you're scared if you don't do this, something terrible is going to happen to him. And you're scared it'll be your fault. But this isn't the way."

Posey stopped when he reached the hallway. He was breathing hard. His eyes were glossy with tears, and the tip of the point made tiny patterns in the air as it trembled near Eli's throat.

"Be smart," I said. "Put it down."

He made a tiny, despairing noise.

Slowly, Eli reached up. His fingers closed lightly around Posey's wrist, and he brought his arm down slowly, the knife drifting away from his neck. He eased the blade from Posey's grip, and then Posey started to cry—huge sobs shaking him.

"It's ok," Eli said, turning to hug him. He held the knife out behind him, and I took it, and he pulled Posey tighter. "It's ok."

ELI (3)

"It is definitely not ok, Eli," Dag said.

We were in the kitchen. Dag had finally allowed me to drag him away—but not until after patting Posey down to make sure he didn't have any more weapons. Then Dag had to get his gun from the safe under the bed, and then he had to give me lots of wounded glances when he saw that I'd topped up Posey's Sugarfield.

I loved my kitchen, although admittedly, I loved it less when I was in the middle of a fight with Dag. It probably didn't look like the kind of kitchen anyone would love: nickel-and-dime pots and pans from the Salvation Army, a total lack of any built-ins, the ancient, rattling Amana, the two tables—one with a skirt to form an improvised pantry. My pride and joy, and the single greatest thing Dagobert LeBlanc has ever done for me, possibly excluding all the times he's saved my life, was the countertop dishwasher. Right then, we were sitting at the drop-leaf table, Dag with his own Sugarfield in front of him, which he was making a point of ignoring. Well, all right. It had been a good try.

"Dag—"

"He tried to kill us."

"He didn't try to kill us. He tried to kidnap me. And, um, stab you? Or maybe just throw you through the wall, which was actually kind of amazing—" Dag's thick eyebrows were climbing, so I hurried to add, "Anyway, it was all misdemeanor stuff."

"No. It wasn't."

"Dag, he's terrified. And for whatever reason, he thinks he needs my help to find Reb."

"I said no, Eli."

"Can we please hear him out? I'm not trying to be contrary—"

"You're always trying to be contrary."

"Only when it's cute! Only when I know you'll like it!"

For a moment, his face stayed stone. Then a smile flickered, and he sipped some of the bourbon to cover it.

"I still don't understand what happened to me," I said. "When Richard—I mean, when the hashok—" I had to start again. "He might know something."

I stopped myself. There was something problematic in hearing myself say, out loud, any variation of *When that swamp-style vampire-type monster we called a hashok, you remember, the one I was living with, tried to rape me to death, oh yeah, and he bit me a bunch of times and injected some kind of venom, and I think it's like a virus because sometimes I can feel it, and I'm always cold now.*

Dag, because he was Dag, understood. He rubbed his eyes, and while he was still rubbing them, he nodded.

"Thank you," I said.

"If he tries anything, I'm going to shoot him."

"That's the sweetest thing anyone has ever said to me."

"I'm serious, Eli. I do not need a smartass right now."

I took his hand across the table. He squeezed my fingers.

"Are you ok? It looked like you hit the wall pretty hard."

Dag nodded. "Couple of Tylenol and a hot bath. I'll be all right."

With a sketch of a smile, I said, "Let's get this over with. We'll try to keep the shooting and stabbing and slaughtering to misdemeanor levels."

"I know you're joking, but do you even know what a misdemeanor is?"

We found Posey with an empty tumbler, his eyes hooded and red as he slumped in the La-Z-Boy. He'd obviously been crying some more. When we sat on the couch, he worked his jaw for a moment and offered a broken, "Sorry."

"It's all right," I said.

"It's not all right," Dag said. "It's felony assault and kidnapping, and on top of that, you touched Eli, which is a much bigger deal for me personally. Any more messing around, and I'm not going to hesitate." He held up the Sig. "Understand?"

Posey nodded.

"You said you needed me to help you." I spread my hands. "Why me?"

The blink had a slight alcohol delay. He leaned forward, touching the prosthetic hand where it was attached, not seeming to realize what he was doing. Right now, it looked like an ordinary hand—well, except for the bottle opener, which actually would have been an awesome evolutionary option for *fratboyicus boozicus*. But there had been a moment earlier when it had looked like something else. I had seen it out of the corner of my eye during the frenzy of the fight, when he and Dag had been struggling together and I, in true Eli fashion, had been trying to save my own sorry ass by literally humping my way backwards over the couch. I didn't have a good word for what I'd seen—something dark, something that turned and twisted.

"You have the gift," Posey said.

"Oh no," I said.

Dag's face tightened.

"I've heard this one before," I said. "A very nice monster that was trying to eat me told me I had some sort of psychic gift. I'm not falling for it again."

Posey's brow furrowed. He tugged absently on the prosthetic hand, as though checking it without really thinking about it. And then he said, "But you do. I mean, I don't know what you want to call it—the sight, the gift, the craft. But Nelda Pie says you do. I've heard her."

I didn't shiver, not on the outside, but I could feel my skin pimpling.

"Those don't even sound like the same thing," Dag said. "The sight and the gift and the craft."

Posey ignored him, staring at me. "She says that's how you found Roger Shaver."

It wasn't technically wrong. It was hard to believe now, a year later—a year of normal life, a year of normal things like cheating (food cheating, with lattes) and hiding the scale in the bedroom from Dag and running ghost tours for groups of corn-fed Kansans and then bitching about the tips with Kennedy, my supervisor-slash-personal librarian-slash-friend, but we didn't talk about the friend part, and she strongly objected to the *personal* in personal librarian. But Nelda Pie was right, although I didn't know how she knew. The year before, I'd done some sort of—ritual? spell? paranormal equivalent of a My First Chemistry Lab experiment?—and I'd summoned a spirit called a lutin. And that spirit had helped me find a man called Roger Shaver.

Outside, a car raced by, chased by the beat of banger rap. Posey's eyes came up slowly to mine, and I forced myself to ask, "Is Reb...different?"

He cracked a smile. "We're all different."

"What does that mean?" Dag asked in what I'd come to think of as his cop voice. "Eli's not different, and neither am I."

"Dag," I said quietly.

Posey played with the end of the prosthesis again. "Have you ever heard of a rougarou?"

I started to shake my head.

Dag burst out laughing. When I glanced over at him, he said, "A rougarou? Get serious. I want to know how you found us. Is Nelda Pie watching us—"

"What's a rougarou?" I asked.

Posey's gaze flicked to Dag. "You were in the news. The police asked questions. They said your names. It's not hard to find someone if you know their name."

"Dag, what's a rougarou?"

He made a helpless noise. "It's a story. My mawmaw used to tell me it would get me if I cheated during Lent. It's not real, Eli."

"Like the hashok," I said. "Like the fifolet. Like the lutin."

Dag set his jaw and looked down. I followed his gaze, tried to see what he was seeing. This was our house. Those were our floorboards. He'd sanded them because I'd asked. He'd stained them a weathered gray because I wanted it to be cute. Days of hot, miserable work, wearing a mask so he wouldn't breathe in the dust and fumes, undressing outside to try not to spread it through the rest of the house. I'd found dust in his ear one time. At the time, it had seemed funny.

I followed his arm to his hand and took it.

"It's a werewolf," Dag said quietly, without looking up. "More or less. The body of a man, the head of a wolf. There're all sorts of stories about it. It hunts down bad Catholics. They ride bats to balls. They roam the bayou, hunting for misbehaving children. A witch can curse you to become one—" He stopped and raised his head.

"A lot of stories," Posey said. "Some truth. He's just—Reb. It's got nothing to do with the moon. He doesn't turn into a wolf, but he does...change. Sometimes. And Nelda Pie didn't make him like that. He didn't get bit or infected or cursed. It's who he is, that's all. There aren't many of them left."

I was trying to reconcile the teenager I'd seen—the petite one, with zero body hair, the one who could have been a mail-order twink—with a werewolf. "Uh," I said. "If you say so."

"Something happened," Dag said in his cop voice. "Something more than Reb disappearing. Otherwise, you wouldn't be here right now. What?"

Posey worked his fingers around the tumbler. The glass caught needles of light from the fixture overhead. "You know Nelda Pie has dogfights? In the Stoplight, I mean. In the basement."

I looked at Dag. "We knew that. Lanny told us. Wait—"

"You let her use your boyfriend in dogfights?" Dag asked.

"I don't let her do anything." Posey lurched up from the seat and began to pace. "And before you ask, she doesn't make Reb do it. He likes doing it. He—he's wild sometimes. It's like somebody else is in there. He'd never hurt anybody—"

"No," Dag said, his voice rising. "Just innocent dogs that didn't have any choice."

"Take it easy," I said, squeezing Dag's fingers.

"I won't take it easy, E. Dogfighting is about the most barbaric thing you can find. What they do to those dogs—"

"I know. I know it's awful. But right now, Posey needs to tell us what happened."

"He liked it," Dag said. "He liked being put in a ring so he could hurt animals that didn't know any better."

"You don't know him," Posey said, rounding on Dag. "And you don't know what he's been through!"

"Enough," I said. "Posey, sit or pace, whatever you want, but tell us what happened. Dag, I know you don't like it, but that's not the point right now."

"The point," Dag said.

I gave him a pleading look and squeezed his hand again.

After a moment, he looked away, but he squeezed back.

Posey took a drink. When he set the tumbler on the console, the glass rattled against the wood. "She has fights on the weekend. People come from all over. They know her fights are different."

"She's got a werewolf. Yeah, I'd say they're different."

"Friday, Reb did real good. I was tending bar, but people tell me. They know I worry. And then, a little later, Nelda Pie and a guy come upstairs. They go to her office, but I can hear them arguing."

"About Reb?"

"He wanted to buy Reb. Like he was a dog, like he wanted to add him to his kennel. At first, I thought, you know, he meant pay for his time." Posey scratched his forehead. "After a fight, when Reb's blood is up—a lot of people want him right then. It's his body, and he can do what he wants with it, and it doesn't—it doesn't mean anything about how we feel about each other. But it wasn't that; Nelda Pie just laughed, and that made this guy mad. Later, I heard somebody say he was in the mob, but if Nelda Pie knew, or if it bothered her, she didn't let it show." Posey hesitated. "I think she knew."

"Why do you say that?" Dag asked.

"Since last year, things are different at the Stoplight. Nelda Pie's still in charge, but the guys who come in are different. Hard guys. Mean guys. And you can tell a lot of them know each other. They're not the coon-ass drunks we used to get. These guys, they're from the city."

"From New Orleans?" I asked. "That's an hour drive, minimum. Why are they going out there?"

"Some of them meet with Nelda Pie in her office. Some of them don't. I don't know."

"This guy," Dag said, "the one who was interested in Reb, did you get a name?"

Posey shook his head.

"What'd he look like?"

"White, dark hair, maybe in his thirties. Nice-looking guy, I guess, except he was such an asshole."

"Do you think he took Reb?" I asked.

Posey shook his head again, but he said, "I don't know." He reached for his pocket, then he stopped. "Can I take out my phone?"

"Of course."

"Two fingers," Dag said, inching to the edge of his cushion. "And slow."

I tried not to roll my eyes, but I must have failed because Dag pinched me. I yelped, rubbed my side, and gave him a sidelong glare.

"Don't undermine me in front of a potential threat," Dag said.

"I'm not undermining you. If anything, I'm overmining you. I gave you that awesome opportunity to save my ass just a few minutes ago."

"Overmining isn't a thing, Eli."

"It could be. Maybe we invented it. Together. As a couple."

Now it was Dag's turn to roll his eyes, and I wasn't sure why that was allowed.

"I think—" Posey stopped himself and held out his phone. I took it as Posey continued, "I think Reb might have messed up."

The headline on the *Times-Picayune* website read VOODOO DOCTOR MURDERED!

"Well," I muttered, "shit."

"Marcel Le Doux," Dag read, "a professor of African-American Studies at Ole Miss and an internationally recognized expert in vodun religions, was found dead Sunday on the north shore of Lake Pontchartrain." He looked up from the phone. "Ok, what's the link?"

"He was at the Stoplight Friday. After the fight—" Posey's throat moved silently. "He talked to Nelda Pie for a while, and then he paid for some of Reb's time."

The man in the picture was black, darker than either Posey or me, and heavyset in middle age. He had a fringe of frizzy white curls, and he wore Malcolm X-style eyeglasses. He might have been a hell of a lay, but if he was, he was doing a great job hiding it.

I looked at Posey's phone. "This article says, quote, 'Investigators say that Le Doux's life-ending injuries consisted primarily of puncture wounds. Manner of death is undetermined at present;

sources close to the investigation say that while the death appears to have been staged as an animal attack, they suspect they are dealing with a homicide.'"

"Puncture wounds like dog bites," Dag said.

Posey was very still for a moment. Then he nodded.

I scanned the rest of the article for relevant information, but all I saw was that Le Doux had been in town to open an exhibit at the Cabildo called *Petwo Lwa, Jean Petro, Marie Leveau, and the Chicken Man: Ascent of the New World Lwa.*

"Do you think Reb killed him?" Dag asked.

In the silence, the living room felt hot, the air close and suffocating.

"The trailer was a mess," Posey said, his voice barely more than a whisper. "Reb hadn't come in for a drink or to tell me he was all right or anything, but sometimes he forgets, so I went to check on him. The place looked like it had been torn apart."

"Do you think Reb did this?" Dag asked. "Do you think Reb killed this man?"

Posey swallowed. He reached for the bourbon blindly and missed and let his hand fall back to his side. "He wouldn't hurt anybody. Not unless he got scared, or they were trying to hurt him."

"Posey—" Dag began.

"Stop asking him." I caught Dag's eye and shook my head. "Please stop."

Dag let out a heavy breath. He looked at me for a long moment, and then he turned toward Posey and said, "When people run, they usually run somewhere they feel safe. Or somewhere familiar. They're not thinking clearly, so old habits take over. If you want us to find Reb, you need to tell us everything you can. Where is he from? What's he like to do in his spare time? Where's his family? Where does he like to go?"

"You'll find him?" The note in Posey's voice made me want to close my eyes. "Oh God, thank you."

"You're welcome," Dag said drily. "Now answer the question, please."

Posey was smiling, but he didn't seem to realize it. He drained the Sugarfield and wiped his mouth with the back of his hand. He started pacing again, his eyes roving, but the movements seemed energized. Hopeful, I thought. Oh God, please don't be hopeful.

"He doesn't have any people around here," Posey said. "I don't think he has any people at all. He was in foster homes until he was seventeen, and then he ran away. He was on his own until Nelda Pie gave him a place."

"In exchange for sex work and dogfighting."

Mid-pace, Posey stopped. He tugged on the prosthetic hand, and when he spoke, he directed the words to the floor. "He's a good person. You don't know the kind of life he had. If it'd been you, you don't know what you would have done."

The silence that came after had a buzzing quality. Then Dag said, "I'm sorry."

Posey nodded. "He likes hunting. There's a fishing camp on the edge of Bayou Pere Rigaud; we'd go there sometimes. I should have gone and checked but—but I think somebody's following me. I know it's crazy, but I see these cars with tinted windows, and—I mean, what if I lead them right to him?"

What if you led them right to us, I wanted to ask. I could see the same thought on Dag's face. Aloud, though, I said, "Give us directions. We'll take a look."

"It's a start, anyway," Dag said.

Posey sent us a pin from his Maps app, and then he wrote out directions in blocky letters that made me think of every athlete in every group project we'd ever done in high school. He added his phone number, the address for his apartment, and then he signed it in a football player scrawl. I don't know why he signed it, but the painstaking sincerity of it made me pull my t-shirt up to wipe my eyes. I caught Dag looking and elbowed him, and that helped me get some of it out of my system.

"Thank you," Posey said as we walked him out onto the gallery. "Thank you so much."

Dag didn't seem to hear; he was scanning the street, probably looking for a car with tinted windows.

"We'll be in touch," I said. "If Reb—"

But I didn't get a chance to finish because, at that moment, a car came around the corner. It was a beat-up Saturn, the side scraped to hell, one of the tires definitely low. Some sort of screamer metal rolled out of the car in waves. The windows were tinted.

Dag still carried the Sig, the gun low and pressed against his thigh. He flexed his fingers once around the grip.

One of the Saturn's windows rolled down.

A pimply, white-boy twentysomething turned the music down—so that now it was only at eardrum-shattering levels—and leaned across the passenger seat. "Any of you guys Eli?"

I raised my hand.

"Cool, man. I've got that edible dildo you ordered."

Posey looked at me.

Dag looked at me.

I learned what it felt like for my body to catch fire by inches.

"Stephen," I said under my breath. "That son of a bitch."

"So, if you could, like, sign here?"

Posey was now trying way too hard not to look at me. Not to look at either of us, actually.

"Well," Dag said, planting a hand between my shoulder blades and, in that moment, betraying every bond of trust and loyalty and boyfriendly goodness. "Go on."

DAG (4)

Heading out to a fishing camp we'd never visited before, in the heart of Cajun redneck country, where a teenage sex worker-slash-werewolf might be hiding didn't seem like a good late-night activity, and Eli and I agreed to wait until the next day. Before we went to bed, Eli made me tie a dime around my neck—an old charm of protection. He wore one as well, the silver flashing in the hollow of his throat.

My classes were over by noon, and while I usually spent the afternoon either studying or working on assignments, instead I drove home and picked up Eli. It was a mild day, pleasant when you were in the sun, chilly when you weren't, but Eli was muffled in my Tulane sweatshirt when he came out of the house. As soon as he got into the car, he angled the vents away from him.

We didn't talk about it. I'd tried—a few times, actually. The first time we'd visited the Stoplight, Nelda Pie had confronted Eli about the hashok's attack, and we had learned that the bite—and more specifically, the venom—had transmitted some kind of virus, something that was now inside Eli. That time, my attempt at talking about it had turned into a fight. And so had the next time. And the next. After that, I stopped trying.

I loved Eli. He was just about the smartest, strongest, best person I knew—and he was definitely the most beautiful. He was absolutely fearless when it came to facing monsters or my insane parents or, for that matter, the kids he'd started calling the Alliteration Gang. But when it came to Eli problems, he was like a wounded animal, trying to hide his hurt, snarling and snapping whenever anyone came near.

Which meant, I spent a lot of time in the library trying to figure it out on my own. And, so far, making absolutely zero progress.

We were driving east through the Garden District, past the double galleries and cottages and the camelbacks, all of them painted in pastels, all of them with hurricane shutters open to let in the beautiful day. The corner of one lot was purple with a massive butterfly bush. On the next block, along the wrought-iron fence, late-blooming birds of paradise wove flickers of red and orange. I looked in the rearview mirror to signal, and that was when I saw the Jag with the tinted windows.

"E," I said.

Something in my tone must have warned him because he twisted around in the seat to look over his shoulder. "Do you think—"

"Let's see."

I signaled and turned down a side street. It was quiet and residential. The Jag appeared a moment later, black and winging its way around the corner.

"Fuck," Eli said.

I turned at the next intersection.

Behind us, the Jag made the turn. It wasn't getting any closer, but it wasn't trying to be subtle either. As a deputy, I'd never had to run a tail on anybody—high-stakes sting operations weren't exactly run-of-the-mill stuff in DuPage Parish. But I'd studied, and I'd tried to learn how to do things right, and I knew that one of two things was true: either the dumbasses behind us had no idea how to follow someone in a car, or they didn't care if we saw them. I was guessing it was the latter.

"Do you have your gun?" Eli asked.

"Yes."

"Can I shoot them?"

I gave him a look.

"I was offering because I know you don't want to be the one in this relationship who does all the shooting. We should share that responsibility."

"Is this what you do all day? Sit around and think up stuff like this?"

"Well, yeah. And eat bonbons." He pinched his waist through the sweatshirt. "Duh."

"Do I have to pull this car over?"

He held up two fingers. "I know, I know. No jokes about my weight or my body or my, uh, figure?"

"You're joking about no jokes."

"It's one of Dag's Rules," Eli said. "I promise, no more. Scout's honor."

"That's not even the Scout salute."

I made another turn, completing the third side of a square, and now I was heading back toward the main road. The Jag drifted behind us. When I reached the main road, I turned out, drove a hundred yards, and pulled onto the shoulder.

"What are you doing?"

"Finding out who's following us. Stay here."

Of course, when I got out of the Ford, so did Eli.

Up close, the Jag was beautiful. The broken asphalt crunched under its tires as it rolled to a stop behind us. Through the tinted windows, I could make out a white guy behind the wheel, but it was hard to say much more than that. He turned like he might open the door, but then he stopped, and a moment later, the back door opened. A man got out.

He was white, in his thirties, with a wave of dark hair across his forehead like an oil spill. He had blue-black stubble and a smile that looked like it had been stitched on. In his knit polo and slacks and penny loafers, some people might have taken him for an office jockey, maybe a lawyer playing casual. Those people hadn't looked closely enough at the smile. I'd seen him before—only in photos, but the other deputies had a name for him you couldn't forget: Joey Jaws.

"Hey," he said as he ambled up the shoulder toward us, hands stuffed in his pockets.

"That's close enough," I said. "Let me see your hands."

That sewn-on grin twitched, and he pulled his hands out and twiddled his fingers like he'd done a magic trick. He kept coming.

"I said that's close enough."

Joey stopped at the Ford's bumper. His eyes lingered on me and then slid to my side. Eli bumped my arm; I hadn't heard him make his way around the car.

"Sorry about the spy stuff," he said, jerking his thumb at the Jag. "If I'd known you'd be willing to talk, we could have done this like normal people."

"Who are you?" Eli asked. "What do you want?"

"Joey Tamborella." He touched two fingers to his chest, and the shape of his hand made a gun. Then he gave me the finger-gun. "Dagobert LeBlanc." He bucked his hand like he'd fired a shot. "Eli Martins." He did some more sharpshooting.

Eli gave me a look that he'd once given me when an old man in a ripped cassock had tried to get him to *give up your sodomite ways* when we'd been holding hands in the park. The politest translation I could think of was *Is this guy serious?* For the record, the guy in the cassock hadn't seemed too worried about the state of my soul; Eli brought that out in people.

"All right," I said. "Why are you following us?"

"Did Posey Rawlins pay you a visit last night?" The grin twitched in place. "You don't have to tell me; it's all over your faces. That's all right. I know he did. Did he tell you about Rebellion, about the deal I made him?"

Eli looked at me again. He didn't have to say it because I knew what he was thinking: Joey Tamborella was the mobbed-up guy, the one who had watched the dogfight and wanted to buy Reb.

"The way I heard it," I said, "you weren't trying to make a deal with Reb. You were trying to buy him from Nelda Pie."

"That was a misunderstanding. I didn't know Reb was his own man." The grin twitched again. "So to speak."

"Mr. Tamborella—"

"Joey. That's what my pals call me, and I want to be pals."

"He wants to be pals," Eli said.

I shot him a sidelong, supportive, respectful, *please shut up right now* look.

"Mr. Tamborella," I said again, "I don't know what's going on—"

"You know how she keeps him? You ever seen the place she's got? I'm not talking about the juke. I'm talking under it, where she makes that boy fight. You turn around too fast, and you're gonna get tetanus or AIDS or some shit."

"She doesn't make Reb do anything," Eli said.

"Is that what his boyfriend told you? What happens if he doesn't fight? What happens if he doesn't roll over and let those fat old men fuck him? You think she's going to let him stay out of the goodness of her heart? You ever see what Rebellion looks like after a fight? Bit and scratched to hell. You think she sits him down and rubs Betadine on him? Jesus, I'd pay him. He wouldn't be sleeping in a tin can. He'd have a house, whatever he wanted to eat, a doctor. He can bring the boyfriend, and they can screw their brains out. I'm an open-minded guy."

"Sure," Eli said. "Werewolves and fags. Too bad they don't have a flag for that yet."

The grin wrinkled up. It smoothed out again like Joey Tamborella was running a hot iron across the back side of it. "You think you're real smart."

"He's just talking," I said.

"Dag's the smart one." Eli did a showgirl gesture, up and down the length of his body. "I'm the pretty one."

"Here I am, trying to be polite, trying to make you a generous offer, and you're mouthing off smart."

"Nobody's trying to be smart," I said. "Look, Mr. Tamborella, I don't know where Reb is, and even if I did, I don't know if he wants to do business with you. If I see him, I'll let him know you want to talk. That's the best I can do."

"I'll save you some time," Eli said. "You want to buy him like an animal, and you want to use him like an animal. The answer is no. Fuck off."

Joey lunged faster than I expected, and he caught Eli's arm. Eli tried to pull away, but Joey must have been stronger than he looked. He dragged Eli toward him, and Eli's sneakers skidded on the broken asphalt.

"You know what I like about the ones who think they're pretty," Joey was saying over Eli's shouts. "You don't even have to work for it. You just go for the face. They go crazy thinking about their face all cut up—"

That was when the side of my arm got Joey in the throat. He choked and wheezed and stumbled back. His arms windmilled once before he clutched at his throat. Then he went down, landing on his ass, then falling onto his back. He flopped once like a fish.

"Come on," I said.

"That's right, asshole!" Eli screamed. "Don't fuck with me because I've got Dag!"

"E, come on!"

I hauled him toward the car, and instead of going around, I just shoved him in the back seat. By the time I was dropping behind the steering wheel, the driver had gotten out of the car and was trying to help Joey. Joey was sitting up again, and I could hear his raspy shouts: "Get them!" Then Joey reached into his pocket, and the driver reached into the car. Both of them came up with guns.

I hit the gas, and tires squealed as we slewed off the shoulder and sped onto the road. Guns fired behind us, but I didn't hear glass break or the whump of a punctured tire.

"I'm sorry," Eli was saying over and over again in the back seat.

In the rearview mirror, the Jag snaked through traffic. I dropped my foot on the accelerator, but the 1988 Ford Escort had never been designed for high-speed maneuvering. The car grumbled and shook and rattled, and the Jag drew toward us like a bead of ink.

"They're catching up!" Eli shouted.

We shot beneath an overpass. The cement belly of the highway was choked with tents and cardboard shelters and people sitting in folding chairs or pushing shopping carts full of their belongings. I turned on the other side of the overpass, almost too late, and narrowly missed being broadsided by a garbage truck. Horns blared. The Jag's tires screeched as the driver tried to follow. Eli's swearing made me glance at the mirror, and I saw the Jag swerve around the garbage truck.

The French Quarter took shape around us. The Ford bounced along the uneven streets and the crumbling pavement. Tourists lined the sidewalks. The Creole townhouses, with their bright stucco and their wrought-iron scrollwork, turned the short, narrow blocks into a maze. It was a weekday morning, and already the tourists clogged the crosswalks—a white girl puking into her go-cup, two kids whaling on each other with foam noodles, three beer-bellied guys in too-tight clothes like they were still in their twenties. It was the usual French Quarter nonsense. It slowed us and the Jag, and it turned the high-speed pursuit into something that, in a movie, might have felt like a gag.

But block by block, the Jag was still gaining.

"Dag," Eli said.

"I know."

"I'm sorry. I'm really sorry."

"Not now, Eli."

A shout behind us made me check the mirror. A red-faced older guy in a MAGA hat was standing in the middle of the street, facing down the Jag, unleashing a stream of expletives. The Jag's driver laid on the horn and inched forward. I watched when the bumper made contact. The MAGA guy stumbled back. Then he recovered and punched the hood of the Jag. I was still watching in the mirror as Joey got out of the Jag. He came down the side of the car, and the MAGA guy was shouting at him. And then, in broad daylight, Joey leaped forward. It looked for a moment like they were kissing. And then the MAGA guy screamed.

The men separated. Gore covered Joey's mouth and chin, and the MAGA guy was pressing a hand to his face, blood leaking between his fingers.

"Holy shit," Eli said shakily. "Did he just bite his face off?"

The crosswalk in front of us cleared, and I hit the gas.

I heard when the Jag started moving again.

I scanned the street, blocks ahead of us, blocks behind.

And then I heard the music moving toward us.

"Please, God," I muttered.

"You've got to be kidding me," Eli whispered.

"Please, God, please."

On a side street, just about at the next intersection, a second line parade—for a wedding, to judge by the Indian man and woman dancing in front—was coming down the street. There had to be at least a hundred people filling the street from wall to wall and taking up the entire block. I didn't even think about it. I goosed the Ford, and we shot in front of the bride and groom, missing them by about six inches. Someone swore. Lots of people swore, actually. But the parade kept moving, blocking the intersection. On the other side of the second line, the Jag was trapped.

I let the Ford roll forward, and a few blocks later, we'd lost them.

Eli leaned over the seat to hug me. He kissed the side of my head. He was shaking. Then I realized he was halfway between laughing and crying as he sat back, wiping his face, and breathed, "I never thought I'd say this, but thank God for tourists."

ELI (5)

We were on the causeway, crossing Lake Pontchartrain, when I broke the silence between us.

"I'm sorry," I said for what was probably the third time in this particular shit-show and, in the course of our relationship, probably number one million.

The thrum of the tires was the only answer. Sawgrass flicked by like a stop-motion film. The glare on the water looked like superheated steel.

"We're all right," Dag finally said. "That's what matters. But could you tell me what happened back there?"

"I don't know."

We kept driving. After a quarter mile, Dag set his elbow on the door and rested his head on his hand.

I scrambled over the seats and buckled myself in, because that was one of Dag's Rules. I watched him in profile. I did that mental arithmetic. It was kind of like tracking macros. A relationship can only tolerate so many fuckups—even a relationship with someone who was practically a saint, like Dag. But it was a little more complicated because you had to multiply the fuckups by how much better Dag was than me. Or maybe you had to divide by how much I didn't deserve him. There might have been a logarithm in there about my total shittiness as a human being. Maybe it wasn't like counting macros, now that I think about it. I wasn't very good at math—Dag was the smart one, so another point in his favor. I think.

"Don't do that," he said.

"What?"

"You know what." He scratched his head. Then he sat up straight, dropped his arm from the window, and said, "I'm trying to be mad at you."

"How's it going?"

"I was doing all right until you started sitting there, looking so sad."

"I can get in the back seat if you want."

"Nah, I lost it."

"You'll get it," I said. "I believe in you. You just need practice."

He looked at me. A Dag look. Which was full of Limitless Love and Weary Patience and with a dash of Please, Throw Me A Rope.

"I'm sorry," I said again. "I don't know. The whole time he was talking, I was thinking about how he saw Reb, how the fact that Reb was different meant that for Joey, Reb wasn't even a person, and it was like this bomb went off inside my head. I felt like I couldn't even hear him."

Dag kept driving.

"I know what you're thinking," I said.

"Ok."

"You're thinking that was really about me. You're thinking I'm still worried about—about whatever Richard, I mean, the hashok did to me. The venom, or the virus, or whatever it is. You're thinking that I'm, I don't know, identifying with Reb because I'm different too, and because Nelda Pie called me a half-breed and Fen wanted to kill me, and I'm definitely not normal and I might not even be human anymore."

"You seem pretty human to me," Dag said. "You seemed pretty human when you hid my laptop because, quote, 'Your homework is your secret boyfriend,' and then I only got a ninety-three on that test."

"And you're thinking I projected all of that onto what Joey was saying, and that's why I reacted that way."

He gazed cautiously at me before looking back at the road. "This feels like a trap. What do I say so this doesn't turn into a fight?"

I laughed in spite of myself, and then I unbuckled myself.

"Seat belt," Dag said.

I stretched over the console and kissed his cheek.

"Thank you," Dag said. "Seat belt, please."

After I was back in my seat—and yes, with my seat belt on—I said, "Did I fuck everything up?"

"I don't think so. If Joey wants Reb that bad, he wasn't going to leave us alone because I asked nicely."

"But he probably wasn't planning on biting our faces off," I said. "Not before you chopped him in the throat, I mean. And he probably didn't like me telling him to fuck off, either."

"You think?" Dag murmured.

I cupped a hand to my ear, and Dag grinned before smothering the expression.

We'd gone another half mile before I said, "Did you see what he did—"

"Yes," he said. "And I don't want to think about it."

We passed Slidell, and we followed the lake west, toward DuPage Parish and Bragg, where Dag and I had met two years before. Where we'd learned that monsters were real. Where we'd learned that the world was much more dangerous than either of us had imagined. We passed a field where they were harvesting sugarcane, men moving like ants in the green brakes. We passed a dairy farm, where the cows lay in the shade of a massive live oak. We passed an old saltbox house that looked totally out of place here, the paint stripped and the wood gray and the gallery sagging like an old man's smile. We followed miles and miles of hayfield, the hay baled and drying in the sun, while the field itself looked so neatly mown it could have been somebody's living room carpet.

The Okhlili was a river that emerged from Bayou Pere Rigaud, and it was a tributary of the Tangipahoa. I know that not because I'm a nerd like Dag (said with tremendous love and full awareness that he could literally bench-press me) but because I used to live in a house that backed up to the Okhlili. I didn't have good memories of that house, or of that river, or of that bayou. Things lived out there, things that hid, things that preyed on people. Even in the sunlight, even bundled up in Dag's Tulane sweatshirt, I was cold. I was always cold. And now, I shivered.

Dag looked over at me.

I slowed my breathing and offered a smile.

"E, maybe I should—"

My phone buzzed. "You're lucky," I said as I took it out of my pocket. "You were about to start a fight."

"Good Lord," Dag muttered with a shocking lack of boyfriendly patience.

Kennedy Sainte-Marie's name appeared on the screen, and I hesitated before swiping to accept the call. Then I said, "You're on speakerphone with Dag, so you can't yell at me."

"Why do I have a patron comment card here that starts with, 'The colored boy was rude and disrespectful'?"

"Because you don't have a good system for weeding out the crazy old racists."

"Eli Prescott Martins!"

"Hi, Kennedy," Dag said.

"Why haven't you broken up with him yet?"

"Funny," I said. "You're a laugh riot."

"It's bad enough that I have to get complaints about you at one job, Eli."

"Oh boy. Here we go again."

"That last gay werewolf FBI book, the one you had for over a year—" The last three words were a bit shouty, in my opinion. "—the one that you blackmailed me into waiving the fine for?"

"I didn't blackmail you. I simply said it would be a shame if anyone found out you own the hardbacks of those gay pirate books—"

"The pages were stuck together from—from—from your abuse! How was I supposed to explain that to the other staff?"

"Eli," Dag said and made a face.

"It was Elmer's glue! I was working on your notecards!"

"It was the pages where they gangbang that intern! And Elmer's glue doesn't spray!"

"Come on," Dag muttered.

"It was glue! I swear!"

"And now," Kennedy said, "now I have to deal with this comment card, where the second sentence is, 'The colored boy told my family that, quote, "Maybe they got it right on *Throw Grandma from the Train.*"'"

"That's not even the title," Dag said.

"I was riffing," I said. "And isn't anyone going to focus on the real issue here, that she keeps calling me 'the colored boy'?"

"Did you," Kennedy said, "or did you not tell the tour group that the movie *Death Becomes Her* was based on this patron?"

"Patron is such a generous term for someone who pays twelve-ninety-nine—"

"Why were you picking movies from the nineties?" Dag asked. "You weren't even alive in the nineties."

"How dare you?"

"And when they were leaving—" Kennedy's voice was rising. "Did you or did you not tell them to, quote, 'strap her to the roof like in *Beverly Hillbillies*'?"

"In my defense, I only know that because Dag watches *Beverly Hillbillies*."

"I watched it once, and that was because you took the batteries out of the remote when you were feeling neglected."

"Eli!" Kennedy barked.

"I'm sorry! She was, well, super racist and super rude and she kept talking over me. And you're an awesome supervisor, Kennedy, and I'm so grateful you hired me to help with the cemetery tours, and you're hands-down my favorite librarian because you always know the porniest books, like that one about Frankenstein's monster, only instead of a human, er, dingus—"

"You cannot talk to patrons that way, Eli. You're going to get fired. And then I'm going to get fired. And I don't have a hunk of white boy waiting for me at home to help pay the bills."

"Oh, you should get one," I said. "Ten out of ten, highly recommend."

Kennedy was making a high-pitched noise on the other end of the call. That was when Dag said, "Kennedy, I'm going to jump in here. We've kind of got a situation." He explained Posey's visit the night before, and when he'd finished, he asked, "Do you know anything about rougarous? Or about this voodoo guy, Le Doux, why he would want Reb?"

"I've never dealt with a rougarou," Kennedy said. Her voice had the clamped-down, unyielding strain that had nothing to do with library books or ghost tour patrons—I'd only ever heard it when she talked about this side of her life, the part she'd wanted to leave behind. "Eli has a copy of the book; he can see if there's anything written about them."

"What about Le Doux?"

Her answer came more slowly this time. "He's a voodoo king. That's the old term for it in New Orleans voodoo. You might call him a priest or a houngan. I've heard the name."

"Good things?" I asked.

"Not exactly," she said drily.

"Why would anybody want a rougarou? I mean, I bet they don't make good pets, and while Reb is pretty—" Something was happening on Dag's face, so I hurried to add, "I mean, that's what I've heard people say—"

"Nice try," Dag muttered.

"—there's got to be another reason this voodoo king was so interested in Reb as soon as he came back to New Orleans."

Dag frowned. "Kennedy, do you ever hear anything about a guy named Joey Jaws? I mean, involved in this kind of stuff. Like, unnatural stuff."

I shot Dag a look, but he shook his head.

After a deep breath, Kennedy said, "I don't know. I don't care. I don't want anything to do with it. I don't want that life. In fact, I try to stay as far away from it as possible."

"But if you know something about voodoo—" I tried.

"I don't, Eli. Voodoo, even New Orleans voodoo, is a religion. I'm Catholic. Some people mix the two. I don't. I happen to belong to a family that's up to their elbows in hoodoo, but that's different, and that's the end of this conversation."

"Could you ask around?" Dag said. "See if anything turns up?"

Her silence practically hummed. Then she said, "I want dinner."

"Ok."

"A nice dinner."

"We can do that."

"And Eli can't come."

"What?" I asked. "Why?"

"Because it'll drive you crazy," she said. "And you make my life impossible three or four days a week, so it serves you right."

"Dag, don't you dare."

"I think we can work something out," Dag said.

Kennedy's breathing sounded smug before she disconnected.

"How dare you?"

"You already asked that."

"I am your boyfriend."

"Well, yeah."

"This is...this is treason, Dagobert."

"Ok," he said.

"Ok?"

"I'm sorry?" It was definitely a question.

I screamed.

Dag made a big show of putting his finger in his ear and shaking his head, but he was smiling and trying to hide it too. As we turned onto the two-lane state highway to follow the Okhlili, I was fairly sure I heard him say under his breath, "She might be on to something."

DAG (6)

We had to cross a culvert and pass through a gate—which was unlocked, fortunately—to reach the fishing camp that Posey had told us about. Fishing camp was one of those Louisiana terms that could mean anything from a stilt shack to a million-dollar home with waterfront property. In this case, it turned out to be closer to the stilt shack: it consisted of a rambling, single-story building, two RVs with rotting tires, and a gravel boat launch sloping down to the Okhlili's dark waters. A pair of fanboats bobbed at the end of a floating dock upstream.

I slowed the Escort, and we parked on a shaggy patch of St. Augustine grass. We sat there as I studied the compound. Nothing moved. Aside from the tires, the RVs looked usable, and they'd probably been parked there and only used whenever they needed extra beds for the camp. The central building had hardboard siding, a corrugated zinc roof, and a shoddily built porch drooping off the front. Someone had laid out astroturf under the porch, and camp chairs surrounded a wood stove.

"I can feel my neck getting redder," Eli said.

"How come you act spoiled," I asked, "but only sometimes, and even though you know I know you're not spoiled?"

"Because I'm drawn to butch, daddy types whose natural response is to make everything better."

I got out of the car.

He was laughing when he caught up to me near the RVs. He looped his arm through mine.

"No," I said.

"It's been a weird couple of days," he said. "I need something to laugh about."

"You're pushing my buttons."

He kissed my shoulder.

I tried to push him away, but somehow it turned into me running my fingers through his perfect, windswept hair. He smiled. I gave a tug.

"Dagobert! Ow!"

"Don't be a brat."

And for some reason I would never understand, his smile got even bigger. Because—of course—he liked that.

I rapped on the first RV's door and called out, "Reb, are you in there? My name's Dag. We met at the Stoplight; Posey sent me to make sure you're all right."

The river murmured, and something moved in the trees. Eli's head snapped toward the sound.

"It's just a nutria or something," I said.

"Sure," Eli said. "That's why you grabbed me so tight."

I tried the door. Inside, the RV was littered with cans of PBR and water bottles cut in half and filled with somebody's tobacco-brown spit. It was a base model, nothing fancy, and it smelled musty. I guessed it was at least thirty years old. The next RV was the same.

"Here we go," Eli said.

The sun was warm on the back of my neck, the air cool enough that the dew soaking through my tennis shoes felt like ice. Eli, still holding my arm, was shivering without seeming to realize it. I needed to start keeping blankets and some spare coats in the car. It was only going to get colder.

In the windows of the camp's central building, the curtains were drawn. When we passed under the porch, astroturf crunched underfoot, and the smell of old wood smoke and pipe tobacco met us. I gave the stove a check and said, "Somebody used it this morning. It's still warm."

I went first, and I ignored the look Eli gave me. The door opened easily. Inside, the air was warmer. It smelled the way closed-up bedrooms did sometimes, like body oils and sweat and polyester that you couldn't ever get all the way clean. We stood in a living room with an uneven tile floor, mismatched furniture, and a massive TV. The interior walls were plywood—some painted, some not.

"Reb?" I called. "We're friends. Posey sent us."

The house's silence swallowed the words. Then, in the distance, I heard something hum to life.

I started forward. The next room was the kitchen, where someone had installed cabinets—kind of. They'd only installed the cabinet boxes, with a plywood countertop tacked into place, probably meant to be temporary. No one had ever come along and done the little things like, you know, leveling the boxes or shimming them or hanging the doors. Canned food lined the shelves, and a loaf of white bread sat on the counter next to an open package of hard salami and a jar of mayo.

"Maybe Reb will cook us dinner if we ask nicely," Eli said. "I'm starving."

"He's a kid, E. It's not his fault. And if you're hungry, we can pick you up something—" I stopped.

Absolutely nothing showed on Eli's face as he whispered, "Big, butch daddy types."

"You're really trying today, huh? Is this because Kennedy got your number in the car?"

"I don't know what you're talking about." But he smirked as he slid his arm free of mine and headed toward a door down the hall.

The bedrooms were crammed with mismatched beds. That sounded stupid in my head, but it was true. Most of them were unmade. The mattresses were squeezed into the rooms, pushed as close together as nominally straight guys would tolerate. Rough openings had been cut in the bedroom walls for window A/C units. I found Eli in one of the bedrooms where the window unit was churning out lukewarm air—the source of the noise I'd heard earlier.

Eli crouched between two of the beds. When I stepped into the room, he looked up. He'd lost the smirk and a lot of the color in his face, and he held up a white t-shirt. It was the kind you buy in five packs for a few dollars at Walmart, and it was soaked in blood.

"It's still wet," he whispered. "I touched it."

I nodded.

"Dag, that's a lot of blood."

"It might be evidence. I'll be right back; don't move."

I found a trash bag in the kitchen, and I helped Eli slide the shirt inside. Then I took Eli to the bathroom and scrubbed his hands clean. No jokes now. When his eyes met mine, they were watery, and so dark they almost didn't look hazel.

"That's how your shirt would look if you—if you killed a man," he said. "They said Le Doux had puncture wounds like he'd been bitten."

I nodded as I dried Eli's hands; even wrapped in the towel, they trembled. "It could be a lot of things," I said. "He was fighting that night. He might have gotten hurt."

Eli bit his lip until a white line appeared under his teeth.

"He might have cut himself shaving," I said. I chafed him a little more roughly with the towel. "That was a joke."

"You knew that guy," Eli said. "Joey Jaws, isn't that what you said? He bit that man's face like he was trying to tear it off."

"Let's talk about this later."

When I tried to lead him out of the bathroom, though, he yanked his hands away. He blinked his hazel eyes clear. "You know who he is. Joey Tamborella. You know him."

"I don't know him. I didn't even realize it was him until, well..."

"He tried to eat that guy's face. Dag, what the hell?"

The house was still so silent. Where's the wind, I thought. Where's the creaks and complaints in a slapped-together place like this?

"You hear stuff," I said, dropping my gaze. "Guys like to talk. The Tamborella family has most of the Northshore action, and that includes DuPage Parish. I'd heard a couple of stories about Joey Tamborella."

"Joey Jaws," Eli said. "What kinds of stories?"

"Come on, E. Not right now."

"What kinds?"

I blew out a breath. I waved a hand the way you'd shoo a fly. "Stuff he did. I mean, they didn't call him Joey Jaws for nothing, Eli. They're not stories worth repeating, and I definitely don't want to talk about it right now."

"Stuff he did to other people. Like he did to that guy?"

"Like that."

"Worse?"

I twisted the towel and pitched it into the sink. In some ways, Eli had seen the worst life had to offer, but in others, he'd been sheltered. I thought about it. Then I nodded.

"Jesus." But weirdly, Eli's voice sounded stronger, and when I checked, his jaw was set in a firm line. "Ok. So, we're dealing with a voodoo king, a legit psychopath backed by the mob, and a werewolf. Anything else?"

"I bet Nelda Pie's involved somehow; she doesn't seem like the type to let Reb run off."

"Great, and an insane witch. Anything else?"

"And Posey—well, he's in a bad spot. I think he'd do just about anything to keep Reb safe, and his judgment is compromised."

"Nutso boyfriend who is freakishly strong. Check. Anything else? Don't answer that."

I smiled in spite of myself. I grabbed the trash bag with the bloody shirt.

Eli's eyes had followed my movement, and he said, "You know, there's somebody else that might have done that kind of damage to Le Doux."

Shifting the bag from hand to hand, I hesitated. "They can identify human bites, E."

"The autopsy hasn't come back yet. I'm saying he could have done it."

I didn't want to think about Joey Jaws killing Le Doux that way—or anybody else for that matter. When I opened my mouth to say something along those lines, though, I heard a noise: the rumble of an engine, the creak of an ancient suspension. It was a bigger vehicle, definitely louder than the Escort, but it didn't sound like the Jag. Besides, I don't know how Joey could have followed us here.

When I tilted my head, Eli nodded, and we crept toward the front of the house. The sound of the engine died, and a door slammed. By the time I got to the front window, I saw a familiar figure stalking through the grass.

I swore under my breath.

"I was joking," Eli said with a breathy laugh. "When I asked, 'Anything else?', I was kidding."

Her name was Fen; if she had a last name, I didn't know it. She was what some people would have called a redbone—the term had fallen out of favor for a while, but now some groups claimed it, and she might have even called herself that. The name came in part from the reddish undertone to her brown skin, in part from the high cheekbones, the shadow of Choctaw or Natchez blood in her eyes. She had her hair cut shorter than mine, and she had almost as much gray as I did. She wore a man's work shirt, jeans, and boots, all under a leather duster. It might have looked funny, but the Browning hanging from a strap around her neck wasn't a joke.

"What's she doing?" Eli whispered.

I shook my head. As I watched, Fen paced a circle in the waist-high grass. She had something in her hand, and she seemed to be studying it, following it. My first thought was a compass, but that didn't make any sense because a compass didn't keep turning like that, and anyway, she wasn't facing north.

Eli shivered, and when I glanced at him, I saw goose bumps where his sleeves were pushed up.

"She's doing something." The color had drained out of him, and he was hugging himself. "She's—it's magic or hoodoo or voodoo or whatever the hell you want to call it, Dag, but she's doing something."

"That doesn't make any sense," I said. "Pretty much the only thing we know about Fen is that her sole purpose in life is to kill monsters and witches and anything she thinks isn't plain old human. There's no way—"

But as I watched, she spun to face upriver. At the tree line, a shape emerged from the shadows, and the next moment the sun fell on Reb. I had a moment where I saw him like a photograph: young, but blond and small and hairless, so he looked even more boyish. He was bare chested, scabbed wounds on his side suggesting recent injuries, and he wore jean cut-offs and pull-on Timberlands that hit him high on the calf. Across his shoulders, almost as big as he was, he was carrying a gator that I was pretty sure he'd killed with his bare hands.

Then everything happened fast.

Fen swung the shotgun up and, carrying it at port arms, sprinted toward Reb.

Reb twisted out from under the gator, letting it fall, and darted toward the river.

Eli threw open the door and raced outside.

I went after him. Eli outdistanced me easily; he was naturally long and lean, built for running, and he clocked anywhere from thirty to sixty miles every week. I worked out at the university's fitness center, and I hadn't let myself get soft, but when it came to running, I wasn't in Eli's league.

Apparently, I wasn't in Fen's league either because that lady hauled ass. She cut through the grass at an angle, and at first, I thought she was trying to head Reb off before he reached the Okhlili. Then she stopped so suddenly it looked like her legs had locked. She brought the stock of the shotgun to her shoulder and drew a bead on Reb.

Fifty yards, I thought. At fifty yards, double-aught buckshot was still considered *effective* by the FBI. They'd drilled that into us at the academy.

I drew the Sig from the holster on my belt and fired. I aimed close to Fen, but not directly at her. The shot cracked the air. Fen dropped into the tall grasses, and I raced toward the river. I kept the gun pointed in her general direction, squeezing off shots, keeping the rate of fire as steady as I could. My hand dipped and bobbed, and if there'd been paper targets, it probably would have looked like I was shooting blind. But Fen stayed down, and that was what mattered.

As I reached the slope that led down to the river, an engine roared to life. Below me, Reb was steering one of the fanboats upriver, toward the wall of cypress and live oak that marked the edge of Bayou Pere Rigaud. The propeller fan drew crescents on the water, forcing a rippling wake behind him. Eli was ten yards ahead of me, almost to the water. I scrambled down after him.

Eli jumped and landed on the near side of the floating dock. The whole thing tilted under his weight, the far side coming up out of the water and threatening to flip over.

"The middle," I shouted, "get to the middle."

Behind me, the shotgun boomed. The buckshot hit the tall grass above me and sounded like tiny pellets of hail.

Eli scrambled forward-slash-up, shifting his weight toward the center of the dock. The floating structure slapped back down and settled into the water. A moment later, I jumped and landed next to him.

"Untie that," I said, sparing a glance for the line securing the second fanboat to the dock.

While Eli worked on the rope, I got on the fanboat and found the pull-start for the engine. I grabbed the handle and yanked. The engine grumbled. Then it sputtered back into silence.

Above us, Fen appeared on the ridge, the shotgun still braced against her shoulder.

I hauled on the pull-start again. The engine made that throaty noise again.

"Dag!" Eli shouted.

"I see her." The line fell into the water. "Get in."

Eli dove into the fanboat. Fen's gun boomed again. Shot splintered the dock where Eli had been a moment before. Some of the tiny beads ricocheted, stinging my arm. Others left concentric circles in the river's darkness.

I ripped the pull-start back, and the engine roared to life. The propeller fan spun, and I grabbed the fanboat's yoke. I gave us too much speed, and the boat lurched forward, almost sending us into a submerged log. It also probably saved our life; Fen's next shot broke the surface of the water behind us. I dragged on the yoke, sending us upriver. Fen fired again, but by that point we were too far out to see where the shot spread. After that, she must have given up, but when I glanced back, she was still standing there, watching us, just a little graphite cutout on the riverbank.

Eli had dragged himself up onto one of the fanboat's seats. He wiped sweat from his face. Then he let out a disbelieving laugh and asked, "What the fuck is going on?"

II

The rougarou's prominent place in contemporary South Louisiana's popular imagination is surprising when one considers its scarcity in the folklore collections.

- *Folklore Figures of French and Creole Louisiana*, Nathan Rabalais

ELI (1)

"We lost him," I said as we reached the mouth of the bayou. Mouth seemed like a good word for it: a dark opening in the line of bald cypress and live oak and willow, broken branches and deadfalls sticking up out of the water like sharp teeth, the moss hanging low enough that I had to part it with one hand as Dag kept us moving forward. Moss like tartar, I thought. Or maybe plaque. And then I thought maybe, just maybe, I was a little too fixated on the mouth metaphor. Maybe because so many things in my life had tried to eat me.

When I looked back, Dag's face was blank, and he seemed to be steering on autopilot.

"Dag, did you hear me? We lost Reb."

He nodded. But what he said was, "She got stabbed. What the heck is she doing?"

"She looked all right to me." The year before, Nelda Pie had stabbed Fen, almost killing her. Of course, that had been after Fen broke into the Stoplight to try to kill Nelda Pie, so it was hard to throw stones. That was the thing about Fen; she got real shooty and stabby and, um, burny about anyone or anything with the slightest hint of the supernatural, me included. That was one reason I hadn't invited her to my birthday party. Her choice in footwear hadn't helped her cause either. "She's obviously recovered."

"Great. That's just great. Why's she after Reb?"

"Because she wants to shoot him. Or stab him. Or burn him. Fen's kind of like a multiple-choice test. The correct answer is D, any of the above."

"But why? I mean, why right now, why come all the way out here for Reb specifically, and how'd she—" He stopped himself. He looked at me. Then, because he was Dag and so gentle, he very carefully did not look at me.

"You can ask," I said.

"What happened?"

Great question, boyfriend dearest, I thought. Great fucking question. What happened, I wanted to say, was I was standing there, watching Fen through the window, and all of a sudden it was like my whole body turned to ice. Not just cold—flashfreeze. It had been the burning cold that I remembered from the hashok's bite, the icy fire of its venom rushing through my body. I had felt it other times. The year before, I had felt it when Nelda Pie used some sort of magic on me. But it had been nothing like this. It's getting worse, Dag, I wanted to say. It's getting so much worse.

All I said, though, was, "I felt something. I've felt it before, around Nelda Pie. Fen was definitely using magic."

"To follow us."

"Maybe, but I don't think so. Did you see her turning in place? And then she was looking right at Reb when he came out of the trees. I think, somehow, she was tracking him."

"That would be useful." It was as close to grumbling as Dag ever came. He was still watching me out of the corner of his eye. He was, after all, smart and attentive, and he'd been trained as a cop, and, in spite of his thoughts to the contrary, had been very good at his job. He hadn't missed my omission when he'd asked me what had happened. But, because he was Dag, he must have decided not to press the issue. "Right about now, for example."

"Can't we, like, track him or something? I mean, we'll look for broken strands of moss, fresh scrapes on the bark of trees, oh, maybe he tied a ribbon around branches so we could follow."

"Good idea," Dag said. "You keep an eye out."

I would have splashed him because of, a) his tone, and b) his total lack of boyfriendly encouragement, but I didn't want a gator chewing off my hand, so I decided I'd just hide the TV remote for a week when we got home.

Because I'd grown up in New Orleans and was, against my wishes and better judgment, a Louisiana native, I'd had to learn about bayous at some point in my illustrious educational career. I think it had been in eleventh-grade environmental science. And what I remembered was that bayous were found in flat, low-lying areas because, basically, they were somewhere between a boggy river and a marshy lake. They were also—fun fact—chock full of awesome things like mosquitos and overgrown rats and things that wanted to get your head in their jaws and drag you underwater. That's an aside. The point was that bayous might have a slow-moving current. They might not. They didn't really have clear boundaries or shores, and they definitely didn't have an easy or clear—well, layout wasn't the right word, but I didn't have a better one.

After another ten minutes of gliding past the knees of cypress trees, the propeller fan filling the air with its droning, I said, "How are we going to find him?"

"I thought you were looking for tangled-up moss or something."

"Dagobert LeBlanc!"

He hid a tiny smile. "Right now, I'm not so worried about finding Reb. You saw him with that gator; the boy can clearly take care of himself. I'm trying to put as much distance as I can between us and Fen. Then we're going to find somewhere to pull out. A couple of state parks take in part of the bayou, and they'll have facilities—launches, parking lots, phones, roads."

"Toilets," I said dreamily. "Showers."

Dag laughed.

"And they'll have vending machines with sour cream-and-onion chips."

"I don't know about that."

"And ice-cold Dr. Pepper."

"I like hearing you have an appetite, but should I have packed you a snack? Oh, Jesus, Eli." He pulled his leg back, too late, from my pinch and massaged it through the jeans. "I bet you gave me a blood blister."

"I'm hiding the remote for two weeks."

"What?"

"The remote. The TV remote. It was going to be one week, but now it's two."

All things considered, it said a lot about our relationship that Dag's only response was a bewildered, "Why?"

I declined to answer.

We kept moving through the bayou. My initial impression that we were alone faded quickly. Something moved in a stand of palmetto, and I flinched. Then a branch creaked overhead, and I was sure it was a snake. The air, fetid with the smell of rotting vegetation, stirred when a bird flapped up out of the water, wings snapping.

"God damn duck," I muttered.

"Coot," Dag said automatically.

"You're a coot. You're the one who owns multiple pairs of slippers."

He laughed. "The bird. And you don't have to keep looking up there; it's a coon, not a snake."

"I didn't say it was a snake."

The worst part was that he looked Gently Supportive, even though I knew he wanted to laugh.

"Is this why you always call yourself a coon-ass? Because you, like, know all this stuff?"

"I know all this stuff because my dad loves fishing almost as much as he loves golf, and he took me out a lot when I was younger." He smiled. "I didn't realize how much of it I remembered."

I pointed to a mostly submerged line that was marked by floating Clorox bottles. "Trot-line."

He nodded.

"You taught me that last year."

His smile got bigger. "I did."

He pointed out a muskrat moving through a clump of buttonbrush, and he said things about sedge and nettle, and he showed me not one, not two, but three armadillos. We passed a houseboat that looked abandoned, and he talked about old Cajun guys who lived out here, trapping for fur. Bream and gar streaked under the water. A heron waded in shallow water, picking each step gingerly. When I asked about the trees with the crooked, praying arms, he had a look like Loving Wonder on his face—which was downright annoying—and told me they were elms. All in all, I almost forgot we were chasing a werewolf and, in turn, being chased by a crazy monster hunter.

Of course, not all of it was beautiful. Go-cups were caught in exposed roots. A plastic can of Grizzly Natural Extra Long Cut floated past. A turtle poked its head out of an overturned foam cooler. Dag touched the trash bag between his feet, the one that held Reb's bloody shirt—or what I hoped was Reb's bloody shirt—and said, "I should have brought the whole roll."

"We don't exactly have time to pick up trash," I said. "We'll do a service project once we're out of this mess."

"We?"

"Yes: you will sail around in a boat, or whatever it's called, picking up trash—"

"It's not called sailing unless it has a sail."

He got his legs out of the way before I could reach him. I settled for continuing, "—and I'll, I don't know, read every article on the internet about 'one weird trick for a flat belly' and practice throwing up."

Leaning forward, he kissed the back of my head. One hand slid around to rest on my stomach. That's all; he didn't say anything.

"I'll stop," I said in a quiet voice.

"It's ok."

But it wasn't, of course.

We must have seen it at the same time: a break in the live oaks to our right, the gravel launch, the fanboat, and approximately a million red-and-black signs that said PRIVATE and NO TRESPASSING. Either Reb couldn't read, or he didn't give a fuck. Maybe he was an all-star like me. Maybe it was both.

"Please God," Dag said as he turned the boat toward the launch, "don't let us get shot by some territorial piney-woods numbnuts."

When the fanboat bumped up against the launch, gravel crunched. Dag killed the engine. He ordered me to hop out, so I did, and I managed to land high and dry on the gravel. He splashed into the water, and between the two of us, we hauled the fanboat up far enough that it wouldn't drift away. Making a face, Dag squished his way up onto dry land and looked around. He reached into the fanboat for the trash bag, and as he straightened, he opened his mouth to say something.

Then the expression on his face flickered. I felt something hot rake my shoulder, and Dag shoved me.

I hit the ground hard and skidded, tearing up my hands and arms even through Dag's sweatshirt. I heard a thud behind me, then a muffled grunt, and then a snapping sound. Dag let out a whistling breath—a compressed sound full of fear and an adrenaline craze. I scrambled to get myself upright and turned.

For a moment, my brain refused to play along. What I was seeing wasn't just impossible—it was at the far end of the scale, where impossible met ridiculous.

Dag was fighting an alligator-man.

There wasn't really any other way to describe our attacker. He wore a pair of New Balance that looked like they were on the brink of dissolving, mesh shorts, and a bro-cut sweatshirt—no sleeves, and the armholes cut open down the sides. His skin was about the same shade as mine, but with a different cast to it—almost a dark green, although that was only at certain angles. He was muscular—legs, chest, arms.

The rest of him was where things got weird. He had fingers, but they sharpened to thick, black claws. It was hard to tell because of the bro-cut sweatshirt, but at some point, his skin transitioned to a leathery hide—thicker, rougher, olive-brown. The hide ran up his neck. His head was some bizarre fusion of man and gator: the long, rounded snout; the upturned nostrils; the upper teeth exposed even though his jaw was shut. His eyes were dark all the way through—no whites. When he and Dag spun in a circle, I saw the ridges—spikes?— on his neck and back, the way a gator has.

As I watched, the gator-man lunged at Dag, snapping his teeth. Dag stumbled back, fell, and landed on his ass.

"Dag!"

The gator-man surged forward, jaw snapping the air. Dag scooped up a handful of gravel and hurled it in the thing's face. The gator man let out a bellowing noise and shook its head. It clawed at its eyes.

Blind, I thought. Everything was still coated by that dazed disbelief. It's blind. Now would be a good time to hit it.

So, I picked up a fallen branch and bashed it on the back of the head.

The gator-man spun toward me, making that strange bellowing noise again. It was still blinking, trying to clear its eyes, but it trundled toward me. It opened its mouth. So many teeth, I thought. So many fucking teeth. And then it launched itself toward me, jaw already closing to catch me and, presumably, bite me in half.

I tried to move backward, but my legs weren't working, and my movements were stiff and uncoordinated.

The gator-man lurched off course, and then it fell face-first onto the ground.

Dag was on its back, arms wrapped around its neck. He was doing something weird with his legs—hooking them around the gator-man's legs, forcing them up, off the ground.

And then I realized that fighting wasn't the best word.

Dag was wrestling it. He was wrestling a gator. Gator-man. Whatever.

The thought snapped me out of my frozen moment. I grabbed another branch, ready to do some more bashing, but there was no way to hit the gator-man without also hitting Dag. While the gator-man thrashed and bucked, trying to throw Dag off—which, I now realized, was why Dag had hooked the gator-man's legs, to keep him from rolling Dag into the water—Dag clung on grimly. Dust and dirt covered his face. He'd gotten a gash on his temple, and blood blackened his cheek. He had one arm around the gator-man's neck. The gator-man was still snapping his jaws and shrieking, the sound outraged. When the jaws shut, Dag clamped one big hand around them.

The gator-man's roar, even with its jaw shut, made my ears ring.

It humped and twisted and writhed, but I saw, now, that it had lost. Dag released his hold around its neck and moved his hand up to join the first, squeezing the gator's mouth shut. Then, slowly, he began to force the gator-man's head up and back. The gator-man tried to fight, but Dag had the leverage—and, now I was beginning to suspect, the advantage of physiology. I felt it when the gator-man's frantic movements took on a different tone: defeat. Surrender.

Dag must have felt it too. He relaxed his hold, allowing the gator-man to lower his head a few inches. Then he reversed the hold: moving one arm down to wrap around the gator-man's neck, and then dropping his other hand from its jaw. I waited for the gator-man to snap and twist again, but instead, in a gravelly voice, it bellowed something.

Words.

I flinched, and the movement sent gravel skittering down the launch. Dag tightened his grip as the creature continued to shout.

"Yeah, yeah," Dag said. "Je me rends, I heard you. You don't speak English?"

"I speak, me." The gator-man's voice had a heavy Cajun accent, and the words sounded like they'd been scraped up off the gravel. "Parlangua speak."

"That's your name, huh? Parlangua?"

The gator-man hissed. "Pascal. Pascal parlangua."

"I think that's what he is, Dag. I think he's telling us what he is. Like a rougarou." At the word, the parlangua hissed again and tried to twist his head to see me. I fought a giggle at the unreality of the moment. "Pascal the Parlangua."

"No fucking way," Dag said. He was silent for a moment. Then he asked, "Why're you looking for Reb?"

"Not looking for nobody, me. Let me go."

"You got all worked up when he brought up the rougarou," Dag said. "You were hiding by Reb's fanboat. I'd say you're interested in Reb."

The gator-man—parlangua—whatever twisted again, but Dag had him in an iron grip. After a moment, he let out a hissing breath. "The witch. She says she wants the pup alive. She says she won't leave Pascal alone until she get the pup. I smell him, me. But I'm too slow. Maybe you know where he is. Maybe then everybody leave Pascal alone."

"Yeah," Dag said. "I bet Nelda Pie will be real happy to leave you alone." He glanced at me, and after a moment, I realized he was waiting to see if I had any questions.

"How'd you know Reb was going to come here?" I asked. "How'd you know to wait for him?"

"Pascal wait."

"Unh-uh," Dag said, forcing his head back. "Answer his question."

"The pup comes up here. The pup looks around. The pup leaves. He comes back."

"He'd been coming up here? How many times? Do you mean the last few days, or before that?"

The parlangua's hesitation had a confused quality. He answered, "The pup leaves. The pup comes back."

Then, in a flash of movement, it bucked, its jaws snapping as it twisted. Dag clung on, his face locked in concentration, and when the parlangua's jaws shut the next time, he clamped down with one hand. Then he got the other hand in place, and he forced the parlangua's head back into the submission hold. Pascal thrashed for a few more seconds, and then he gave up. His body was limp, but it was hard to ignore that densely coiled strength waiting to move again.

"Uh, Dag—" I stopped because I had no idea how to ask what I was thinking, which was something along the lines of: *How the fuck are you going to get off that thing?*

"Get the rope from the boat," Dag grunted. The muscles in his arms and shoulders were corded with effort, and his back was bowed, his legs flexed to keep the parlangua from rolling him. It had only been a few minutes, but I realized he must be exhausted.

I stumbled down the launch and worked the rope free from the fanboat. I grabbed the bag with the bloody shirt while I was at it and scrambled back to Dag.

"Can you tie him?" he asked. "Around the snout. I wouldn't ask, but—"

"But you're literally restraining a gator-man in a submission hold." My laugh sounded bright and broken and a little insane. "Yeah, extenuating circumstances."

Even with Dag holding the parlangua's jaws shut, it took me about ten seconds to work up the courage. I inched closer. Huge teeth poked out, and they were thick and yellow and looked incredibly sharp. The hide was cool and pebbled when my hand brushed it. I jerked back, and Pascal made a noise and tried to thrash again before Dag forced him into stillness.

"E," Dag said, weariness drawing his voice.

"Can't you just shoot him or something?" I asked as I looped the rope around his snout a few more times. I didn't know any knots—something which was an endless source of disappointment to Dag, I knew, even though he'd never said anything—so I did a granny knot and then another one. I backed away.

"I'm not going to shoot him. He's just protecting his territory. Well, maybe a little more than that." Dag drew a breath. "Follow the road and run."

"We're not getting back in the boat?"

"Eli, run."

I opened my mouth to say, *Not without you,* but Dag apparently already knew that. In a smooth movement he unhooked his legs from the parlangua's. Then he scooted backward. Last, he released the parlangua's head and sprang up.

We ran.

Behind us, Pascal bellowed, although the sound was muffled because he couldn't open his mouth. Then heavy footsteps thudded after us. I tried to look, but Dag's hand closed around my arm, urging my attention forward again.

Since cardio was one of my love languages—or, at least, one of the few Dag-approved ways to try to get rid of my belly—I settled into an easy stride, my long legs eating up the rutted dirt road. Dag ran alongside me. After a couple of minutes, he started huffing for breath. He wasn't in bad shape. The opposite, actually; he had a fucking rock of a body. But since he was a normal person and didn't use running on the levee as a release valve for all his self-loathing, he also wasn't used to running this fast for more than a couple hundred yards.

When he stumbled the first time, I risked a glance. The parlangua was nowhere to be seen.

I caught Dag's arm and slowed him. He looked over his shoulder, and when he looked back at me, I shook my head. He sucked in air. I got a few deep lungfuls myself.

"They can't run far," Dag said between breaths. Then his brow furrowed. "Well, gators can't. I guess I didn't think about the fact that he might be able to."

"I can't respond to that," I said. "I'll never be able to respond to that."

He put a hand at the small of my back. His touch was hot, and it was the first time I'd felt warm in weeks.

Then I said, "What the fuck was that?"

He was wiping his face with his shirt, exposing the hard planes of his chest and stomach. Through the cotton, he said, "Some kind of gator-man. You heard it—a parlangua, or something like that."

"Not that, dummy. What was that stunt about jumping on its back and, I don't know, wrestling it like Crocodile Dundee?"

"Crocodile Dundee wrestled crocodiles, I think—"

"Dagobert!

"Don't yell at me, please." He dropped his shirt. "It hurt you—oh God, Eli, let me see."

Until then, I'd forgotten about my shoulder. I'd been occupied with little things like watching my boyfriend fight a human-alligator hybrid and then running for my life only to discover that, while my boyfriend apparently knew how to wrestle gators, he hadn't considered the possibility that a parlangua might be able to run a five-minute mile.

I tried to look, but I couldn't turn my head far enough. Dag stepped behind me. When he pulled on the sweatshirt, the wound stung.

"That's your good sweatshirt," I said.

"It's a sweatshirt, Eli."

"It's your favorite."

"It's not bad, I don't think. I'd like a doctor to look at it, but it's barely more than a slice. It's already stopped bleeding."

"It's not bad because you pushed me out of the way and then made that thing into your one-man bucking bronco. I'm sorry about your sweatshirt, Dag. I'll get you a new one. I'll get you a bunch of them, and I'll wash them a hundred times so they're soft and you can sleep in them and you can wear them on Saturdays when you don't want to do anything except read."

His fingers fell away from the cut. They brushed the outline of my shoulder blade. It felt like a long time before he said, "Aren't all bucking broncos designed for only one person?"

I turned around to glare at him.

"What?" he asked with a laugh.

"Don't think I didn't realize you dodged my question. Explain yourself, mister."

Color came into his cheeks. He shrugged. He toed the rut in the dirt road. I'd seen five-year-olds act less embarrassed. Well, I wasn't sure I even knew what a five-year-old actually looked like, but I had a general impression.

"Lanny liked gator wrestling," he said, and his tone was a closed door. "He made me watch, I don't know, a million videos about it. He was crazy about it."

I studied him for a moment. Lanny was his ex, and he had died the year before, and in some ways, I was pretty sure Dag blamed himself. He'd been an annoying-as-hell combination of fuckboy and overgrown child, and he'd spent most of the short time I'd known him trying to steal Dag away from me. He'd been something of a sweetheart, and the world was a lesser place without him.

"I'm too tired right now," I said, "but I want you to know I'm going to build up my strength, and then I'm going to be so mean to you about this."

Dag knuckled his eyes. Then he cupped my face and kissed me.

"It's like you don't even hear me," I said. "So mean, Dagobert. Like, the time I threw away your leftover lobster mac and cheese? That'll be nothing. The time I put all the sofa cushions under the bed so you couldn't study in the living room? Nothing, nothing compared to this."

"I'm glad you're ok too," he said quietly.

I turned into his hand to hide my tears. Then I let him kiss me again.

When we separated, I looked around at the sprawl of live oak and cypress and tatters of moss. "What now?"

"We couldn't get back in the boat," Dag said, turning me by the shoulders. "You never want to deal with a gator in the water if you don't have to. Besides, Fen has probably found a boat by now and is coming this way. So, I guess we're going to find out where this road leads."

"Great plan."

He smacked my ass to get me moving.

DAG (2)

The dirt road connected up with a state highway, it turned out. We'd seen no sign of Reb, and we had no idea where he might have gone after abandoning the fanboat. But at least we had phone service. I called Posey, and when I started to tell him what had happened, he asked where we were and said he was coming to pick us up.

"Ride-share," I said to Eli.

Eli gave me a flat look and plucked at a twig that had gotten caught in his admittedly now less-than-windswept hair. The day had warmed, and we were both sweating. "This motherfucker better have A/C."

It turned out Posey did, in fact, have A/C. He had plenty of it. He was driving a Ram Power Wagon, cobalt blue, which had to have been about eighty-thousand dollars' worth of luxury trim. The inside was as big as our house.

As Posey drove us around the bayou and back to the fishing camp, I caught him up on events—Joey Jaws, Fen, the parlangua, and what the parlangua had said about Nelda Pie.

"He didn't say her name, though," Posey said as he pulled up next to the Escort. Fen's truck was gone, and the fishing camp looked abandoned again. "He said, 'the witch.' That could be anybody."

Eli caught my eye. I tried not to think what he was thinking.

"We'll keep an open mind," I said. "But Nelda Pie is most likely who he meant. She had a hold of Reb, and now everybody wants him. It makes sense that she'd want him back."

"He looked ok, though?" Posey's voice caught. "Reb. When you saw him, he was ok?"

"He'd murdered an alligator with his bare hands," Eli said. "It was as big as he is, and it wasn't slowing him down at all. Oh, he was shirtless, and he has great nips. I don't know what you consider ok, but that's what we saw."

For a long moment, Posey stared out the windshield. "He wasn't hurt, though?"

"Dag, I can't."

"He was fine," I said. "I'm sure he's still fine."

Posey adjusted the prosthesis. Then he said, "What are you doing now?"

"Now we're going home," Eli said. "We're going to shower. And eat. And shower again. And sleep. And shower again."

I squeezed his hand, and he flopped back on the seat.

"I should go with you," Posey said.

"There's not really anything you can do," I said. "We appreciate the ride, and we'll keep you updated."

Posey leaned over the steering wheel. The powerful muscles in his neck and shoulders looked tight. I opened the door and helped Eli out. When I turned to shut the door, Posey said, "You might be in danger."

"Might?" Eli said loudly enough that I gave him a look.

"I'm coming with you," Posey said. "I can help."

I opened my mouth, but Eli reached past me and shut the door. When I turned around, he said, "He's crazy with worry, Dag. He's not listening, not really. If you tell him no, he'll park on our street and sit there until somebody calls the cops."

We drove home. Eli made a big show of playing with the vents and the air and plucking at the front of his shirt. When he reached over for the thirteenth time to try to force the temperature colder—even though the dial was already all the way to cold—I caught his hand and said, "E."

And because I will never understand him, even though I love him, for some reason that made him smile and settle down while the causeway thrummed under our tires.

"I'm too cold now," he said as we were turning onto our street.

I flexed my fingers. I wrapped my hands around the steering wheel again.

He turned into his shoulder and started to laugh.

Eli took the first turn in the shower. He was still hopping out of his clothes, leaving a trail of the ruined sweatshirt and the jeans and a crisp white jock on his way, when Posey opened the front door. He stared for a moment at Eli: his long, lean body; the soft brown of his skin that lightened on his ass; the sharp vee of his torso; the muscles of his back. I stepped in front of Posey and put my hand on the doorjamb at eye level, and Posey blinked and pulled his gaze away. A moment later, I heard the bathroom door click shut.

"Last year, at the Stoplight, I let it slide," I said. "But this is our home. Are we going to have a problem?"

Posey shook his head.

I stayed there a moment longer, which I'm sure would have made Eli roll his eyes. Then I stepped back to let Posey into the house.

In the kitchen, I inspected the fridge, trying to figure out something halfway healthy to eat. It was late afternoon, and Eli didn't eat breakfast, and I'd settled for a granola bar because I'd thought maybe we'd get an early lunch. I found a bowl of leftover quinoa salad that Eli had made up, and I added more feta, and I added more olives, and then I thought about it, and I found the half a rotisserie chicken we'd gotten, and I shredded that and put that in the salad too. I added some more cheese, just in case.

When I turned around, Posey was watching me.

"You add cheese instead of salt," I said. "The cheese makes it salty."

Posey didn't even blink. He slumped against the wall.

I served the salad into three wide, shallow bowls, and I made Posey sit. I couldn't make him eat; he poked around with a spoon, the stainless steel chiming against the tempered glass. The salad was good. I added some Italian dressing, and then it was really good. I added some to Eli's bowl too. He wouldn't know, and he needed the calories.

"All right," I said after another bite exploding with feta. "Spill it."

Posey brought his head up. "What?"

"Whatever you're holding back."

"How long is he going to shower? He's been in there half an hour."

"He hasn't been in there twenty minutes, and it's our house and our shower, and he can take as long as he wants. What's going on? What haven't you told us?"

"Reb's out there. You realize that, right? He's out there, and he might be hurt, and those people are looking for him—"

"That's what I don't get." When I went for another bite of salad, I was surprised to see that my bowl was empty. I set the spoon down. I spotted some quinoa that had made it onto my shirt and wiped it away. "That's where I'm hoping you can start filling in some blanks. Why are all these people looking for Rebellion?"

"I don't know."

"Oh yeah? It was one thing when you came here, when you told me you were worried Reb might have done something, when you said you just wanted to know that he was ok. But that's not what's going on here—"

"I do want to know that he's ok. I'm scared out of my fucking mind."

"—and I'm tired of being lied to. Joey Jaws sees Reb fight, and because Joey is a psycho, he wants Reb for himself. Ok, I believe that. Le Doux pays for time with Reb, and maybe Le Doux gets too rough, or he tries something else, and he ends up dead. Reb runs and ditches the body. I'll believe that too—or I'm willing to entertain the possibility, anyway. So tell me, Posey. Where does a monster hunter come into the picture? Why is Nelda Pie scaring up gator-men monsters to hunt Reb, and telling those monsters to spread the word to other monsters—"

"Quit using that fucking word!" The shout erupted from Posey, and he slapped the table hard enough that the bowls rattled. After a heartbeat, he subsided, his chin sinking to his chest, but he was still breathing hard.

I waited. Then I said, "What? You don't like the word monster?"

He sat there, meeting my stare. Then he jerked his head to the side and pushed back from the table, the legs of his chair scraping on the boards.

"Hold on," I said. "We're having a conversation."

Posey started down the hallway.

I caught up to him as he hammered on the bathroom door. "Hurry up," he called. "We've got to get out there and look for Reb."

"Leave him alone," I said.

"Dag?" Eli called over the spray of the shower.

"You're fine; take your time." To Posey, in a lower voice, I said, "You don't know where Reb is or what to do next. If you did, you wouldn't have asked us to help. You sure as heck wouldn't have let us drive all the way back to the city."

Making a face, Posey reached for the doorknob.

I grabbed his wrist, and the next thing I knew, he had a hand planted in my gut. He forced me up against the wall hard enough that the plaster shivered. My breath blew out of my lungs. I had a moment where I thought, Not a hand. It was something else: dense and fingerless and rubbery, and even through my shirt, it felt slick. But when I looked down, he had the prosthesis awkwardly angled against my stomach.

"Yeah," I said. "That's what I thought. What's really going on?"

Posey's chest rose and fell like he'd been sprinting. He pulled his hand away from me. He tried for a smirk. I remembered this guy—a more convincing version of him, anyway—the one with the cool eyes and the laid-back shoulders, from the year before when he'd tried to pick up Eli right in front of me. He rattled the doorknob like he might go in again, but when I didn't move, his smirk just got bigger. "You don't trust me with your boy? Or you don't trust your boy?"

"You pulled a knife on me. You laid hands on me in our home. You tried to kidnap Eli, for heck's sake. No, Posey. I don't trust you. And I think you're keeping a lot of secrets, the kind that are going to get somebody hurt."

He stared at me for a long moment. Something snuffed out the smirk, and he dropped his hand to his side. "You wouldn't understand. You're not the type."

"Wouldn't understand what?"

"What'd you do," he asked, "when I put a knife to his throat and was dragging him out of here?"

The water in the shower changed quality, the sound of it coming from the tub spout now. Then the water stopped entirely.

"You stood there," Posey said. "He had to get himself out of trouble while you watched."

"Eli knows how to take care of himself."

"What'd you do when that gator thing tried to kill him?"

"I handled it."

"You had your gun. Why the fuck didn't you put two in its head?"

I stared at him. I heard a noise in my skull like a fan blowing. Then I realized it was Eli's hair dryer, and my knuckles cracked when I flexed my fingers.

"Dag," Eli said from inside the bathroom. His voice was muffled—he was drying his hair, I guessed. "I had an idea. Dag?"

"Right here," I said loud enough to carry through the door.

"Somebody did that to Reb," Posey whispered. "I'd have ripped his fucking head off."

I folded my arms across my chest.

"Some guys don't have what it takes," Posey continued in that whisper. He checked the prosthesis where it met his arm, tugging. His eyes came back. "You wanted to keep him safe? You should have broken my fucking neck."

Eli was moving around inside the bathroom. The hair dryer clicked on again. The whoosh of it sounded like a wind running hard through the house. I thought I could feel it tugging on me, pulling on my clothes.

"Get out of our house."

Posey cut his eyes away. His lips parted.

The bathroom door opened, and Eli stood there, the towel slung low on his hips. He'd been diligent over the last year, stripping away any extra padding. You could see the tracework of abdominal muscles now, the definition to his pecs, the artwork of biceps and triceps. He was sculpted, not built, everything from the slice of his jaw to the long, narrow feet.

This time, Posey had the good manners to stare at the floor. "I've got an idea," Eli said, "where to look for Reb."

ELI (3)

After Dag reloaded the Sig and grabbed a couple of spare magazines, I checked that he was still wearing his silver dime, double checked my own, and we snuck out of the house through the back. We crossed two streets to where Posey had parked his truck, and we headed back across the lake. Dag kept checking behind us to see if somehow we'd been followed. At one point, when we were crossing the causeway, there was a black SUV that had me a little worried. But when we got to Slidell, the SUV exited, and we drove the rest of the way without spotting anyone suspicious.

The house was a fading Queen Anne bristling with dormers and a corner turret. Whatever color it had originally been painted, it was now a lusterless gray in the slanting, late-afternoon light. It sat on a gravel road out at the end of DuPage Parish, with trees on three sides. Across the road, an ag field had been abandoned and was overgrown with waist-high tangles of weeds.

"Do they still do flip-or-flop, or whatever that home reno show is called?" I asked.

Neither Dag nor Posey answered. They had been silent since I had stepped out of the bathroom, the tension between them like steel. I didn't have to guess to know what it was about; Posey hadn't been shy about checking me out a year ago, and while Dag wasn't exactly the type to fly into jealous rages, he also wasn't shy about speaking his mind. Exhibit A: the lengthy conversations Dag had with me about stupid stuff like calorie deficits and stress fractures. And when Dag did say something, it tended to be...effective. Which was why I now ran ten miles a day instead of twenty.

There had been one exception to their silence: while I'd been busy on my phone, dropping into Facebook groups connected to adoption and fostering in every parish for a hundred miles, I'd heard them in the kitchen. Posey said, "I shouldn't have said what I did." And Dag hadn't said anything, which was about as bad as it got with Dag.

Fortunately, my idea to try to track down Reb's foster family through the miracle of the InterWebz had panned out. Someone had recognized Reb—from a photo I'd posted, provided by Posey—and pointed us to a woman named Juniper Ortiz.

Now, as Posey's truck rumbled to a stop on the gravel, I was starting to wonder if it was a good thing that someone had recognized and remembered Reb so easily. I mean, he was striking—too pretty to forget, maybe. But people tended to remember trouble, too, and the last couple of days had proven that Reb was a hell of a lot of trouble in a twinkie wrapper.

"You wait here," Dag said as he unbuckled himself. He'd insisted on riding in the front seat. Probably, I figured, so he and Posey could murder each other at the appointed moment.

"I'm not waiting—" I began.

"Not you," Dag said and slid out of the truck.

I met Posey's eyes in the rearview mirror. "Do you want to tell me what happened between the two of you?"

He looked away first.

When I got out of the truck, Dag started up the walk, and I had to hurry to keep up. "Ok," I asked, "what happened while I was in the shower?"

He shook his head.

"Unh-uh," I said. "I kept waiting for him to pull over so you could duke it out on the side of the road."

The treads creaked as Dag took the steps up onto the gallery.

"Was it about my honor?" I asked.

"Will you drop it, please?"

He said *please* because he was Dag and Gloria would have spanked him with a wooden spoon if he hadn't, but the tone was all barbed wire and jangled piano strings.

"Hey—"

"It's fine," Dag said, turning to avoid my touch. "Believe it or not, Eli, I can handle this on my own."

I stopped on the second step as he continued up onto the gallery. He knocked on the door. He put his hands on his hips. Juniper Ortiz— or whoever—kept their recycling bin by the front door, and it was full of Pepsi twenty-ounces. A couple of ancient rockers were pulled up to the rail. What looked like a length of surplus carpet was rolled and tucked up against the side of the house, and somebody had planted mums in Pedialyte jugs with the tops cut off.

Dag knocked again. He put his hands on his hips again. Then he turned around.

"Wow," I said.

"I'm sorry," he mumbled.

"Oh, I know you're sorry. I'm just still trying to process all that."

"I'm not mad at you; I shouldn't have gone after you. I'm mad at Posey."

"I did kind of figure that out. But if you are mad at me, you should tell me. I probably deserve it."

He had the softest brown eyes, and right then, they got even softer. He shook his head.

"What happened?" I asked.

"He's being a—a dick."

"You can do better than that."

"He's being a fucking knob."

I burst out laughing.

Dag's eyebrows drew together.

"No, that was good," I said, fighting more laughter. "That was really good."

"Go sit in the truck," he said, trying to shoulder past me. "You two can keep each other company."

Instead, I took his arm, and we moved off around the side of the house. The day was cooling, the gold evaporating into blue. I'd stolen another of Dag's sweatshirts and layered it over a thermal Henley, and I was shivering again. The sweetness of laundry detergent floated on the air. I wondered if I should threaten to wash Dag's mouth out for saying knob.

"If you threaten to wash my mouth out," Dag said, "I'll spank you, and I'm not joking."

I had to bury my face in his sleeve to hide my grin. When I trusted myself, I pulled back and said, "I know you can handle things."

He grunted.

"But if this is serious, whatever it is with Posey, you'll tell me, right? Because the whole point of being, um—"

Sometimes when Dag looked at me, it was like old war movies, with the flashing red lights and the klaxons sounding.

"Boyfriends," I said with what I considered Enthusiastic Commitment and Everlasting Love.

"Good Lord," Dag muttered.

"The whole point is that you don't have to handle things yourself, you know? We're a team. I want to help you. You basically spend your whole life helping me."

He grunted again, but it had some of the edges knocked off this time. I kissed his cheek, and he squeezed my arm.

Behind the house, a woman was hanging laundry on a sagging clothesline. She was white, probably in her sixties, her hair crimped into crinkle-cut frizz, and she wore pearl earrings that turned her lobes into stretched-out pendulums. Her housedress hit her at mid-calf and rose a few more inches every time she bent to retrieve clothes from the tub—what appeared to be children's clothes, I realized on closer inspection. The backyard gave way to a canebrake that rippled when the breeze picked up, dark lines combing through it as the cane whistled.

"Can I help you?" she asked as she grabbed unicorn-printed underwear and clipped it onto the line.

"I hope so," I said. "I'm Eli; this is Dag. We wanted to talk to you about someone who used to live here. He's in trouble, and we hoped you could help us."

"Half the kids who come through here end up in trouble," she said. "If it's Bobby, he's eighteen, and you can talk to him yourself when they get back from the corn maze."

"His name's Reb," Dag said. "Rebellion."

She pulled out a Ninja Turtles t-shirt that had to have been meant for a five- or six-year-old and hung it. She had red knuckles, and I thought I should recommend a good hand cream.

"Ma'am—Ms. Ortiz—"

"Missus," she said. "I heard you. You can dump that along the canebrake; there's a ditch, you see?"

Dag and I shared a look. Dag pointed to a tub of gray water, which had a bottle of something called Mrs. Stewart's Liquid Bluing wedged into one of the handles. Mrs. Ortiz didn't acknowledge his silent question, so Dag shrugged and walked over to the tub. He slid the bottle of bluing out of the handle.

"That's a job for two people," she said as she picked up an identical Ninja Turtles t-shirt. I was starting to wonder how many kids she had. A pack? If there were more than three, was that technically a horde?

"Dag's really strong."

She looked at me.

My mom had been dead for several years at that point. I had forgotten how quickly and hard I could blush and what it felt like to have absolutely nothing smart to say.

Together, Dag and I carried the tub to a ditch running along the canebrake. We emptied the tub. Then, per Mrs. Ortiz's instructions, we rinsed it out and dumped that water in the ditch too. By the time we'd finished, she was done hanging clothes, and she had the empty basket under one arm. She was eying the clothes and indicated for us to lean the washtub against the house. Then she said, "They'll get a little sun tonight, and there's a breeze, low humidity. They'll be all right after a few hours in the morning."

I nodded.

Dag was looking at me.

I couldn't stop nodding, and Dag was starting to smile, and I realized I was probably going to have to break up with him or cut him off sexually or mix up his notecards before a test.

"You wanted to talk about Rebellion," she said, and she sounded tired. "What's he gotten himself into this time?"

"We're not sure, actually," Dag said. "He's disappeared, and we think he's in danger."

"But you think he did something, too. Well, you're not wrong—he probably did. That boy." Her red knuckles moved as she opened and closed her fingers around the basket. "It's a good thing Dave and Bobby took the kids to the maze. That boy broke Bobby's heart." She must have caught something of what Eli was thinking on his face because a hard smile cracked her expression. "Bobby and Rebellion might have had something going on. I don't know. I tried to catch them, and I told them what's what more than once, but when they're that age, and after what most of them have been through—well, give them a who, and they'll find the when and the how, even if they don't have a clue about the why or sometimes the what."

"Dag sometimes doesn't know the what," I said.

She gave me another look, and I was starting to remember what it felt like when my face caught on fire.

"We thought Reb might be here," Dag said. "If he is, I want you to know that we only want to make sure he's ok. His boyfriend is waiting in the truck, and he's worried sick."

The clothesline creaked as the breeze dragged on the wet clothes.

"You could tell him," Dag said. "After we leave. You could let him know we're worried. Posey is worried. He might not recognize our names, but he'll know Posey. Even if he could just call."

I thought she might not say anything. Then, massaging the small of her back, she said, "A boyfriend. Well, I guess I was wrong."

"I thought you said—I mean, Bobby is a boy, right? So you knew Reb was, um, gay?"

She snorted. "Do you know how long Rebellion was with us?"

I shook my head.

"Six months. That's five months longer than anywhere else. He was a runner, that's the thing. Couldn't hardly keep him in the house without tying him to a chair. I told him as long as he came back once a day, as long as he let me know he was ok and ate something, he could do whatever he wanted. Maybe that's wrong. But I've been doing this a long time, and the ones like Rebellion, well, there's nothing else you can do for them. He never went far. He took his meals on the gallery, and then he was off again. After a couple of months, he started sleeping inside. He liked the laundry room. He had a way of getting behind the dryer; I think he ran it sometimes to keep himself warm. And before you say anything, he had a bed."

"It sounds like you took care of him the way he needed," Dag said.

The slashing line of her mouth wasn't quite a smile.

"What—what happened to him?" I asked.

"Young man," she said, "I stopped asking that so I could close my eyes at night." She started toward the house, her gait uneven, and she used the weight of the basket as a counterbalance. "He's not here, and he hasn't come back here. I'll ask Bobby; if he knows anything, well, I'll see what I can do. But this wasn't home for Rebellion. You've got to understand that. He was out tramping in sheds and barns as often as he was here, even if I wish it were different. Six months later, he got himself arrested for attacking that man, and I haven't seen him since. I'm sorry I can't help you."

With that, she stepped up to the rear gallery, let herself into the house, and shut the door.

"Well," I said, "fuck."

Dag was frowning.

"Maybe we can find a way to talk to Bobby," I said. "And I'll keep trying to find people online who knew him. They might be able to tell us something about him—friends, favorite places. That's what the cops would do, right?"

Nodding, Dag said, "One of the basics, when you're trying to find someone, is that people run to places they're familiar with, especially places they feel safe. You assume when they run, they're not thinking clearly, and so routine takes over."

"Ok, so that's what we'll do."

I took a step toward the side of the house, but Dag looked toward the canebrake.

"Dag?"

"He liked it here," Dag said. "He felt safe here. He was here six months, when everywhere else he barely lasted four weeks. He ate her food. He slept inside. He might have had a relationship with that boy."

"But he's not here," I said. "Or she says he's not here, anyway. Do you think she's lying? Or do you think Bobby's—what? Hiding him in the basement?"

"I think you're right," Dag said, turning slowly in a circle. "I think he ran somewhere he felt safe."

It took me a moment. Then I said, "Oh shit."

I started turning around like Dag—like I was going to spot something he hadn't, for fuck's sake—but by then, Dag was already pulling out his phone. He had the Maps app open, and he was looking at a satellite view of the Ortiz property and the surrounding area. With one blunt finger, he started pointing. "East, you run into the interstate. And north takes him back into the bayou. See here? This is the private property where he ditched the airboat. Maybe a mile from here. South, you've got new developments—subdivisions, mostly, with lots of people close together."

"So, he ran west," I said. "Into these fields."

"Ag fields," Dag said with a satisfied smile. "Fields that have been worked for a couple of hundred years, with plenty of sheds and barns and cribs, a lot of them probably abandoned."

"Dag, that was amazing."

He blushed. "It was pretty obvious."

"Uh, no, it wasn't. I mean, not to me, anyway. Can you be bad at something, please? Just once. It would be a huge relief."

"I'm bad at plenty of things. Come on; I guess we should get Posey and take a look while there's still some light."

"Name one thing you're bad at," I said as I followed him around the house.

"Putting my foot down with you seems like a good start."

"Oh, I thought of one. Fighting. Not, like, actual combat because you're really, really good at that. But relationship fights. Just one time if you would please get in my face and scream, boy, howdy—"

Dag looked over his shoulder, and I thought the *boy, howdy* might have been a little much.

After explaining to Posey what we thought might be happening, we started west. The first field after the canebrake looked abandoned, with weeds and wild grasses growing waist high and whispering against the denim of my jeans. Then we hit a tree line, and from the other side came the rumble of a big engine. Through the branches, I could see a tractor trundling down a tilled field. It was towing some other machine behind it, and it was spraying something everywhere.

"Broadcast spreader," Dag said, nudging me to get me moving again. "They're seeding winter rye."

"Reb wouldn't have hung around if somebody was working a field," Posey said. He was craning his neck like he might get a glimpse of Reb anyhow, and I was still having a hard time deciding his particular ratio of dumb to desperate.

Dag nodded, and we started walking again.

The day's last light felt good on my face, and when the occasional eddy kicked up, stirring dust around my tennis shoes, it brought the smell of diesel and sun-warm dirt. The shower and the food had helped push back the nightmare of the parlangua, but in some ways, this helped more: the quiet, the easy movement of my body, the shadows of the trees, the fields of what Dag insisted on telling me— even when I threatened not to glitter up his notecards for a month if he didn't stop—were probably chard and onion and kale. It was like a part of my brain could go to sleep. Stop worrying.

I was holding hands with Dag, kicking a clod of dirt ahead of us, watching it break apart, when the memory came again: the pain in my shoulder, Dag pushing me to the ground, dragging myself up to see Dag and the parlangua fighting. But the rush of old fear didn't come this time. Instead, my thoughts were cool, detached. I imagined what it would have been like, when it opened its jaws, to shove a branch in there. To keep shoving until the wood tore at the sensitive tissue of its throat. I could see it in my head, the splintered end of the branch driven with such force that it tore through the leathery hide, ripping its way free of the parlangua's neck. The spray of blood. Folds of flesh sagging outward. I rolled my head on my neck. I felt flushed. I felt like I weighed as much as the sunlight. I thought, in that moment, it would have looked like a flower.

"Eli, Christ!" Dag said, and he yanked his hand away.

For a moment, I didn't know where I was: the furrowed soil, the line of the sky, the outstretched arms of the trees. Then, pieces of it started to come back together. I turned, opening my mouth to ask if I'd fallen asleep, and stared.

Dag was holding one hand with the other. On the back of his hand, in a clear line where my fingers had rested, were puncture marks. Where, I realized after a moment, I'd driven my nails into the flesh.

"Jeez," Posey said.

"I didn't do that," I said automatically.

The hurt on Dag's face had nothing to do with the wounds on his hand.

"I didn't mean to do that," I said, so quickly I felt like I was talking over myself. "Oh my God, Dag, I'm so sorry. I—I don't know, I think it was a muscle spasm."

Dag just stood there, supporting his injured hand.

"Oh my God," I said again. "I am so, so sorry."

"A muscle spasm," Posey said.

"Will you shut up?" I said to him. "Dag, are you ok?"

73

He watched me for a moment longer, and I couldn't read whatever was in his eyes—disbelief, confusion, fear. Maybe none of those. Maybe all of them.

"I'm fine," he said. "You startled me is all."

"Let me see—"

But when I took a step, Dag rotated his body, his injured hand dropping behind him.

I stared at him.

He colored, but all he said was, "I'm fine, E."

The taste of diesel wafted on the wind, and I felt like I was going to be sick. "Can we—can we go back? I think we should go back."

"We can't go back," Posey said. "Not if Reb's hiding out here."

"If he's hiding out here," I said, my voice getting pitchy, "it's because he wants to. He doesn't want to be found. What's so hard to understand about that?"

"You don't know what you're talking about," Posey said, his volume rising to meet mine. He turned to face me, tugging at his prosthesis. "He's scared, and he might be hurt, and he's alone. He doesn't have anybody else in the world except me."

"You?" I laughed. This was the old Eli, winging up darkly, wanting to hurt because I was hurting so bad myself. "What the fuck does he care about you? You're the one he fucks when he can't get anybody else to pay for it."

The punch probably would have broken my nose, except Dag got hold of my sweatshirt and yanked me backward. Posey's fist whistled through the air. I stumbled and fell against Dag, who wrapped an arm—the one with the injured hand—around my waist. For a moment, my mind was bright and blank, like sunlight through quartz. I lunged at Posey. I thought what his eye would sound like when it popped. I thought I'd use my thumb. But Dag dragged me backward.

"Walk it off," Dag said.

Posey took a step toward us.

"Posey!" Dag barked. "Take a walk!"

After a moment, Posey shook his head like he was the one who'd gotten his bell rung. He turned and staggered away from us. Against the sunset, his outline looked like a paper doll with its edges burned black.

"What's going on with you?" Dag asked. He gave me a little shake as he released me. "What the hell, Eli?"

"I'm sorry about your hand—"

"I asked you a question! What's going on?"

"Nothing." I touched my mouth, surprised to see blood. My lip was starting to ache dully where I'd bitten it. I turned into my shoulder to wipe my forehead on the sweatshirt. Sweat dampened the cotton, even though the day was cool slipping toward chilly. Maybe I had a fever, I thought. Maybe I'm sick. I wanted to laugh. And I wanted to throw up. Maybe? Who was I kidding?

"E," Dag said softly, touching my arm. "I'm sorry I yelled, but you're scaring me. What's happening? That's not like you, hurting Posey like that. You're the kindest, sweetest person I've ever met—when you're not threatening to put my phone on the streetcar tracks." He said the last part with a tentative smile. "You like to act bitchy when there's nothing on the line, but as soon as somebody needs you—I mean, I've seen you do it. The whole reason we're helping Posey is because you wanted to. But today—help me understand this."

I dashed at my eyes and shook my head, and for a moment, I couldn't say anything. Then I turned and started after Posey and called back, "We'll never find him out here if we lose him."

His steps came after me, hard and clipped against the dirt. I had this image of him grabbing me by the arm, swinging me around, and—

I made myself stop there. I focused on breathing. The only sounds were the two of us trudging across fields of winter vegetables. And then something else—a high, whirring sound. I glanced up and saw a drone—a kid playing with his new toy, I guessed. Or, as seemed to be the case with a lot of electronics, a grown-up kid. Or maybe there was some legitimate use for drones in farming. Maybe this was how they caught trespassers, and the farmer was about to release his mean old hound.

It would come snapping and snarling, but its skin would be so soft—

I went back to my breathing. And by the time we reached the next line of trees, I was cold again. Frozen all the way through. Eli Martins, everyone. Ice queen.

Posey was waiting on the other side of the trees, and after a moment, I saw why. Ahead of us, a series of large, man-made ponds ran in two rows. A small pontoon boat was drydocked in a sun-bleached shed. At the far end of the ponds, a small brick house sat, a dirt road curling off from it like a tail. The sun had started to set, and it gave everything warm colors—red and orange and gold—but when I exhaled, I expected to see my breath.

"Reb?" Posey called. He put his hands to his mouth and tried again: "Reb!"

The shouts echoed back to us and faded to stillness.

"Come on," Dag said, shouldering between us. "We're going home after this, and we'll pick up tomorrow."

I caught up with Dag, walking at his side, but he didn't look at me. The sun layered copper across the surface of the water. One time, I wanted to say, when I locked myself in the bathroom, you took the door off its hinges. That's what I needed, and somehow you knew. All I heard was the sound of my tennis shoes flexing with each step, the rustle of dry grass, the skitter of a pebble.

"Why would somebody dig themselves eight ponds instead of one big one?" I asked in a low voice. "And what's the point of a fucking boat? I could jump across these. Ok, I couldn't, but you know what I mean."

Twenty seconds of silence felt pretty damn long. Then Dag said, "They're for crawfish. This is a crawfish farm. Well, these are rice paddies in the spring and summer. Then they harvest the rice, and they stock crawfish." The coiled spring of his voice relaxed somewhat. "See? They leave the rice stalks after the harvest; that's for the crawfish to eat. And you need the boat for when it's time to harvest the crawfish."

"I never thought about a crawfish farm," I said. "I thought—I mean, don't you just catch them in the river?"

Dag laughed, and I could hear more of the spring decompressing. "Sure, plenty of people do. But it's like anything else—there's a demand, and so people figure out ways to meet that demand. It's a good business, I think. You get the rice crop and the crawfish. You can do it on land that's no good for planting. Of course, you can't mind getting wet."

"I don't mind getting wet."

He mimed something on his head that, in an indignant flash, I realized was supposed to be my hair.

"Dagobert LeBlanc!"

He smiled and dropped his hand to his side

"I cannot believe you!"

He shrugged. "There aren't enough hair dryers in the world."

"You are—" I stared at him. "You are being savage! I love it!"

He shrugged again. The angle of the light was perfect to bring out the texture in that short, stiff gunmetal hair. From behind the tree line came the sound of an engine—surprisingly close, which meant we were near a road, although I hadn't heard any other cars.

"Do you ever get tired of me?" I asked quietly.

"I could do without that time you cancelled cable to teach me a lesson."

"It wasn't to teach you a lesson. It was to teach the cable company a lesson. Or maybe you. I forget." I swallowed. "Dag, I'm serious."

"I love you," he said. And because he was Dagobert LeBlanc, that was actually enough.

I opened my mouth to say something, and then I stopped. Over Dag's shoulder, where the drydocked pontoon boat was stored, I thought I saw movement. I caught Dag's sleeve and nodded toward the shed. Now, everything was completely still. I grimaced, and I started to shake my head, but Dag held up a finger. He waited until Posey was looking at us and waved and held a finger to his lips. Then he started toward the boatshed.

The pontoon boat wasn't big, and it had a protective canvas cover in addition to the sun-bleached wood of the shed. I strained to hear, but all I got was my own heartbeat and the slight sounds of Posey shifting.

Then Dag said, "You can come out now."

Still nothing.

"We're all friends, Reb," he said. It was his cop voice—firm, controlled, even. "Posey's here. You might not know my name, but you remember me from the Stoplight, I bet. I'm Dag, and this is Eli."

"Reb?" Posey asked. A tremor ran through the name. "Reb, baby, are you in there?"

The answer was the stutter of a zipper on the canvas cover. It moved slowly. Posey drew in a sharp breath, and then he wiped his eyes and dried his hands on his jeans. A pale hand parted the canvas flaps, and then Reb slipped out from his hiding spot aboard the pontoon.

He was as beautiful as I remembered: shorter than the rest of us, built lithe and muscular, his white-blond hair matted and snarled with broken pieces of leaves. He was wearing a too-large Red Man Chewing Tobacco t-shirt, along with the cut-offs and the Timberlands from before. He looked like the summer catalogue model for pretty peckerwood boys, and if the cold bothered him, he gave no sign of it. He looked at me and Dag and bared his teeth.

"Don't worry about them," Posey said, sliding in front of us. He held his arms out—somewhere between an embrace and a way to hold Reb's attention. "Hey, baby. Hey, sweetheart. Are you ok? I missed you. I've been so worried about you."

Reb offered Dag and me another warning glance before slipping into Posey's arms. He buried his face in Posey's chest. Posey held him tight, whispering to him. It might have been my imagination, but after a moment, I thought Reb relaxed slightly. I thought maybe I even saw him start to shake.

"We can bring the truck down that road," Dag said to me in a low voice, "and then we've got to decide where we can take him."

Before I could answer, an Explorer with dark windows—the one I remembered from the causeway—drove out down the road, appearing from behind a windbreak of brush and trees. It came to a stop near the old brick house, and the doors opened, and men got out, drawing their weapons, making a big show of it.

And Joey Jaws was one of them.

DAG (4)

"Posey," I said, trying to keep my voice steady—what Eli called my cop voice. "Trouble."

Reb made a noise that, from an animal, I would have called a growl. He spun around, his back to Posey, and a little knife flashed in his hand. Little—it was three inches of steel, and I figured that was enough to do plenty of damage. Posey had a hand on Reb's shoulder, and he was still whispering to him, calming him, but he flicked a look at me, and the look had a question.

"We can go back the way we came," Eli said. He was clutching my arm. "They can't follow us as easily, and we might be able to lose them."

"Call the police," I said.

Eli took out his phone and placed the call. I tried to keep my face neutral. We wouldn't be able to lose Joey and his thugs. The tree lines and windbreaks weren't thick enough for that, and we'd be running across miles of open ground. Besides, I was starting to suspect Joey Jaws—or someone on his team—was smarter than I'd given them credit for. After all, they'd had a pretty good idea to follow us with that drone.

Reb stretched up on tiptoe to whisper something in Posey's ear.

Posey shook his head. "No. No fucking way."

Reb's brow tightened.

"I said no."

"Dag," Eli said, plucking at my sleeve again, "we have to go—"

The gunshot blew away the rest of the words. Part of the shed's roof exploded out; dust and splinters and the light of sunset rained down on us, and the sound of the wood being torn away overlapped with the distant clap of the shot.

"I just want to talk to the boy," Joey Jaws said. I hadn't spent much time going to gay bars—I never got how you were supposed to hit it off with someone while you had Cher screaming in your ear, and the badge bucks were out of control—but I'd learned, after a few visits, to recognize the guys who thought they were entitled to whatever they wanted. You heard it in straight guys too, of course. It was a way of talking. Like everything was ok, everything was easy. Or it would be, as long as you gave them what they wanted. "How about that? How about you let me talk to him?"

"Fuck off!" Posey shouted back. He had a hand clamped around Reb's shoulder.

Joey laughed. "Kid, you listening?"

"I said fuck off!"

"Kid, I'm trying to do right by you. Your own place, a good doctor, money—whatever you want. I've seen you fight. Hell, I'm not even asking you to do anything you don't want to do. That's why I want you—you've got it in you. You love it. You can bring your boyfriend if you want. You can bring the whole gang and get stuffed from hole to hole, if that's your thing. Hey, I'm an open-minded guy."

"You're a loudmouth, that's what you are," I said under my breath. I was trying to think. I hadn't been a good deputy—never mind what Eli thought—but I'd been decent at tactics, and right then, I was trying to think tactically. If I'd been Joey Jaws, I would have worried that we'd try to cut towards the closest road. If we got to a road, and if we could flag down a vehicle, if we could get to Bragg, we'd have a chance.

"How about this?" Joey shouted. He was twirling the pistol like he was a gunslinger, a huge smile on his face as he strutted up and down a stretch of dirt road. "How about you tell me what you want, kid? Whatever you want, you got it. You want a car? How about that? Kids love cars. You want somebody who will cook and clean? I got a cousin, you wouldn't fucking believe her ziti. You want somebody to scratch your back? Kid, you're looking at him; I'm a hell of a back scratcher."

"Asshole," Posey said and shook his head.

"Let Reb talk to him," I said.

Posey, Reb, and Eli stared at me.

"We need to buy time until the police can get here," I said. "Reb can—"

"Reb isn't going anywhere near that prick," Posey said, drawing Reb against him.

"Maybe you missed it, but that prick took a shot at us. We're lucky he hit the roof; at that distance, with a pistol, he's practically shooting blind."

"It's like I told you." Posey was breathing hard, a ruddy glow under the dark skin of his cheeks. "You're not the type, so you don't understand. You can pussy out if you want, but I'm not going to let anything happen to Reb."

"Come on," Eli muttered. "Why aren't they answering?"

I tried to tune them all out; five seconds of silence would have been nice, five seconds when I didn't have Posey reminding me that I'd been a shit deputy and now I was a shit boyfriend, five seconds when Joey Jaws wasn't yammering nonstop like—

Like he wanted to keep our attention.

Several things happened at once.

I spun around.

Reb growled and twisted out from under Posey's hand to follow my gaze.

"Yes, there are men holding us at gunpoint," Eli glanced at me as he spoke into the phone.

If he said more, I didn't hear it. Three men had come up behind us; their trail was a dark break in the overgrown weeds, and it snaked back toward—I guessed—the road. All three were white. Two of them in their thirties. One had sandy hair and a round face, with a beard that was doing nothing to hide his bad complexion. The second had his head shaved, and he was heavyset in a blue polo and khakis and loafers, like he had to go to an all-dads meeting right after this. I heard that thought, heard how much like Eli it sounded, and realized a hysterical laugh was trying to escape. The third one was younger, with olive skin and his dark hair moussed, and he obviously thought he was pretty. You could tell because he wore his windbreaker too tight, to show off all that beef, and the outline of the holster was visible under the nylon. All three of them had guns pointed at us.

"Don't," the one with the shaved head said when I reached for the Sig.

I stopped and eased my hand away from the weapon.

"Everybody be smart," Shaved Head said. "Joey just wants to talk to the kid."

"You'd better get lost," Posey said. He was touching his prosthesis again. For a moment, I thought I saw something else— twisting, braided shadows.

The pretty one laughed. "Yeah? Or what?"

It was Eli who answered: "Fuck around and find out."

The pretty one started to laugh again. That was when Reb pounced. There was something different about the boy—something my eyes couldn't quite keep up with—but I had the impression of bristling fur and huge teeth. The pretty one screamed, and he and Reb hit the ground and rolled across the packed dirt.

Shaved Head and Bad Beard turned, following Reb and Pretty Boy, and both raised their guns. But they didn't shoot. Reb and Pretty Boy were tangled together, and they couldn't shoot Reb without shooting their friend too. Or maybe he wasn't their friend, and they were just worried about damaging Joey Jaws's new pet. Either way, they hesitated. Pretty Boy's screams rose, getting higher and louder, and Reb snarled and snapped and growled.

In that moment of hesitation, Posey launched himself at Shaved Head. He landed a punch on the side of that gleaming dome, and it rocked the man sideways. The man staggered in a quarter circle, bringing his pistol around, and Posey grabbed his arm.

I was still drawing my Sig when Eli threw himself on Bad Beard's back.

For a moment, I couldn't believe what I was seeing. Eli clung to him like a spider monkey, raining blows down with his fists, screaming at the top of his lungs. Bad Beard staggered under his weight, lurching into the boatshed as he tried to shake Eli off. Then my body rebooted, and I drew the Sig, but I had the same problem as Pretty Boy's friends—I couldn't shoot any of the men without endangering Eli, Posey, or Reb.

Then Bad Beard screamed. I looked over to see Eli gripping the man's ears and pulling. Blood streamed down Bad Beard's neck, and he had the blind, terrified look of a man pushed beyond reason. He crashed into the pontoon boat, cracking Eli's head against the frame of the canvas covering. Eli sagged, and then he and Bad Beard tumbled further into the shed—behind the boat, and out of sight.

Vaguely aware of Reb's snaps and snarls and of Posey's labored breathing, I went after Eli. I heard a shot behind me—distant, my brain registered, and I guessed Joey or one of his buddies had fired, probably out of sheer frustration. Then another shot came, and this one had to have been from either Shaved Head or Pretty Boy. Pretty Boy's screams continued to escalate, and the sounds from Reb made me think of documentaries, the tearing of flesh, the grunts and growls—all the noises of a predator savaging prey.

Then I cleared the boat and got a line of sight on Eli, and I forgot about what was happening behind me.

One of Bad Beard's ears hung from a thread of cartilage, and blood soaked his neck and t-shirt. His gun lay on the ground where he must have dropped it while struggling with Eli. Eli was in a strange, half-kneeling position, like he'd been caught in the act of getting up from the ground. His legs were bent, and his feet scraped the dirt. He had one hand planted on the pontoon like he was using it to brace himself. Bad Beard had a docking line wrapped around Eli's neck, the muscles in his forearms popping as he yanked the improvised noose tighter.

They trained us to shoot to kill. That was the whole point of having a gun. And I'd killed before. But those had been supernatural things, things that there had been no other way to deal with.

Bad Beard drew the line tighter and grinned as Eli clawed at the rope biting into his neck.

For a moment, Eli's eyes weren't darkly hazel, bloodshot and slightly protruding from the blood trapped by the noose. For a moment—only a moment—I was sure they flashed blue.

I fired. The shot caught Bad Beard in the shoulder, and he moved like I'd shoved him. He bent to reach for his fallen gun. This was when he would be the most dangerous, my brain told me, before the pain had caught up to him, while he still thought he was invincible.

In reaching for the gun, though, he dropped the dock line. Eli hit the ground on his ass and then, faster than I could believe, scrambled onto his knees. He grabbed the gun first, pivoted at the waist, and shot Bad Beard in the gut.

Bad Beard let out a shocked breath.

Eli shot him again.

Bad Beard reached for the pontoon boat. His hand brushed a long crimson streak down the canvas cover as his knees buckled.

Eli began firing rapidly, squeezing off shot after shot. Bad Beard fell halfway through the volley of shots, and Eli rose up on his knees and kept firing into the dead man's body until the slide locked back.

My ears echoed with the thunder of gunfire as I holstered the Sig. Distantly, the sounds of Reb and Posey struggling reached me, but the world felt strangely silent as I crouched next to Eli. I put one hand around his, around the gun. He started. Then he twisted, trying to hit me. With my other hand, I grabbed his jaw and held his head, forcing him to meet my eyes. In that first instant, I thought I saw cold blue fire. And then they were Eli's eyes—wide and hazel and brimming with tears. He started to shake. Then he started to cry.

"Come on," I said, although I could barely hear my own words. "We need to go."

I got an arm around Eli and helped him up, and I walked him toward the mouth of the shed. Then I stopped.

Posey lay on the ground, trapped under the dad-bod bulk of Shaved Head. He was trying to protect himself as Shaved Head rained down blows, but his face was a bloody mess, and it was obvious that Posey was starting to slow down.

Reb and Pretty Boy were nowhere to be seen, but then I heard Pretty Boy's scream, and it sounded like it was coming from behind the shed. It rose in pitch to a squeal, and then there was a shot. Reb yelped, the noise full of surprise and pain.

Posey's eyes flashed open. They were totally dark, without any white to them. He sat up, batting aside the blows from Shaved Head, and reached. I thought I saw something that wasn't his prosthesis, something like smoke curling, indistinct in the dusk. Eli cried out, his eyes huge like he'd seen something too. And then, without even seeming to try, Posey ripped the head off the man straddling him.

Blood fountained up from the shredded ruin of his neck. Then Posey pushed himself up, and the body fell off him, the blood geysering into the dirt and the crawfish ponds.

"Reb," he bellowed. He staggered in a circle, and it was obvious that he was keeping himself up by sheer force of will. "Reb!"

A moment later, Reb slunk into view. Blood pasted the Red Man t-shirt to his slender frame, and he moved in a limping, loping stride that I'd never seen from a human before.

He was five yards from Posey when a gun went off, and Posey stumbled and went down.

Reb sprinted to him and dropped onto his knees. He bent over Posey. Over the lingering hammer of gunfire in my ears, I couldn't hear what they said—if they said anything. Posey's eyes were wide, brittle-hard like glass. He was panting. Reb pressed his forehead to Posey's, and Posey stroked Reb's white-blond hair with a bloody hand.

Then Reb was up, running in spite of his limp, darting toward the line of trees and the road. I heard one more gunshot, and when I turned, I saw Joey Jaws paralyzed with rage. Then he shouted something I couldn't hear, and the men with him piled back into the Explorer. A moment later, they were tearing down the dirt road, a rooster tail of dust following them.

Eli turned into me, face pressed against my neck, shaking.

I gripped Eli's wrist once, tightly, until he nodded. Then I stepped away and moved toward Posey. I felt like part of me—my soul or my spirit or my brain, whatever you wanted to call it—lagged a step behind my body. Everything was delayed. Everything out of frame. I squatted next to Posey, who had his eyes half-closed and was crying.

"I need to turn you over," I said, my words muffled inside my own head.

He nodded.

The shot was clean through the shoulder, which was a miracle only partially explained by the fact that Joey—or whoever had fired on Posey—had been almost a hundred yards away. I tore strips from

Posey's shirt and packed the wound as best I could, ignoring Posey's howls.

When I'd finished, Posey caught my arm, his hand tacky with drying blood, his grip impossibly strong. "No police," he said. I could hear him, but only barely.

"You need a hospital."

"No hospital. No police."

I glanced at Eli. Eli grimaced. Then his head came up, and he stared at the old brick house with the peeling roof.

"Dag." His voice was rough. He stopped and rubbed his throat; red marks showed where the dock line had bit into his skin. He cocked his head as though trying to listen. "Somebody's in there."

I could barely hear him, and he was standing right next to me; I had no idea how he could hear anything that far away. But I trusted his judgment, and as I watched the house, movement flickered behind the old, dirty windows.

"We need to move," Posey said. He was trying to sit up. "They're going after Reb."

"Be quiet," Eli said.

I held out a hand for him to stay, and I started toward the house.

Eli followed, of course.

"He ripped his head off," Eli said and touched his neck. "Dag, did you—"

"Not right now."

Eli swallowed and nodded.

"Whoever's in there," I said, looking at the house, "they aren't after Reb. If it were Fen, she would have come charging out by now to blow our heads off, and if it were Nelda Pie, she would have stabbed us in the back the minute we turned around."

"They're hiding," Eli said. "And they didn't help us."

"Reb could have gone somewhere else," I said. "A toolshed in the middle of a canebrake. A corn crib ten miles past nowhere. But he came here."

"He lived here. Or close by, anyway."

I nodded, but I kept walking.

It was one of those Montgomery Ward houses, the kind they used to ship on the railroads in kits. The brick was crumbling at the corners, and the tuck-pointing looked like dirty ice. Strips of the tar-paper roof fluttered in tattered pennants. When I tried the door, it opened an inch and then stuck on warped flooring.

Frantic, scrabbling sounds came from inside.

"Dag," Eli said.

I shoved, and then I shoved again, and the door skidded open.

A hallway offered a view of the far side of the house where two people were trying to force the boards out of a window. Light spilled in around me, and when it touched them, they stopped and turned.

It was hard not to see the resemblance: the fair hair; the slenderness—part of my brain said, the wolfishness—of fine features; even the way they held themselves. The two women were different ages, but although it was clear they were related, I had a hard time guessing exactly how. Sisters, maybe, with a long gap between them. Or mother and daughter, but if so, the mother couldn't have been more than thirty, and the daughter had to be in her late teens.

"Hey," I said. "Stop right there."

They gave up on the window and stared at me, fear tightening their faces. Nothing changed in their posture, but now they looked poised, the way Reb had crouched before he'd launched himself at Joey's pretty thug.

"Why don't you come outside," I said, "nice and slow, and you can tell me who you are and what you're doing here?"

Eli's touch startled me, and when I glanced sidelong, his face was open in wonder. "Dag," he said. "I think they're why Reb was here. Why he came here, I mean."

My jaw loosened as understanding hit me, and I turned to consider them again. I said it aloud because I still couldn't quite believe it, but Eli was already nodding.

"They're his pack."

ELI (5)

Because Dag and I had absolutely zero clue what to do, we fell back on our standard: we went to his parents.

Getting away from the farm turned out to be easier than I'd expected. Reb's packmates—their names, they told us, were Dutch and Lurnice—had an ancient Toyota hatchback hidden a quarter mile from the crawfish farm, tucked up a coulee off the same road Joey Jaws must have used. Dag drove us back to the farm, and we got Posey in the front seat, and I crammed in the back with the werewolf Bobbsey Twins. We saw no sign of Reb or Joey or, for that matter, the sheriff's department. I wondered if Joey had something to do with that. I thought maybe Dag was wondering too.

The only point of friction came when we reached Posey's truck.

"He needs a hospital," Dag said. He and I had gotten out of the hatchback, and he was leaning on the driver's door.

"I'm not going to a fucking hospital," Posey shouted.

Dag shut the door.

"He got shot," Dag said in a quieter voice.

"And the hospital will be required to report a gunshot wound," I said. "And how long do you think it'll take Joey to hear about that?" I knew that look, the way Dag's eyebrows drew together, the uncharacteristic tightness of his jaw. "Dag, something—something isn't normal about Posey."

I didn't want to say more. Apparently, I didn't need to because Dag blew out a breath and nodded. Then he looked at me, and he touched my neck. Tender skin stung when his fingertips brushed it. "You should be in a hospital," he said.

"I'm fine."

"Try that again. See if you can say it without sounding like you screamed yourself hoarse at a rock concert."

"Oh my God," I murmured as I took his hand and kissed his fingers. "Nobody says rock concert anymore. How old are you?"

He cleared his throat. Then he held out the Toyota's keys. "Don't speed and don't stop for anything until we get to my parents. I'll be right behind you."

I stared at the keys. "I can drive a truck."

"I know you can drive a truck."

"It's emasculating, giving me the keys to the hatchback automatically, like you think I can't drive a big, manly truck."

"Eli," he said, "are you really trying to pick a fight with me right now?"

"Just keeping in practice. Oh, you know what? Maybe you can work on getting physical. Grab my shirt. Jerk me around."

Instead, he kissed me and gave me a gentle push toward the truck.

"Oh, God no," I said. "I can't drive that."

And somehow, ladies and gentlemen, I still have a boyfriend.

Dag's parents lived in a section of Bragg known as Fogmile—lower middle class, with small houses and sagging chain-link fences, older-model trucks and cars, everything maintained but, you could tell, with an effort.

When we got to Dag's parents' house, the air smelled like simmering onions and shrimp and the muddled heat of Cajun spices. The usual cooing picked up. Gloria, Dag's mother, was in her sixties, and she had iron-gray hair in a set that would have been perfectly appropriate for the Republican National Convention.

"Hello, Dagobert," she said, bussing his cheek. "Eli, you're skin and bones. Get into the kitchen right this instant; you need to eat."

"Hi, Gloria," I said, accepting a kiss as well.

"And what happened to your neck? And you're covered in blood! Dagobert, have you been trying breath play? We talked about this—you said you'd FaceTime your father or me so we could make sure nothing went wrong."

Dag was supporting Posey, and he adjusted his grip and made a face. Posey let out a weird noise that—for a guy who had been shot—sounded suspiciously like a laugh.

"That's 'cause I told you ten different ways we weren't going to try breath play, and you wouldn't listen. It was the only way to get you to stop talking about it. And in case you didn't notice, this is Posey, and somebody shot him, so can we please stop talking about my sex life for five minutes?"

"Well, get him on the couch, dear," Gloria said. "Why are you standing here talking about breath play?"

"That's what I was wondering, Gloria," I said in what I thought of as my most helpful tone.

Dag glared at me as he helped Posey into the house.

"And your father's in the kitchen," Gloria said. "He needs help with someone who wants him to come on their face. And who are these treasures?"

I was still clearing my airway from the spit-choke as Gloria hugged first Lurnice and then Dutch. The two girls stood stiffly, arms at their sides, and let the hugs happen—which was good thinking on their part. My experience with Dag's parents over the last couple of years had taught me that the best thing to do was to just let it happen, whatever it was.

As I introduced the girls, movement came from the kitchen, and Hubert appeared in the hallway, phone in hand. Dag's father was a big, bearded man who was one hundred percent straight, had been with the Knights of Columbus longer than I'd been alive, and, without a doubt, knew more about being gay than Dag and I put together. "He's definitely a twink, Gloria, but I don't think—well, what in the world? Hello, Eli. What happened to your neck? And what's all that blood? Dagobert, I thought we talked about breath play."

"We did talk about breath play, Hubert," I said. "We talked at great length, and Dag promised he'd FaceTime you."

"I'm leaving," Dag said. "You can figure this out yourselves."

"And who are these beautiful young ladies?"

"Nobody," Dag said. "Don't talk to them. Don't even look at them. At this point, they can still leave and be nice, normal people once they get away from this house."

"He's hungry," Gloria confided to the girls. "He always gets grumpy when he hasn't eaten."

"I'm not grumpy!" Dag said.

"Eli, when did he eat?"

"Well, I think he had some quinoa a few hours ago."

"Quinoa," Gloria said to herself. "Skin and bones, and you're eating quinoa. I've got an etouffee on. Let's get the two of you freshened up. Eli, you and Dagobert and your friend can use the hall bath."

"This strapping young man?" Hubert said, eyeing Posey, who now lay with his eyes closed. "He's a grade-A piece of meat, definitely hunk material, but good luck trying to get all three of you in that tub."

"Not at the same time," Dag said. "This isn't a threesome. Not everything, despite my parents' belief to the contrary, is a threesome."

"Why not?" Hubert asked.

"Ok," I said when Dag's face started to turn red. I rubbed his shoulder and nudged him toward the hall. "Posey, are you all right for a few minutes?"

After a moment, he gave a tiny nod.

"Boys," Hubert called, "could you rinse the tub out when you're done? Your mother cleans that bathroom, you know."

"I'm going to kill myself," Dag said as I shut the bathroom door behind us. "That's the only way out. They're never going to die, and I'm never going to be able to have an orgasm again, so I might as well end it now."

I laughed as I helped him out of his shirt and pants and boxers. He returned the favor for me. As the adrenaline from the fight had died down, the aches had started up, reminding me that I'd been very stupid and, as a result, gotten my ass handed to me. Dag, of course, was gentle, but I still gasped a few times.

"Your shoulder?" he asked once he'd finished easing my shirt off.

I nodded.

He probed it gently and made a dissatisfied noise. Then he turned me. I was facing the mirror, which wasn't as much of a trigger as it would have been a year ago. I'd been struggling with Prozac weight for a couple of years, and it was nice to finally see some progress. Not enough, of course. And not quickly. I still didn't have much of a chest, and my legs—

"Stop it," Dag murmured. He examined me slowly, and when he pressed on my hip, I hissed. "You deserve it," he said in that same low voice. "You're going to have a bruise the size of California here. Otherwise, you look all right."

"All right?" I asked and turned to face him.

"Eli, what happened today?"

I knew what he was asking about. He was asking about those moments I'd lost track of. One minute, I'd been standing there, staring at Joey's thugs, thinking these weird thoughts that I couldn't shake—how the guy with the patchy beard would look with his throat torn open, arterial spray filling the air like confetti. Weird, messed-up shit like that. And the next, it was like someone had turned on a spotlight and shone it right in my eyes, the blue glare making it impossible to see. I'd come back to myself kneeling on the ground, a pistol in my hands, the smell of gunpowder in my nose, and the guy with the beard on the ground, dead.

"I killed that guy, didn't I?"

"He was trying to kill you."

I shook my head.

Dag pulled me against him, his arms warm and firm around me. "How are you doing?"

"Not good." I spoke into his chest, smelling his sweat and the hint of talcum powder and the woodsy aftershave he liked. "I don't know.

I don't feel anything, I guess. I don't remember it, and—God, Dag, I killed someone."

"If you hadn't, he would have killed you and me and Posey." He kissed my temple. "I'm sorry you had to do that; it's a terrible thing. But you didn't have any other choice." And then, in a tone I didn't quite understand, he said, "I shouldn't have let that happen."

I pushed back from him, widening the circle of his arms, to look into his eyes. He looked away. Through the door, Hubert's voice filtered down the hall. It sounded like he was talking about golf. Good luck, Posey.

I kissed Dag on the lips, my mouth dry, and then I pulled him toward the shower.

The water was hot. Dag took his time with the soap, and the water that sluiced around our feet was pink at first, and then it wasn't. I tilted my face into the spray when I started to cry so Dag wouldn't notice. He knelt and washed my legs, my feet. He stayed there between my legs, his forehead against my belly, the wet bristles of his hair pleasantly rough and silky at the same time.

When he took me into his mouth, I was still soft, but that didn't last long. I planted one hand on the tile and tried not to make any noise, my palm sliding on the wet ceramic. I reached out with my other hand and caught the curtain, jangling it on its rings. Dag wasn't doing anything fancy, just slowly moving his head up and down, pausing to curl his tongue around the head of my dick, alternating the sucking wet with that velvet contact.

"I want to fuck your face," I whispered. My cheeks were on fire, but when Dag nodded around my cock, I grabbed a handful of that gunmetal hair. My body was a bundle of cut wires, sparking and crackling. The cold that had been with me for months was receding, driven back by hot water and what Dag was doing to me, and I realized I was warm. Then I was beyond warm—I was hot, and it was like being awake, suddenly feeling the difference.

I only lasted a few seconds, twisting my fingers in his hair and thrusting. He choked, but he stayed on, and then I lost it. The orgasm hit me like another klieg light, so bright that I couldn't see anything, and I went away from myself again. When I came back, terror floated under the backwash of pleasure—how long had I been gone? What had I done? But chill, water-slick tile was still under my palm, and my fingers ached around a fistful of Dag's hair.

"Oh shit," I whispered, easing my fingers open. "I'm sorry. I'm sorry, baby."

Dag shook his head. He still had my dick in his mouth, suckling softly now, and he adjusted his position, widening his knees. The spray hammered the broad, chiseled muscles of his back, and those muscles moved now as he jerked himself off. I couldn't hear him over the spray, but I felt the sound he made when he came to the edge, the vibrations transmitting themselves through his mouth into my body. His jaw tightened, and he sucked harder as the muscles in his back flexed and froze, and then his body surrendered. I heard the sound of his load hitting the fiberglass, shot after shot. For another moment, he stayed where he was. Then he eased himself off me, and he knelt there, head hanging, water combing his hair into his face.

I crouched next to him and put my arms around him. "I love you," I said into his ear. "Thank you."

Voice rough, he said, "I love you too." He stroked my flank, the water making his fingers stutter along my skin. "E—"

I heard it in his voice. The guilt. The self-blame. In our relationship, self-loathing was actually my realm of expertise; Dagobert LeBlanc—who had loving and supportive parents, who only ever did good things, and who was pure as the driven snow—was an absolute rookie.

"We're both safe," I said. "You got us here. You kept us safe."

I thought, for a moment, he'd say more. That he'd argue. Or that he'd press for an answer about what had happened, why I had done what I had done. The answer wouldn't satisfy him; I didn't know, because I didn't remember. But instead, all he did was wipe his face and nod.

I tried to put a grin in my voice as I tickled his neck. "But seriously, Dag, how much did you shoot?"

He looked up at me. After a moment, he wiped water away again. Deliberately.

"You get sex all the time," I said. "It's not like you're backed up."

"Ok, thanks. I'm turning the water off now."

"Without rinsing the tub?"

"E, don't—"

"Think of your mother."

The slap to my flank sounded so much louder because of the water.

"That's it," Dag said, coming after me as I scrambled backward, yelping and massaging my flank. "That did it. No more sex. I'm officially never having sex again."

But for the record, he did chub up a little when I was drying him off. I didn't say anything, but I think he noticed me noticing because he definitely gave me the stink eye.

He got clothes for us from his bedroom—which his parents had left untouched after we moved out. I was swimming in one of his old

Braxton Bragg Memorial High football sweatshirts, and the matching track pants were the right length but kept sliding off my ass. Dag, on the other hand, looked like a dream in sweats and a t-shirt, finger-combing his hair as he stood barefoot in front of the mirror.

"I'm going to cut all your hair off again," I said from the bed. "I'm tired of you being so handsome. I'm going to buzz it while you're asleep."

"I don't think I'd sleep through that."

"I'm going to roofie you. Not for sex, so don't get any ideas."

"I will not get any ideas about you roofying me for sex I wouldn't remember anyway."

"If you're going to be a smartass, I'll shave your head bald."

Gloria and Hubert, of course, were beaming when we went out into the kitchen.

"Don't say anything," Dag said. "If you don't want me to put you in a nursing home, then don't even open your mouths."

"You're so awful sometimes, Dagobert," Gloria said. "Eli, isn't he simply awful?"

"He's got a wicked mouth," I said and waggled my eyebrows.

Both his parents laughed. Gloria actually blushed and touched Hubert's arm.

"You like him so much?" Dag said. "You think he's so funny? Fine, you can date him."

"Dagobert," Hubert said. "Don't talk about your partner like that. And don't talk to your mother and father in that tone. It's disrespectful."

"Disrespectful? He said he was going to roofie me and cut off all my hair."

"That sounds very nice, dear," Gloria said, rising from her seat at the table. "Now, who wants etouffee?"

Apparently, we both did.

"The girls are resting in the guest room," Gloria said as she loaded a plate—so much food that, in spite of what my stomach was saying, I hoped it was meant for Dag. "But that young man in the living room needs a hospital. Your third—Hubert, is that the right word?"

"I think he's called a hinge. Or maybe Eli is the hinge. I'm not sure."

"Nobody's a hinge," Dag said. "Or a third. Or whatever. And are you really only going to give me eight shrimp?"

Gloria rolled her eyes and picked a few more shrimp out of the pot. And then, floating the plate past Dag, she said, "This one is for Eli."

Dag turned a betrayed look on me as she set the plate in front of me. I mimed helplessness.

"Eli is probably the hinge," Hubert said. "He's a natural ten, so it makes sense that two randy young bucks would both connect strongly with him."

"Doesn't anybody listen to me?" Dag asked. "It's like I'm not even here. There's no threesome. And you'd better give me as many shrimp as you gave Eli."

"I'm speaking hypothetically, Dagobert," Hubert said. "It's a hypothetical scenario."

"Hypothetically," I said around a mouthful of shrimp, "thank you, Hubert."

"You're welcome, Eli."

"I'd make an excellent hinge."

"Oh, sure," Dag said. "Then you could roofie both your boyfriends. Stop encouraging them."

"Don't you have any manners at all?" Gloria asked as she set a plate down in front of Dag. "Eli is a wonderful young man."

"You're lucky to have Eli," Hubert said.

"And Eli's lucky to have Dagobert," Gloria said.

"Nobody's talking about Eli, Gloria."

"You were," I said. "A minute ago. About how I'm a perfect ten and I'd make a natural hinge."

"Well, yes, Eli, but that was a separate conversation. Try to keep up."

"Dagobert always liked them simple," Gloria said.

"I'm going to run away from home," Dag said. "That's what I should do. I'm going to put some clothes and a toothbrush in my pillowcase, and I'm just going to walk out the front door. I bet you'd all feel pretty lousy if I did that."

"Probably, dear," Gloria said. "Now see if your third—I'm sorry, your hinge—wants to eat, and then you need to help your father with this young man on the phone. Something about getting his rocks off, I think."

It was probably a good thing that Dag wasn't in the process of swallowing anything at that particular moment because he might have choked to death.

Since I was a kind, patient, sensitive, and understanding boyfriend, I told Gloria we were going to save the rocks-getting-off operation for later and would, right then, eat in the living room. Posey was still lying on the sofa, eyes closed. The bloody strip of cloth packing the wound looked rust-colored in the dim light.

"All right," Dag said between bites. "Talk."

Posey stayed still.

"Either you stop faking, or I'm hauling your butt to the hospital. Your call."

After a moment, Posey's eyes opened to slits. He had dark eyes, but they weren't the inked-out black orbs that I'd seen earlier—more specifically, in the moment before he'd ripped a man's head off. His prosthesis looked normal too. When I turned my head, I thought something rippled at the corner of my vision, but that could have been the exhaustion. I was trying not to remember what I'd seen at the crawfish farm, the—what? tentacles?—that had flashed into view for a moment as he tore that man's head from his neck. But I was having a hard time forgetting, and the etouffee didn't taste like anything in my mouth now.

"How bad was it?" Posey asked, the words dull and dead. "Reb's leg?" He struggled to speak and then swallowed. "He heals fast. If he can hide, he'll be ok."

"Reb's fine," I said. "He can take care of himself. We're worried about you."

Posey let out a broken noise that might have been a laugh. "I heal fast too. We all do." He turned his head into the pillow, shifting around, and I thought I saw dark spots on the fabric where he had wiped away tears. "He can take care of himself, but not if it's him against the whole world. He needs me. Christ, I fucked up. He was counting on me, and I really fucked up."

"If you're talking about the fight," Dag said, "then you handled yourself better than most people, and if you're talking about the rest of it, well, we all should have been paying better attention. I don't know if it would have helped. Joey has money and resources we don't; he could have had twenty different cars following us, and there's no way to beat a tail like that."

Posey tightened his grip around the pillow and stared emptily in the middle distance.

"What did you mean," I asked, "when you said, 'We all do'?"

He squeezed his eyes shut.

"Posey, this is important."

Dag leaned forward in his seat; his etouffee was gone, I noticed, and he set the empty plate aside. "You want us to help Reb? This is the way to do it. Tell us what you've been holding back."

"You saw." He opened his eyes and looked at me. Then he waited.

"I don't know." I scraped my fork against the plate. "Maybe I saw something. I don't know. I don't know what I saw."

Making a face as the movement pulled at his injured shoulder, Posey sat up. He touched the polymer prosthesis. His fingers played lightly at it. And then they settled where it was attached to his arm. "It's a never-you-mind charm. That's one of the reasons we stay with her. We can go out in the world without everybody and their mother either screaming their heads off or trying to kill us."

My mouth was dry, but I said, "Nelda Pie?"

He nodded. "She...wants people like me. Looks for them. And then she holds on to them, uses them. She's smart like that; she never lets anything useful go to waste."

"What do you mean," Dag asked, "people like you?"

"People like us." Posey looked at me again. "Half-breeds."

In the kitchen, Gloria was asking Hubert about a crossword puzzle clue—six across, *like a door when it's*—and Hubert was mumbling distracted answers, probably still dealing with the internet boy and whatever the hell that situation was.

"Eli's not a half-breed," Dag said. "That witch said that to confuse him—"

"Dag," I said, barely more than a whisper, and put a hand on his arm. I was remembering the strange people at the Stoplight, the bizarre stories—the tiger-woman, and the boy playing pin-finger, the wait staff who walked like they had hooves instead of feet, the old woman who might have stepped out of a Civil War photograph. I remembered Nelda Pie asking me about the hashok's bite, if I'd purged myself or washed myself or something. I remembered the look in her eyes when she realized I had no idea what she was talking about. I cleared my throat, but the words still broke in my mouth when I said, "Tell me."

"Half-breeds are made," Posey said. "All of them. That's what makes us different from, well, somebody like Reb. You're attacked, or you're tricked, or you make a deal. Some of the ones in the Stoplight, Nelda Pie did that to them. She's got loads of them—that's what people say, anyway. The worst ones, you never see, but she's got them."

"And they stay?" Dag asked.

"Where are they going to go?"

"What happened to you?" I asked. Posey glanced down at his lap, and a fire went through my face. "I'm sorry, you don't have to—"

"I was fishing. Out on the salt. Perfect day, middle of June." He swallowed. "It came up and took me. It had me for—for days. I was in and out for a lot of it. I woke up on the shore, not a mark on me. I thought it'd been, I don't know, maybe one of my buddies had dropped a couple of tabs of acid in my beer. A few months later, I started to change. Little things at first. And then—" He stopped, and he shut his mouth, the knuckle of his thumb pressing against his lips until they turned white.

Little things, I thought. You got a weird chill on a hot day. You had a strange thought, something you couldn't explain. You blacked out, lost time, and when your boyfriend asked, you didn't have any answers.

"Rebellion is different?" Dag asked.

"He's a rougarou," Posey said. "That's who he is, how he was born. The rest of us, we got...infected."

"What happens?" I asked.

Out of the corner of my eye, I saw the change in Dag's face when he understood the question, but I kept my gaze on Posey.

"Don't answer that," Dag said.

"What happens, Posey? What happens to half-breeds? Does it keep going? Does it get worse and worse?"

"Keep your mouth shut," Dag said, and he caught my upper arm. "Eli, can I talk to you?"

"No, I'm asking—"

"Thank you," Dag said, and he hauled me up from the love seat and dragged me down the hall and into his bedroom.

"Let go of me," I whispered savagely, aware of Hubert and Gloria just down the hall and, even in the midst of this, unwilling to involve them. "Let go of me! Let go!" I tried to pull away. Then I struck out at Dag—wide, open-handed blows on his chest and shoulders and arms. I could hear my shrill gasps for breath. He absorbed the blows, grunting once in a while, and when I slowed down, he pulled me into a hug and held me until I stopped struggling, one hand stroking the back of my neck. After a while, my body went limp, and I dried my face on his shoulder and wiggled until he let go of me.

"Can you just—can you leave me alone, please? For a minute?"

Dag didn't go anywhere, of course. In a quiet voice, he said, "He doesn't know what happens, Eli. And if you ask him, he's going to tell you a story he's heard, and I don't want that in your head."

I was crying again in spite of my best efforts, and I had a hand over my eyes. "Please go away. I just want you to go away."

"Would you like to lie down for a while?"

"No. I want you to go away."

He was silent for what felt like a long time. "Let's lie down."

And since he apparently wasn't going anywhere, I let him herd me to the bed. We stretched out next to each other. Our breathing was out of sync, mine shallow and rapid and catching in my throat, his slow and deep. The first time I'd come here, he'd had a blue light, and it had rippled on the wall so that it felt like we were underwater. I tried to breathe myself back to that place and that time when things made sense, even though part of my brain knew that back then, we'd been fighting a monster we hadn't understood, and nothing had made sense. Maybe nothing had ever made sense.

When I shivered, he put his arm around me and drew a blanket up. I was still cold. I was always cold. I was going to be cold forever, I realized, getting colder and colder, losing pieces of myself as whatever the hashok had put inside me slowly took over. And then I started to cry all over again, but this time was different, like something had come unmoored inside me.

I pressed my face into his side and, as the tears came harder, choked out, "Dag, I'm going to die."

I don't know how long it took for me to really cry myself out. When I was done, he was still running his fingers through my hair and talking softly—nonsense stuff, plans for the future, stuff he was studying at school, stats for the Saints, things that didn't chain up in any logical order. I dried my face on his quilt, and he handed me some tissues, and I blew my nose. My eyes were hot and raw when I made myself sit up.

"Sorry," I said scratchily.

"You don't have anything to be sorry for." He was still lying down, one arm behind his head, biceps looking fucking huge. He rubbed my leg with his other hand. "That's a lot to hear. That's a lot to take in."

"It's better, you know," I said, pressing the tissues under my nose for a moment. "It's better to know, to actually have a, you know, an explanation, and like, a term for it." I wiped over the tender skin where I'd already rubbed the tissues too many times. "Who the fuck am I kidding, Dag? It's not better. It's a million times worse. I wish I'd never asked."

"It's better to know," he said. "Now we can do something about it."

"Great. We can get me one of those Hannibal Lecter mouth things. That way, as I slowly and inevitably turn into a fucking monster, we're prepared."

"You didn't even watch *The Silence of the Lambs*. You said like ten different things about how bad Buffalo Bill was at sewing, and then you took a nap."

In spite of everything, I smiled.

"So far," Dag said slowly, "everything we've learned about supernatural creatures has been, well, also true about natural creatures. The way they live, I mean. The principles of zoology."

"I will burn your flashcards right now," I said. "I will ask your dad to lend me his chainsaw and I'll cut your textbooks in half."

"This happens in nature, too. We talked about this like it was a virus before. And now we know more, about how people change. They've got a word for organisms with two sets of DNA—a better word than half-breed. They're called chimeras. They happen in nature. They even happen in people, like when one twin absorbs another, and then they have two sets of DNA." My mouth made a horrified O, and Dag stopped and asked, "What?"

"Not. Helping."

He grinned. "It can happen if you get a bone marrow transplant. It even happens to pregnant women. And it happens in plants all the time. A lot of the plants we eat are chimeras."

"Oh good, so you'll be able to eat me."

"I already did today." He just laughed when I hit him in the face with the pillow. Pushing it aside, he said, "There's so much we don't know, Eli. The more we learn, the better chance we have of beating this thing."

I wanted to lie down, close my eyes, and sleep for a year. But I nodded. "I'm only agreeing because I honestly can't stand any more of your unconditional love and support."

"That's all right. I'm only being unconditionally loving and supporting because I know it annoys you."

I stared at him.

He was trying not to smile.

"How dare you?"

"Come on." As he sat up, a little more of the smile slipped out.

"Dagobert LeBlanc! Don't you dare become snarky and bitchy and—and snarky with me!"

"You already said snarky." He caught my hand and tugged me up. "Let's go talk to those girls."

"I'm going to borrow your mother's wooden spoon. I'm going to spank your ass until you can't sit down."

"She has a million wooden spoons, so you'll have to be more specific, and anyway, my parents would love that."

"I'm the bitchy one. I'm the mean one. I'm the one who gets to undermine our relationship and be passive-aggressive and be—" I barely caught it in time.

"Snarky?" he asked as he led me out into the hall.

"Gloria," I shouted toward the kitchen, "where do you keep the wooden spoons?"

"The ones for spanking Dagobert?" she called back. "Or for cooking?"

"She has two sets?" I whispered.

"Eli," Hubert bellowed, "if you're interested in a discipline kink, I printed off a very informative article. Apparently, the gays love discipline."

"We do?" I whispered.

"We can compare notes!"

"You deserve that," Dag told me. "You really do."

After a quick stop to wash my face and check for any incipient monster changes, I joined Dag outside the guest room. I could hear Hubert asking Gloria where he'd put that printout.

"Hurry," I said under my breath.

It might have been my imagination, but it seemed like Dag took extra long to knock on the door.

"Come in," one of the girls said.

It was a small room, barely big enough for a queen-sized bed, a trestle table that had been pressed into service as a desk, and a hard-backed chair. The girls sat on their bed. It was clear that they'd showered, and both of them wore borrowed clothes. Lurnice, the younger, was rawboned, her skin tight and pink, and she had long, strawberry-blond hair that was straight and fine. She wore a sweatshirt that said simply SAUSAGE STUFFERS, INC. with a picture of an enormous, phallic sausage. Dutch, the older, had the same gossamer hair as her sister—er, daughter, maybe?—and the same prominent cheekbones and jaw. She had gotten a sweatshirt that showed a naked man's behind, dusted with what I seriously hoped was powdered sugar but might have been cocaine, and the words SWEET CHEEKS—ALL NIGHT LONG.

"Good God," I said.

"Please be nice to me," Dag said.

"If your parents had been any less supportive, I honestly think you might have died from neglect."

"I said be nice."

The two women shared a look and then turned identical stares back on us.

"Mind if I sit?" I asked. Neither responded, so I sat in the hard-backed chair. Dag stood behind me, his hand warm and heavy on my shoulder. "We need to talk about Reb," I said. "Where do you want to start?"

They shared another look. Dutch had a deep voice for a woman, but there was an unsteadiness in it as she asked, "What you said about pack, how did you—why did you say that?"

"Well, I don't know. You were there, hiding. And it was obvious Reb chose that spot for a reason."

"He chose it because he was sentimental," Lurnice said. Dutch threw her a look, but Lurnice didn't seem to notice. "It made him easy to track."

Dutch turned her attention to me again. "What else?"

"I mean, you look like you could be related to Reb," I said. "Your features, and the way you're built. Although you don't look like siblings, so maybe cousins? And there's something about how you move." I hesitated. "Don't take this the wrong way, but it made me think of him, the way he moved. It's not quite...human."

Dutch and Lurnice shared another long look.

"He was trying to protect us," Lurnice finally said quietly. She looked down, one hand playing with the stitching around the sausage on her shirt.

"Protect you from what?" Dag asked.

The silence stretched out—ten seconds, then twenty. Lurnice shifted on the bed, color seeping into her cheeks, while Dutch set her jaw and stared at a spot on the wall. As a connoisseur of lying, guilt, and shame, I could see that I was dealing with a couple of amateurs.

"You feel bad because he was trying to keep you safe from Nelda Pie and Joey Jaws, and instead, he got himself taken, is that it?" I made my voice as gentle as I could. "He saved all of us, you know, leading them away like that. That's why we're all alive right now."

Dag's fingers tightened on my shoulder. He bent, his mouth to my ear, and in his cop voice whispered, "Don't answer the questions for them."

"I've got this," I whispered back.

"Why don't you tell us what's going on?" Dag asked as he straightened.

Dutch's head swiveled toward us, her eyes glittering like a bird of prey's. "You're the ones who killed the hashok."

I didn't say anything, and neither did Dag.

"They're supposed to live in the bayous," she said. "In swamps and marshlands and wetlands. Did you know that?"

"We know," Dag said. "These were different."

"But didn't you ever wonder why they were different?"

Lurnice looked up, surprise etched on her face before her features smoothed out again.

"What do you mean?" I asked.

"Why they changed their behavior? Did you ever ask yourself why?"

"Animals change their behavior for all sorts of reasons," Dag said slowly. "Changes to the environment, usually. A disruption of their food source, climate change—" He stopped. In a different voice, he said, "Pressure from a new predator."

Dutch held his gaze.

"Oh my God," Dag said.

"What?" I asked. "What am I missing?"

"For creatures like us," Dutch said, drawing a circle on the quilt, "the world is changing. And we have to change with it, or we will die."

"The hashok was, like—what would you call it, Dag? An apex predator? Trust me, it didn't have to change."

"Apex predators do change their behavior," Dag said, squeezing my shoulder in excitement. "Not often, but they do. Almost always, the behavioral modifications are because of human expansion and compromised ecosystems. Pressure from humans triggers a cascade of changes, starting with apex predators. You see it with wolves, for example, the way humans hunted them almost to extinction. And here, you've got hunters, right?"

"I don't think—" I tried.

"Like Fen," Dag said in a rush. "Apex predators are rare, relatively speaking, and their populations aren't controlled by other predators. That means, on the one hand, they've got fewer antipredator adaptations than other species. And on the other hand, it means when humans start putting pressure on apex predators— either because they're hunting them or because they're disrupting their environment, destroying their habitats, etcetera—those predators start exhibiting prey-like responses. They adapt. The hashok, for example, started disguising themselves as people and hiding in human communities, which they'd never done before. In fact—" He stopped so quickly that in a cartoon, he would have gulped.

"In fact what?" I asked, twisting to look up at him.

He didn't quite meet my eyes. "Those changes would have trickled throughout the entire ecosystem. So, you wouldn't only see changes in the apex predators, like the hashok. You'd see changes in mesopredators and in prey species too."

"Like the fifolet," I said. "So, what? Humans have been living in Louisiana for hundreds of years. Why the change now?"

"There are more people now," Dutch said.

"And weapons are better," Dag said, "technology is better. There are fewer places to hide. But if I had to guess, I'd say it's about Nelda Pie and Fen and people like them—people actively applying pressure to supernatural creatures. Nelda Pie wants to control them and use them. Fen wants to kill them. It amounts to the same thing: more direct, focused pressure from people with really powerful tools."

I turned back to Lurnice and Dutch. Lurnice was staring at her sister/mom, and Dutch's cheeks were pink as she studied the quilt.

"You still haven't answered Dag," I said. "What's going on?"

Lurnice made a soft noise and pulled on her sweatshirt. Dutch grimaced.

"I asked you a question." I sat forward. "Don't sit there and ignore me."

"We don't know," Lurnice said.

"Bullshit."

"We don't!" Dutch barked. Her head came up, and for a moment, an afterimage ghosted behind her: an impression of snapping jaws, a blood-flecked muzzle. It wasn't like anything I'd seen around Reb, but then, I'd only been around Reb a couple of times, and then only briefly. A day before, I might have convinced myself it was my imagination, but now I wasn't so sure. Her expression tightened, as though she were locking something down, and in a quieter voice, she said, "We don't know what's going on."

"You don't know why people are looking for Reb?" Dag asked.

They shook their heads.

"Do you know where he is?" Dag asked.

They shook their heads again.

"You've got to do better than that," I said.

Dag squeezed my shoulder, and when I glanced back at him, he nodded to the hall.

"You can stay in your room and think about your choices, young ladies," I said as Dag hustled me into the hall. "And you can come out when you're ready to tell us the truth." When Dag pulled the door shut, I said, "And you're in trouble too. Spankings all around."

"Eli."

"They're lying. Or they're hiding something. Or both. They're not even very good at it—you can tell they haven't had time to make up a coherent story."

"They're scared. The person who was keeping them safe is gone, and they don't know where he is or if he's alive or who we are. We're lucky they didn't pop the screen out of the window and bolt."

"Did you see when she just about attacked us? Even in the fight, Reb didn't get like that; she must have been about to lose her mind."

"I didn't see anything except a couple of scared girls, Eli." He hesitated. "When you say you saw something—"

"Don't change the subject. What didn't you want to tell me in there? Why did I practically hear brakes squealing as you tried to stop whatever was about to come out of your mouth?"

"It's nothing. It's something I read, and it doesn't apply—"

"Dagobert, do not make me march you into that kitchen, sit you down in front of your parents, and describe to them, in excruciating detail, how considerate and gentle and tender you are as a lover."

"You threaten that all the time."

"I'm going to tell them about that time you stopped in the middle of riding me so you could fix the pillows."

"Oh my God."

"You were worried I was getting a crick in my neck."

"You were getting a crick in your neck! And you cannot tell my parents that."

"They'll be so proud."

He dry-washed his face and let out a long breath. When he dropped his hands, he had a line between his eyebrows. "Historically," he said, "in a few, limited cases that I've read—"

"Spit it out, cowboy. That's a line from the Western porno your mom and I are scripting, by the way."

"I wasn't kidding about running away. You'd never find me."

"Dag!"

"One of the prey-behavior adaptations researchers have seen? In apex predators, I mean, in human-dominated areas? Hybridization."

"Half-breeds," I said. "Chimeras. Like me."

"This is why I didn't say anything. There are only a few examples—wolves and dogs are one—and that's not necessarily applicable here. In fact, it's actually a positive sign that non-lethal control methods—"

He stopped at whatever he saw on my face. Outside, a car with a blown muffler drove past, breaking the evening's stillness. Dag rubbed my arm. I let him for a few minutes until I couldn't stand it anymore and pulled away.

"What are we going to do now?"

"We're going to rest," Dag said. "We're exhausted, and we're not thinking clearly. We'll spend the night, and in the morning, we'll figure out what to do next."

"What to do with the crazy monster hunter who's after us? Or the crazy mobster? Or the crazy witch? Or the crazy wolfman? Wolfmen? Wolfpeople? What's the non-sexist way of talking about wolfpeople?"

He held my eyes, and I broke first.

"I'm scared too," he said, the words so low they barely reached me.

I nodded.

Instead of his bedroom, though, we headed toward the kitchen; I don't think either of us was ready to try to sleep, and Dag's parents would provide a welcome distraction. We found them both seated at the table, Gloria playing Candy Crush on her phone, Hubert on Prowler—after two years of this kind of thing, I barely even thought about the fact that it was a gay hookup app.

"What's going on with those girls?" Hubert asked without looking up from the phone.

"They're in trouble," Dag said, taking ice cream from the freezer. "We'll be out of here tomorrow."

"Did Eli get one of them pregnant?" Gloria asked. Her phone chimed with some sort of victory, and she glanced up.

The ice cream thunked onto the counter. "Eli? Did Eli get one of them pregnant?"

"Twinks can be very assertive tops, son," Hubert said. "Although Eli's really more of a twunk these days."

"Thank you, Hubert."

"What about me?" Dag asked. "You're not worried I got them pregnant?"

Hubert snorted. "That'd be the day."

"Excuse me?"

Laying a hand on Hubert's arm, Gloria wore a look of parental indulgence. "All right, dear. Did you or Eli—" She stressed *you*. "—get those girls pregnant?" Then she sat back, a hint of a smile on her lips at this triumphant moment in parenting history.

I pulled my sweatshirt over my face and tried not to die in my boyfriend's parents' kitchen.

That was when my phone buzzed. I worked it out of Dag's giant-assed sweats, saw Kennedy's name on it, and answered.

"We need to talk," she said over my hello. "I think I know why he wanted the rougarou."

DAG (6)

I'd grown up walking to the Fogmile branch of the DuPage Parish Library; it was half a mile from my parents' house, and the neighborhood had always been quiet and residential and safe. We decided to walk tonight. Night had snuffed out the last bit of dusk, and the darkness was broken only by the streetlamps and the humidity-ringed smears of amber porch lights. The air had cooled, and even with my arm around him, Eli hugged himself and shivered. I could smell rain coming and the chill of the old concrete sidewalk and fresh-fallen leaves.

The library had been built sometime in the '70s, with brick walls and skinny, floor-to-ceiling windows that made the inside bright and warm during the day. It was built into the side of a hill, and instead of the main entrance, we made our way down to the lower parking lot and entered there. This section of the library held classrooms and multipurpose rooms and the behind-the-scenes rooms where librarians did all the work that went into maintaining a library. We'd come here once on a field trip in third grade, and Patrick Westerman had pushed Marquel Hodge into a book truck and knocked it over because Marquel said Patrick had a pizza face, on account of all his freckles. Then we'd had to go back to school early.

"You don't have to make that face," Eli said. "I'm not going to get in trouble again."

"No, I was thinking about—wait, when did you get in trouble?"

"I didn't tell you? Remember last year, when Lanny attacked me in the parking lot? Well, before that, I'd been trying to get someone to help me find a book, only everyone was too busy, and I only needed a tiny bit of help, like five seconds—"

"Oh my God, you were the code 090.1167?"

"You heard about that? And you remember that dumbass code and number and everything?"

"Eli, they put it in the library newsletter—in the next four library newsletters, as a matter of fact. It's all they could talk about. It was above the fold."

"Why do you look so disappointed? It was a misunderstanding, and I think it was totally reasonable for me to want someone to help me—hey, hold on. You read the library newsletter?"

"My parents read the library newsletter," I said. "Religiously. My mom called me when she read about the code 090.1167."

"Why are you two still out here playing grab-ass?" Kennedy Sainte-Marie stood at the end of the hall, arms folded, offering a masterful example of the Pissed-Off Librarian. She was black, younger than I was but older than Eli, and stunning in a copper-colored blouse and dark jeans. "I told you to meet me in the bookbinding room."

"Sorry—" Eli began.

"Are you sorry that you aren't in the bookbinding room?" she asked. "Or are you sorry that you can't read a sign that tells you this is the bookbinding room? Or are you sorry that you are once again fucking up my life in ways that go beyond the usual, day-to-day fuckups you create in both of my jobs?"

"Since I can't tell if those were really questions—it got a bit shouty at the end—I'm going to go with, 'Yes.' No, wait, I changed my answer to 'Maybe.' No, sorry, I've got to stick with 'Yes.'"

She did this little scream thing in her throat, which I'd gotten to hear a lot of times in the context of: a) books Eli had forgotten to return; b) books Eli had damaged (the most innocent reason was keeping them folded open to his favorite part, but there were others); and c) pretty much everything to do with the cemetery tours where Kennedy and Eli worked together. Then she stepped into the bookbinding room and shut the door.

"It's a little-known fact that librarians are genetically incapable of slamming a door," Eli said. "That gene got replaced by the gene that loves stamping things like date due cards. But you've got to give her credit for trying her best. She did manage to shut it very firmly."

"Can you please try not to antagonize her?" I asked as I started down the hall. "Since, you know, we need her to help us, and she's your boss—"

"She's not my boss. She's my shift supervisor, which is, like, the person at McDonald's who wears a different-colored hat. Wait, do the shift supervisors at McDonald's wear the same hat? Does anyone at McDonald's wear a hat?"

"Running away isn't my only option. I could join the merchant-marines. I could probably still find a circus."

"You'd hate the circus. You'd spend your whole day talking about animals and animal cruelty and cages, and then you'd probably get eaten by a lion. Here's an idea: why don't we stand out here and argue about the circus just to see how mad we can make Kennedy—"

I grabbed his arm and pulled him into the bookbinding room. It was small—too small for the three of us, in fact—with a table, two stools, and a wall of cabinets. It smelled like beeswax and binding glue and cardboard, and even with the door shut, the distant hum and lurch of a copier filled the silence. Someone had left a book mid-repair on the table: the cover lay to one side, next to an awl and a strip of leather.

"Why do you repair books?" Eli asked. "Why don't you just throw them away and buy new ones? Oh, or you could be charitable—"

"Stop talking," Kennedy said.

"—and give them to people who are homeless, and they could burn them in barrels to, um, stay warm."

Kennedy's eyes narrowed. Eli stepped back into me, and then we bumped the table, and the awl started to roll. The sound of it scraping against the wood was enormous in that tiny space. Kennedy caught the awl a moment before it fell, made that wild noise in her throat again, and slammed the awl back where it had started.

"It's not my fault," Eli whispered. "It's Dag. He's too big, and he takes up too much room."

"Why haven't you divorced him yet?" Kennedy asked.

"We're actually not married," I said. "We've talked about it, but then Eli cuts up all the window screens or puts the weed-eater under my back tires."

"Then why are you still with him? You can still get away. You can still have a happy, safe, normal life."

"It's interesting that you think so highly of Dag," Eli said, "because he was just saying in the hall that you're basically the equivalent of a shift supervisor at McDonald's, with the hat and everything—ah, Christ!"

"Stop trying to get under her skin."

He muttered and grumped and checked the elastic waistband of his briefs, which I'd snapped. Then he bumped into me until I put an arm around him.

"He's actually really happy to see you," I told Kennedy. "This is his way of showing it."

Kennedy stared at us for what might have been twenty seconds. It felt a lot longer.

"You said you know why people are looking for the rougarou?" I said. "For Reb, I mean."

She gave us another twenty seconds. Then, letting out a controlled breath, she said, "Possibly." She opened one of the cabinets, drew out a newspaper, and laid it on the desk. "Look familiar?"

It was the print edition of the *Times-Picayune* from the day before. I recognized the headline—VOODOO DOCTOR MURDERED!—and the photo and article; they were the ones that Posey had shown us the night he had come to ask for our help. "Ok," I said. "I've seen this—"

"Here," Kennedy said, pointing at the photograph.

I bent closer, bonked heads with Eli, and let his grumble become background noise. Marcel Le Doux looked how I remembered him: black, middle-aged, the fringe of white curls and the thick black glasses. But now I focused on where Kennedy had pointed. Something hung on a necklace, barely visible where it had slipped out from behind the placket of his shirt.

"What is it?" Eli asked. "A charm or something?"

"Have you ever heard of a veve?"

I shook my head, and Eli frowned.

"It's a symbol," Kennedy said. "It has two roles. At least two roles. I'm not exactly an expert on this, so bear with me; I'm doing my best. On the one hand, it's a beacon for the lwa. On the other, it serves as their—proxy, I guess. In a ritual sense, anyway."

The silence had a packed, insulated quality inside the tiny room, like we'd been boxed away from the rest of the world. When Eli spoke, his voice was tight. "What is a lwa?"

"Well," Kennedy said with a strange smile, "funny you should ask."

"What does that mean?" I said.

"What do you know about voodoo?"

Eli bit his lip and shook his head. I said, "Not much. I mean, I know it's not how they make it look on TV, voodoo dolls and that nonsense."

"In vodou or vodun religions, including New Orleans voodoo, a lwa is a spirit. A powerful spirit, actually, and an intermediary."

"An intermediary like a saint?" I said.

"That's a good comparison; Catholicism and African religions have intermingled and influenced each other for a long time, especially in places like Louisiana, where they coexisted. Like the saints, the lwa communicate with humans. They receive offerings. If they are propitiated, they might help."

"Might?" Eli said.

"They have personalities, minds. In fact, all lwa were once people. That's part of what makes them so complicated. It still happens, although not as often. The best-known example for people around here is Marie Laveau, the Voodoo Queen of New Orleans. After her death, practitioners of New Orleans voodoo believe she ascended to become a lwa. You'll find altars to her around the city, people who make offerings, invoke her aid. There are others—the Chicken Man is a recent one. Jean Petro is an older example; depending on who's telling the story, he was either a slave or the owner of slaves in the New World."

"I know that name," Dag said. "Why do I know that name?"

"Because it's in the title of the exhibit Le Doux was opening: *Petwo Lwa, Jean Petro, Marie Leveau, and the Chicken Man: Ascent of the New World Lwa*. From what I can tell, the exhibit focused on biographical details of these New World lwa. Before they ascended, obviously."

"How do you go from being a person to a semidivine intercessory spirit?" I asked. "Because that would be a nice level-up for me. Oh, and maybe for Dag if he's interested."

"I don't know," Kennedy said. "But if half the stories are true, nobody makes that kind of transition without a lot of power. It doesn't end there, either. They're still...people in a way. Mortal would be a better way to say it. They need offerings and attention to survive, and without them, they wither away and die. That's part of what's going on here, I think."

A silent heartbeat passed, and I asked, "How so?"

"This veve, the one Le Doux is wearing? It marks him as a houngan—a voodoo priest. And not just any priest. A priest of Kalfu. Kalfu must be his patron or his master—what a voodoo practitioner calls his *met tet*."

"I'm going out on a limb here," Eli said, "but Kalfu, is he the lwa of puppies and rainbows and the sappy stuff people write in greeting cards?"

"Eli, you might like Kalfu. Among other things, he's the lwa of transformation—specifically, humans transforming into animals. He'd be the right one to ask if you wanted your werewolf porn—"

"FBI novels," Eli said.

"—to come true. Although with Kalfu, the wolves would probably eat you alive at the end; he's not exactly the most approachable lwa."

"Could he turn Dag into a werewolf? Just, you know, when Dag wanted to change. Or if I wanted him to. Like if he'd been busy studying all week, and my, er, needs weren't being met—"

"Tell us about him," I said.

"Kalfu, Kafou, Carrefour." Kennedy shivered. "You understand this isn't really my area of expertise, but I did as much research as I could—"

"Oh, God, so nerdy," Eli said, his voice too high, the words too fast. "Why couldn't you be like that badass dom librarian with a whip? There's a whole series. He whips everybody. He whips the circulation boy. He whips the facilities administrator. He whips this twink who only works at the library for one semester because he's doing a practicum, and of course he's in charge of the return chute."

"Eli," I said.

He bit his lip and nodded. Then he slid under my arm and pressed himself against me; he was shaking, and I thought about what he'd learned—what we'd both learned—only a couple of hours ago. Now, we were adding in a dangerous demigod. No wonder he couldn't keep quiet.

I gave Kennedy a nod. "Go on."

"Among other things," she said, "Kalfu is the lwa of evil spirits, bad luck, misfortune, the moon, and darkness. Oh, and magic. Of all the lwa, he is supposed to be the strongest with charms and sorcery. Hence, his association with transformations. He is the lwa of the crossroads—in fact, if I'm understanding this correctly, he is the crossroads. But unlike Papa Legba, who is also associated with crossroads, Kalfu holds the in-between points, the off-center corners of the intersection. It's all elaborately metaphorical, but at the same time—" She took a breath. "At the same time, I'm not sure it's metaphorical at all."

"He sounds bad."

"I'm not sure he's bad. Or at least, not in a cosmic-morality sense. Supposedly, he was a powerful sorcerer in life, before he ascended to become a lwa, and now he controls the flow of magic. The comparison people make is to a crossroads—good and evil people pass through the crossroads, and the crossroads isn't good or evil because of it. Kalfu is dangerous, but he's not evil simply because he is a—a channel for power that some people choose to misuse."

"So—" I studied the picture. "—we've got a lwa connected to werewolves, and his dead voodoo priest, and a werewolf on the run, and a lot of nasty people trying to find that werewolf. That fills in some of the picture, but it still doesn't tell us why."

"Kalfu is not a popular lwa," Kennedy said. "And a houngan with Kalfu as his *met tet* is not common."

"Why not?" I asked.

"You've been spending too much time with this one; your brain is getting soft. Did you not hear the part about sorcery and bad luck and evil spirits?"

"People want power. And they want their enemies punished. And they want to avert bad luck. Those all sound like good reasons to make an offering to Kalfu."

"Sure," Kennedy said. "Unless you get the opposite result because you annoyed him, and Kalfu shows up and eats you. That's not a metaphor, by the way. He is...hungry."

Eli shuddered against me, and when he spoke, his voice cracked. "Nelda Pie wants power."

After a moment, Kennedy rubbed her temples and nodded. "That's what I was afraid of."

I frowned down at my boyfriend. "You think Nelda Pie wants Reb—why? To offer him to Kalfu?"

"Think about it, Dag. Last year, someone walked into Nelda Pie's stronghold and almost killed her. Would have killed her, actually, if we hadn't showed up. For someone like Nelda Pie, that's unacceptable. As soon as she recovered, she would have tried to find a way to make herself stronger, to prevent that from ever happening again."

"Voodoo isn't like hoodoo, though," Kennedy said. "Hoodoo, any skinny mixed boy can pick up a book and follow the steps and get a result."

"First of all," Eli said, "rude."

"And witchcraft is something else entirely. Voodoo, though, you have to be initiated. You have to have a guide. You have to build a relationship with the lwa, especially with your *met tet*. I suppose it's possible Nelda Pie started that process last year, but it would have been rushed to say the least."

Eli's words picked up speed. "What if she'd been practicing for longer? What if she's been a houngan, one of Kalfu's houngan, for a long time?"

"A female priest is a mambo," Kennedy said.

"Think about it. We know she's fascinated with chimeras—collecting them, keeping them, even creating them. That's Kalfu's domain. What if she's been doing this for a long time, offering him the occasional—will I get my hot stud muffin card pulled if I say 'were-creature'?"

"Sometimes," I told Kennedy. "It's better to pretend you didn't hear him."

"Hey!"

"Is he right? Could that be the case?"

"Nelda Pie has always been ambitious," Kennedy said slowly. "And the lwa are a path to power. I don't know; I've tried to keep my distance from her. I suppose it's possible."

"She wants to offer Reb as a sacrifice," Eli said slowly. "If Kalfu is the lwa of transformation, a rougarou would make sense as an offering, right? Maybe a very special offering. But we don't know what she wants or why."

"Whatever it is, knowing Nelda Pie, it won't be good." Kennedy swallowed. "There's also the way Le Doux died. Did you read that?"

"They thought it was an animal."

"No, they said he'd been torn up. It wasn't an animal, trust me; it was torture. I'd put money on it. Le Doux knew something that someone else wanted, and he didn't give it up easily. If I had to guess, it was a ritual—voodoo isn't like hoodoo or even certain aspects of witchcraft. Nothing is written down; it's all passed word of mouth. Whatever Le Doux knew, someone else wanted to know it too."

"Nelda Pie," I said. They both looked at me. "He was at the Stoplight the night he was killed; Posey said he was talking to Nelda Pie. Joey Jaws doesn't know his head from a hole in the ground, and Fen's whole purpose in life is to eradicate anything supernatural. That leaves Nelda Pie. She must have figured out Le Doux knew something she didn't. She's the one who tortured and killed him—put money on it."

Kennedy made a face and nodded.

"Reb's got a sixth sense for danger," I said. "I bet he was out the door five seconds after Le Doux approached him; that's why he ran. He didn't just need to keep himself safe. He had to think about Dutch and Lurnice—they'd be targets too."

"Then Fen gets wind of it," Eli said, "because she keeps her ear to the ground. As soon as Le Doux turned up murdered, she must have started putting this together—a lot faster than we did, by the way. So, being Fen, she sets out to blow Reb's head off. You know, because that is definitely one way to prevent him becoming a sacrifice."

"And Joey Jaws is bumbling along the whole time, thinking he's going to get a rougarou for his kennel." I shook my head. "That guy doesn't have any idea what he's messing with."

"Sounds about right," Kennedy said sourly.

"What do we do now?" Eli asked. "I mean, it was bad enough when Nelda Pie was a witch with her own private army of—for lack of a polite word—monsters. Now, she's got unholy powers as the cleric of a dark deity."

I looked at Eli. I looked at Kennedy.

"We have a group that meets on the weekends," Kennedy said with a dramatic roll of her eyes. "Dungeons and Dragons. He's taken eight of their flyers, by my count."

"It's called nerd-baiting," Eli said. "I invented it."

"I think Fen has the right idea," I said. "The way to stop Nelda Pie is to keep her from getting her hands on a rougarou. We've got two of the three—"

"What?" Kennedy said.

"Don't ask," Eli said. "Dag's parents are so disappointed in me for not getting them pregnant, and they used all the hot water, and they took the best sweatshirts. I ended up with this one, which is so basic I want to stick my head in that paper cutter."

"Here, let me get this out of your way."

When Eli opened his mouth in outrage, I tightened my arm around his shoulders. "I mean, we need to find Reb, and then we need to get the three of them away from here. Whatever Nelda Pie wants, it must have some real specific requirements—otherwise, she wouldn't have put out that bounty on Reb."

"The timing matters too," Kennedy said. "On Halloween, the barriers between worlds are thin."

"We don't know where Reb went," I said. "He's injured, so we could call hospitals and urgent care clinics, but if Posey is right, if he heals quickly, he might just hole up and wait."

"Can't you just, you know?" Eli twiddled his fingers in the air. "Please?"

"Not unless you have some of his blood," Kennedy said drily. "You have to have the right blood, or there are consequences. In this case, the wrong blood would just lead you to the wrong person, but in a bigger ritual, it could have, well, disastrous effects."

"We do have some of his blood, actually," Eli looked at me and then at Kennedy. "Is it weird if I tell you we have a lot of it?"

ELI (7)

At the next intersection, Dag let the Escort roll to a stop. We were lucky it was night, and we were on the outskirts of Bragg. Traffic was minimal—well, it was nonexistent—and the streetlights were spaced far apart. On one side of us, Bragg huddled under the dome of its own light pollution, a gray skin stretched out over the night. On the other, the lake was an empty space, as though someone had cut out part of the world. And then, even farther, like neon brambles, New Orleans.

After a moment, the jack around my neck swung right, and I pointed.

Dag turned right.

Along with other valuable traits like finding really porny books for me and getting me a job and recommending a great hand lotion—ok, I found it in her purse, and then she refused to tell me where she'd bought it, but thank you, Internet—Miss Kennedy was apparently really good at hoodoo.

Like, really damn good.

All that whining and moaning about family legacies and not wanting to be involved, etcetera? When the rubber hit the road, it turned out that Miss Kennedy seriously knew her shit.

The jack was, she had explained, essentially a modified flannel. I'd had about as much as I wanted to do with flannels the year before, but I understood the general principle. Flannels—or mojo bags, as they were also called—were typically made out of flannel. Hence the name. You added the right items inside, and if you knew how to shape the energy, they could produce certain effects. How's that for woo-woo? Of course, an all-around genius-slash-perfect-physical-specimen like me was also, it turned out, naturally good at woo-woo. Big surprise, right? It's my curse, being able to—as my fellow bros would say—crush everything. Ask Dag. I'm so good at getting stains out of his shirts that sometimes the whole shirt disappears.

For a jack, you needed the following: red flannel, a silver dime (pre-1965, for those playing along at home), some High John the

Conqueror (the root, not the leaves), goofer dust (which, when I pressed Miss Kennedy, meant graveyard dust), the wishbone from a chicken, a lodestone pair (fancy word for magnets, which both Kennedy and Dag refused to explain, so thank you, Internet), blood (from the shirt we'd found at the fishing camp), and musk. Animal magnetism, Miss Kennedy had said.

Thank you for noticing, I had said.

That was when Dag sent me to sit in the car.

Miss Kennedy had all this stuff in her trunk, by the way, most of it organized in old tackle boxes. Which really makes you think, when was the last time she went on a date?

I got out of the car to ask her, and Dag made me get in the back seat, and I think I saw him set the child locks.

Fast-forward, and now we were following the jack as it led us to Reb.

At the next intersection, Dag had to pull over while a Silverado blasted past us. The truck had—at my estimate—eighteen frat boys crammed into the cab, and as the taillights faded, it trailed a Justin Bieber beat and the boys' drunken cheers. When the street was clear, Dag swung the Escort into the center of the intersection, and I leaned forward. The jack, which hung from my neck on a shoelace liberated from Miss Kennedy's Lady Nikes, swung in the air. After a moment, it pulled left.

I pointed left, and Dag drove.

When I saw the whitewashed wall of the cemetery, I said, "Motherfucker."

Dag nodded tightly. He eased the Escort onto the grassy verge and turned off the engine. When the headlights snapped off, I blinked, trying to adjust to the darkness. The moon was still coming up, and it was huge—only a day or two from being full. It made the whitewashed plaster gleam. I spent a wonderful thirty seconds reliving every horror movie I'd ever seen. And I worked here.

This was St. Guillaume de Verceil Cemetery No. 3, where I had the pleasure, five days a week, of shepherding red-faced, corn-fed tourists in their fanny packs and Birkenstocks and hilarious tees—I'M WITH STUPID. Yeah, buddy, you sure are.

"Give me the jack," Dag said. "And you hold on to the car keys."

"Oh my God," I muttered and pushed open the door.

We crossed the street in silence. The only sound, aside from our tennis shoes on the asphalt, was the occasional breeze that whistled in the grass and made branches clack. The gates were already chained shut, so when we reached the wall, Dag crouched and laced his fingers into a stirrup. He boosted me up. Fortunately, Bragg had never gotten the same kind of tourists as New Orleans, which meant that, at no point in its history had anyone decided that broken glass on the top of the wall would be a lovely deterrent. Plaster crumbled, powdery and at the same time strangely damp against my palms, and I pulled myself up to straddle the wall.

Bending, I offered Dag a hand. He did something annoyingly athletic and coordinated that basically looked like running straight up the wall, and then he grabbed my hand. Between all the muscles I'd built folding my bikini briefs and Dag's momentum, we got my much more substantially built boyfriend onto the wall. I caught a glimpse of his grin, his teeth white in the moonlight.

"No comments about my arms, please. I'm well aware that I need to do more strength training."

If he heard me, it didn't register—Dag was usually quick to remind me of Rule 497, or whatever number it was, about not saying anything bad about myself. Instead, he said, "Mason and I had to do this about every weekend in high school. His parents had an old house with a wall like this."

Mason had been Dag's best friend, and in some ways, his first love—although, since Mason had been straight and as emotionally developed as a tube sock, the love had mostly gone in one direction. Maybe some of those thoughts showed on my face because Dag's expression changed, the softness of memory sloughing away. He slid across the wall, lowered himself onto his belly, and dropped out of sight.

When I joined him, Dag steadied me, and we were nothing more than touches in the deeper darkness of the wall's shadow. I couldn't see his face, and as soon as I was standing straight, he released me. In the gloom, he felt like he was a mile off. Then Dag turned, his tennis shoes whispering against the concrete walk as he moved into the cemetery.

Anyone who's ever visited a Louisiana cemetery—the old ones, anyway, around New Orleans—has probably had the same thought. It looked like a little city: the tombs and mausoleums like buildings of all different shapes and heights, the paths that crossed and turned and dead-ended like city streets, the broken sightlines and blind alleys. A city of the dead. Not original, like I said, but hard to escape.

But it was a real place, too. Real in the broken plaster, the crumbling brick, the weeds that grew up where the concrete walk gave way to gravel or, in places, dirt. Real in the little things: plastic flowers next to a vault, the petals emptied of their color by the moonlight; three large X's scrawled across the back of a tomb; a bronze plaque from the DuPage Parish Historical Society, commemorating Claude-

Joseph-Andre Laverdure, who I guessed in life had been a colossal twat. Some of the newer tombs—well, relatively newer—were low, flat blocks of concrete, and on one of these, someone had left what I took for a figurine of a Catholic saint. Its face had been melted down to a soot-stained nub, as though someone had held it in a fire.

Fuck me, I thought, and I hurried after Dag.

The air seemed colder in here—but then, I'd been cold, more or less, for the last year—and the breeze carried the smell of chilled stone and rust and, occasionally, a whiff of trampled peppermint. When I caught up with Dag, he glanced over at me, his face a mask of shadows, and kept walking. Our soles crunched loose stones. One of them slipped underfoot, and I stumbled, and Dag caught my arm without even looking.

We'd gone five more paces before he said, "We shouldn't have done that, sneaking out like that. His parents trusted us. My parents trusted us."

"You were kids."

"I'm not talking about being kids."

The moon had cleared the cemetery's wall, and it balanced now on top of a cross mounted on the roof of a tomb ahead of us. Where the light reached, the avenues and alleys of the cemetery had a pallid brilliance, like they'd been painted onto a black canvas.

"What are you talking about, then?" I asked. "Because this doesn't sound like you."

"I'm talking about my whole life. Mason bossing me around. Me being the worst deputy to ever put on a badge. I'm talking about seeing things that are wrong and not doing anything to stop them."

"Where is this coming from?"

"You know what it's like? It's like that was all practice, all the times we snuck out of his parents' house, all the times I let him copy my homework, the times I sprayed a whole can of Lysol because he got real paranoid after smoking some weed and was sure his parents could smell it."

"To be fair, they probably could smell it."

"And then when he needed me, I couldn't do it. I couldn't stop him."

He was talking about two years ago, when the hashok had broken Mason's mind, infected him, and then turned Mason loose—sending him to kill me. Dag had stopped him, which I intended to point out. But I also knew that Dag was talking about how it had ended, in that confused struggle over the gun when Mason had gotten shot.

I opened my mouth, but instead of what I had intended to say— something about how Dag's strength had nothing to do with being strict or authoritarian, how it had nothing to do with physical power, even though I was the number one fan of all those lovely muscles—different words rose in my throat: *Because you're not strong enough. You let me get hurt, didn't you? By the parlangua. By Joey Jaws's thug.*

Biting back the words took everything I had. For a moment, the taste of them—hot and ripe and metallic—lingered in my mouth, and I could imagine the hurt that would rush into Dag's face. It would be like pressing both thumbs into a wound and forcing it open even further. The pleasure, even in prospect, made me put out a hand to the pebbled plaster of the tomb next to me.

Dag looked over at me, and the moment vanished. Hurt did show in his face—not the agony that some messed-up part of my brain had pictured, but hurt nonetheless. I had waited too long to respond, and he had taken my silence as its own kind of corroboration. I opened my mouth to say something, but before I could, the jack jerked right.

We both came to a stop in the middle of a tiny crossroads. Dag slouched under the dark bulk of a mausoleum, barely more than an outline, face set resolutely away from me.

"Dag—" I started.

"Guess we go that way," he said at the same time, and he brushed past me, moving in the direction the jack had indicated.

I went after him.

The jack led us in jerks and fits toward the edge of the cemetery. This was one of the older sections, perhaps the oldest. Some of the people buried here had lived and died hundreds of years ago, and that age fell on me like the darkness, both of them with their own particular weight. Most of the tombs were clearly untended, their plaster gone and the bricks softening, the structures themselves squat and unassuming. In the walls of the cemetery, smaller vaults were built into the brick, and they looked like old-fashioned ovens. From giving a hell of a lot of cemetery tours myself, I knew they were called wall vaults, and they'd been cheaper than a tomb or a mausoleum. You know—for the discerning deceased on a budget.

Ahead, on one of the older tombs, the topmost vault gaped open. It had been that way for a while—at some point, someone had broken down the brick wall used to seal the vault, probably with the intent to inter another ancestor. And then, instead, the vault had been left open and neglected. We used it on tours to show people what the vaults looked like on the inside; the ghoulish ones were always disappointed that there were no rotting bones or gaping skulls. One woman had suggested I try Rutland Brick and Stone to clean it—"I think the next group would appreciate that."

The jack jerked toward the opening, and I grabbed Dag's arm.

He pulled away, but he glanced at me and asked, "What—"

I shook my head and held a finger to my lips. Then I pointed at the open vault. It was big enough that, on occasion, we had to roust drunks who had decided that any shelter was better than the rain. And Reb, who was built small and who—in my mind, anyway—had a wounded animal's desire to hide in its den, would have fit perfectly. It was too dark to see anything, and I realized how stupid we'd been, trusting to a bit of folk magic instead of, well, bringing one of those high-powered flashlights that can blast your eyeballs out if you look straight at them.

Dag must have caught what I was thinking because he made a faintly amused noise and unclipped a flashlight from his keyring.

Of course.

He handed it to me, but then the sound of leather scuffing stone reached us, and we both froze. I strained to listen. The breeze picked up, rattling a few dry leaves down the corridor of tombs. Then the breeze died, and there was nothing.

Dag moved slightly. I followed his gaze back to the tomb with the open vault. Reb was squirming out of the opening, and he landed softly in the dirt and weeds. Crouching, he turned his head, almost as though scenting the air. In my peripheral vision, something moved, and I craned my head.

The shape of the person was hidden in shadow, but there was no mistaking the barrel of the gun. Reb was still crouched, head swiveling.

Without thinking about it, I scooped up a handful of pebbles from the ground and flung them at the person with the gun. Some of the stones struck home, and the shooter jerked backward. Other stones clattered against the tomb. Some disappeared, ruffling the weeds. I thought I recognized Fen's voice in the sound of surprise and annoyance the woman made. An instant later, the shotgun boomed. A sheet of plaster on a tomb near us buckled and then began to fall in huge slabs.

Reb was gone.

"Get Reb," I said, shoving Dag in the direction I thought the boy had gone. I turned and sprinted in the other direction.

The gun boomed again, and this time, I was close enough to hear the shot tinkle as it struck the mausoleum next to me.

"Half-breed!" Fen shouted.

I kept running, my hand clutching the mini-flashlight so hard that it bit into my palm. The slap of leather on stone came after me, and I put on the gas. I darted between tombs. I vaulted a sagging iron fence, my ass getting a good poke from one of the pointed tips—and not the fun kind. My tennis shoes came down hard on concrete, jolting me all the way to my teeth, and I took off again.

I didn't want to lose her—if she stopped to think, she'd realize she needed to go after Reb, not me. But I also didn't want her to catch up with me; that was really high on my personal list of no-no's. I forced myself to slow. As Dag liked to point out, I spent way too much time running, and on top of that, I wasn't wearing boots and a duster and carrying the kind of gun that gave straight boys wet dreams. I turned on the flashlight, and I made sure that the beam pointed backward as I ran, so that she could see the bouncing light. It's like tag, plus hide-and-seek, plus murder, I thought as I ran. Murder-tag-seek. It's the latest craze.

But it turned out, I hadn't needed to bother. The sound of leather on stone was getting closer. Apparently boots and a duster and a massive shotgun weren't much of a hindrance when you were a stone-cold badass like Fen. She was a monster hunter, and she wasn't going to let a mixed boy with fantastic hair and a jiggly-in-a-good-way ass outrun her. She was going to track me down and kill me. And just when I was getting abs.

I threw on a little speed, and at the next intersection, I glanced back to make sure Fen wasn't in sight. I tossed the flashlight to the right, and I jinked left. I was shaking with the combination of adrenaline and the need for air, and it took me two tries to get the jack over my head. I doubled the flannel strip around my hand, and I forced myself to take long, slow breaths. Quiet breaths, I hoped. Hell, at this point, I'd settle for not sounding like a rhinoceros in heat.

Footsteps pounded toward me. I bent my legs at the knees, timed Fen's pace in my head, and tried not to throw up.

When she reached the intersection, the duster billowed behind her. I had a glimpse of the work shirt, the heavy-duty jeans, the ass-kicking boots. She was wearing some kind of cowboy hat tonight, and it looked dope, which only pissed me off more. She swung toward the flashlight, which had landed in a clump of bushes. It looked—maybe—like I was trying to hide and was too dumb to turn off my flashlight.

I stepped away from the tomb where I'd been leaning. Fen started to turn toward me. Either she hadn't fallen for the ruse, or she'd heard me. My arm was already cocked, though, and I hit her as hard as I could with the jack.

It probably didn't do much damage—it didn't weigh hardly anything—but getting popped in the eye unexpectedly is nobody's idea of a good time. Unless there's a kink for that. Which there probably was. Which I'd search for on Dag's phone and leave all the tabs open, just to mess with his head, the next time I got a chance.

For now, I settled for the satisfying whap of flannel hitting eyeball.

Fen jerked her head back, her body instinctively trying to pull away from the threat. She was carrying the shotgun in both hands, holding it across her body the way I'd seen soldiers run with guns in the movies Dag made me watch sometimes. She pulled it tighter to her, as though expecting me to try to wrestle it away.

Instead, I punched her in the throat.

She staggered, made a retching noise, and tried to suck in air. Instead, she made that retching noise again. One eye—not the one I'd whapped—was huge.

Now, I did grab the shotgun. She clawed at my face, and when I reared back, she raked her nails on my arm. She was still wheezing. I yanked on the shotgun, using my relative height and weight advantage to drag her off balance. She stumbled, and then she started to fall. I wrenched the shotgun away and threw it like a javelin.

"I'm sorry," I said. Fen was on hands and knees, hacking, her whole body shaking. I turned, started to run again, and called over my shoulder, "I'm really sorry!"

I had almost reached the next turn when a gunshot cracked the air, and a plaster cornice exploded above my head.

Ok, that one was on me. I should have guessed the crazy monster hunter packed a backup.

Picking plaster out of my hair, I sprinted in the direction I had come, back toward the oldest section of the cemetery. The breeze raised goose bumps on my chest and arms, in spite of Dag's sweatshirt, but I felt warm. Hot, actually. A good, loose, relaxed feeling, like I'd just had the world's best combination sauna-massage-sex. I thought about going back and putting the barrel of the shotgun in Fen's mouth. I thought of what it would sound like, the noises she'd make, with her tongue and cheeks and teeth jammed against all that steel. Sweat broke out on my forehead, and a wave of dizziness washed over me.

It's getting worse, I thought, and the words had a lighthouse clarity, spinning brightly and then lost in the red surf pounding in my brain. You're getting worse.

A soft whump came from my right, and then Reb hollered. I turned, following a cramped gravel path between two crumbling tombs, and crashed into Dag. He grabbed me, steadied me, and dragged me into a deeper patch of shadow.

Our position let us look out on a relatively clear area of the cemetery, where the tombs were all low, and I could see for almost a hundred yards. Reb leaned hipshot against one of the tombs, his hand against his neck. As I watched, Joey Jaws emerged from between a pair of larger tombs on the far side of the open area. He had a rifle shouldered, and when he fired, the gun rocked in his hands.

I opened my mouth, but Dag squeezed my hand hard.

Something was sticking out of Reb's shoulder—something with a fluffy feather that looked blue in the moonlight. Not a bullet, I realized. A dart. And then my brain clicked: a tranquilizer dart.

Joey fired again. This dart struck Reb in the stomach, hanging there, wobbling when the boy made a desperate, throaty noise and tried to drag himself along the tomb.

I made a move toward him, and Dag dragged me back. I couldn't see him shake his head, not in the dark, but I could feel the movement, and his arms tightened around me. A moment later, two more of Joey's guys emerged. One of them said something, and the other laughed, and then a moment too late, Joey laughed too, like he'd just gotten the joke.

Reb took another disoriented step. He looked so young, his face turned up to the sky, his breathing erratic. He looked lost. In the moon's pale glare, his skin had a blue tinge just like the fletching on the darts. Then he crumpled, and Joey made an annoyed noise.

"If that motherfucker hurt himself playing games, I'm going to be seriously pissed." Joey waved his men forward, and Dag and I shuffled back into the darkness. I didn't see what happened next, but Joey barked, "Careful, careful. Jesus, you fuck him up, you want to take his place? Like your grandmother's fucking china, you dumb fuck. Yeah. Thank you, Christ."

I twisted in Dag's arms. I pointed to his gun.

"He's got ten more guys in here," Dag whispered in my ear. "E, we have to go."

And because I'm a coward, after a moment, I nodded, and we made our escape.

DAG (8)

The next morning, the mood was tense in my parents' house. Eli had barely spoken to me after we'd gotten away from the cemetery, and although we'd shared a bed, he'd slept with his nose against the wall, doing just about everything except crawling under the mattress to get away from me. When I started moving around in the morning, he stayed that way, pretending to be asleep until I finally gave up.

Nobody else seemed to be doing any better. Dutch and Lurnice refused to come out of the guest room. I could hear them talking—low, worried talk—every time I walked past, but when I stopped and tried to listen, they immediately went silent. Which I guess made sense—super-hearing was probably one of the perks when you were a rougarou. Posey was physically much better—he hadn't been lying about his accelerated healing—but all he wanted to do was ask about Reb, talk about Reb, or sit by the window in my dad's recliner, silently worrying about Reb. After ten minutes, I'd had so much silent worrying about Reb that I went into the kitchen and pretended to read my textbook. My dad puttered around for five minutes before announcing in a too-loud voice that he was going to meet friends for a morning coffee, and five minutes after that, my mom claimed she needed to go grocery shopping, even though the fridge was completely full.

"We can play Scrabble," I said. "Or Bananagrams. We can do a crossword puzzle together."

My mother, who was supposed to be the one person in the world I could trust, laughed for way too long and then said, "Dagobert, don't be a goose. You need to study."

"I don't need to—"

She was out the door so fast, I swear her Crocs left skid marks.

I sat there, thinking about the classes I was missing, wondering if I was going to have to ask Sal if I could copy his notes—Sal being my nemesis on account of he thought he was hot stuff because he'd been in an episode of one of those teen vampire TV shows, and who always made sure I was in his study groups because he knew I'd do the work. I lined up my highlighters on the kitchen table. I wondered if my parents still had any posterboard, and then I wondered if you were even supposed to use posterboard when you did presentations in college. After a while of sitting there, watching a squirrel through the window, I admitted I wasn't going to get any schoolwork done. I could try to get Eli to eat something. Or I could check on Posey, see if I could stop his worrying. Or I could drag the girls out of their hidey-hole. But I figured if I was going to do something impossible, I might as well go big, so I took out my phone and did a search for Joey Tamborella.

There wasn't much, which made me think the Tamborella family paid good money to keep it that way. There was a LinkedIn page—apparently Joey Jaws was Vice President of Operations for Tamborella Holdings, which sounded like a great name for a company without telling you anything about what they actually did. There was an old fraternity bio from his days at Tulane. And then a news story from five or six years back about a car accident, and I'd been a deputy long enough not to believe it had been any kind of accident. In other words, I found nothing—no address on the free white-page lookups, no obvious list of favorite places, no hint of where I might find Joey. Tamborella Holdings had nothing more than a PO box.

It would have been a lot easier if I'd still been with the deputy's department. We had access to all kinds of databases where I could have looked for Joey's address—heck, I could have started with his driver's license. And if those leads didn't pan out, I could have put out a BOLO, had every deputy in the parish looking for Joey and his Jag.

I thought about that for a while. And then I figured if I didn't at least try, we'd never find Reb. So, I took out my phone and placed the call.

"DuPage Parish Sheriff's Department," a woman's voice said. She didn't actually pop the gum in my ear, but it still sounded like a firecracker going off. "If this is an emergency, please hang up and dial 911."

"I'd like to speak to Sergeant Kimmons."

"Let me see if he's available. Who may I say is calling?"

"Dag LeBlanc."

Silence. She popped the gum again. "He's busy."

"Sherlene, either put him on the phone, or I'll drive up there right now and talk to him in person. And if I have to do that, I'm going to tell him about your Instagram account where you upload all those mug shots."

I must have caught her mid-pop because she made a strangled noise like the gum had gotten stuck in her blowhole. As she coughed, she got out something about trying to find Amrey, and then the call went to hold. Department-approved soft jazz whispered in my ear. A moment later, the hold music ended, and a man's gruff voice said, "Mr. LeBlanc, how may I help you?"

Amrey had been my sergeant, and he'd been a good one—he was smart, he was tough, and he was fair, which were three things you couldn't say about half of the DuPage Parish Sheriff's Department. I hesitated, not sure how to start, and jumped in with, "I need to find Joey Jaws."

In the background, the bullpen was full of its usual noises: raised voices, chairs scraping linoleum, phones ringing.

"Why is that?" Amrey asked.

"I think he has someone. A friend of mine."

"What are we talking about here? A kidnapping?"

"Something like that. It's complicated."

Rustling noises came as Amrey adjusted the handset. "Let's make it simple, then. If it's a kidnapping, or if it's any other kind of illegal activity, you either call the emergency line, or you come in and talk to an officer. If it's something else, Mr. LeBlanc, then it's not police business."

"You know it's not that easy. You send somebody out there, and Joey will know as soon as you do, and they'll never find Reb."

"I'm sorry you feel that way about this department, Mr. LeBlanc. If you have an official complaint, you can file it—"

"It wasn't a bear. You know it wasn't a bear, so why are we still dancing around it?"

Amrey's breathing was slow and deep. "I don't understand—"

"Yes, you do. Two years ago, when I left the department. That murder out by Bayou Pere Rigaud. The bodies they found in the house. Richard didn't have some disease that made his bones look different. And the other body wasn't a bear. You know that. You're smart enough that you know something was weird about that, and something was weird about how the bodies disappeared. And last year, you knew something was wrong then too. You know Roger Shaver didn't kill Ivy. For heaven's sake, he was in the parish lock-up. You know something bad happened at the Stoplight the night Lanny died, even if nobody will tell you. You're not stupid, so don't act like you are."

More of the slow, deep breathing. Like he was counting each breath in his head.

"It's like that," I said quietly. "It's going to be worse if I can't stop it. I just need to know where to find him."

In the background, someone must have been jackassing around because McCormick, who was tender as beef jerky, shouted, "Sit your ass down."

"Even if I wanted too," Amrey said stiffly, "I couldn't provide you with the address for Dauphin House."

I heard the no first, and then I heard the rest of it. I flexed stiff fingers around the phone. Then I said, "Ok."

Amrey's silence held a kind of helpless tension. Then the call disconnected.

I searched Dauphin House as fast as I could type it.

It was a historic plantation house, privately owned and not open to the public. A couple of more searches told me the company that owned Dauphin House was owned by another company, which, in turn, was owned by Tamborella Holdings.

"Hot shit." I dropped my phone on the table and stared at it. "Hot fucking shit."

"I know it shouldn't be such a turn-on when you swear," Eli said from the opening to the hallway. He had found a gag sweatshirt Mason had given me when I turned seventeen—it had a picture of my head on it, and it looked like my body was in the middle of a po'boy. We'd seen shirts like that in a tourist shop in Moulinbas, and Mason had laughed so hard he'd peed himself, even though he swore he hadn't. The dumbass had gone back later and gotten one for me. That was the kind of thing he did. Frowning at whatever he saw on my face, Eli twisted the hem of the sweatshirt. "So, uh, if you could help me with something in the bedroom? I know it's traditional to ask you to look at my etchings, but—"

"E, I found him." I remembered too late Posey moping in the living room, and I lowered my voice. "Reb—I found him. Well, I found Joey, but he's got Reb."

"Holy shit. How?"

"I'll tell you later. Come on, we've got work to do."

ELI (9)

"He's asleep," I said, trying to settle the binoculars in the optimal, I-can-actually-see-through-these-damn-things-but-they're-not-leaving-red-marks-on-my-nose position. "Or he's dead."

"Let me see."

Dauphin House was gorgeous; there wasn't any other way to describe it. Sure, I felt a little bad admitting that—after all, the beauty had come at the expense of generations of slaves, and I felt a little complicit admiring the results. But it was hard not to be impressed. An avenue of live oaks, their branches trailing Spanish moss, led up to the house, which was a huge structure of stucco bleached by the moonlight, with wings extending off to either side. A double gallery at the front was supported by Greek columns—Dag would have known the name for them. The floor-to-ceiling windows and French doors glowed with yellow light, their louvered shutters open. Nothing moved inside—nothing had moved inside for the two hours we'd been sitting there and getting eaten alive by mosquitos.

"It's my turn," I said.

"E, let me see."

"You had your turn. And why do you need to look anyway?" I lowered the binoculars. "You don't trust me? I can't be trusted to report what I see with my own eyes?"

"Stop trying to pick a fight because you're bored," Dag said as he eased the strap over my head. "You stared at that tree for five minutes and told me it was a guard. You said he had a gun."

"It was a guard-shaped tree," I said. "Anyone could have made that mistake."

Dag said something under his breath that sounded suspiciously like, "Anyone who was holding binoculars backwards after I tried to help him and he told me, 'I know how to use binoculars, Dag'." But I knew that was too treacherous and unboyfriendly even for him, so I decided I must have misheard him. And besides, I didn't sound like that.

Picking a fight because I was bored was an ungenerous but accurate assessment of my current status. We'd spent the day rummaging through Dag's parents' shed for various pieces of hunting equipment, including the godawful camo coveralls and rain jacket and boots I was currently wearing, as well as the binoculars, high-powered flashlights, and a rifle. Then Dag had wanted to spend time studying old survey maps and parish property records, including an ancient floor plan of Dauphin House that had been printed in a turn-of-the-century guide to DuPage Parish's few plantations. It had been a lot of reading.

"We're turning into nerds," I said. "I'm realizing that right now."

"Could you realize a little more quietly, please?"

"My hair is too good to belong to a nerd."

Dag shook his head, but what he said was, "What kind of help is Joey hiring? That guy's totally passed out."

"See?" I said. And then, hearing the need for validation, I added, "Told you."

Dag made a frustrated noise as he swept the binoculars across the face of the building again. "Doesn't anybody live here? That place might as well be empty."

"Let's move closer."

"We can't get any closer."

"We could go on the property. That guard isn't going to bother us, and we could check the house. Nobody's going to see us in this." I plucked at the camo rain jacket, and it sounded plasticky between my fingers.

Dag made a face. "It's camo, Eli. It's not an invisibility cloak."

"That's five nerd points."

"It's too dangerous. There's no tree cover to approach from the back, but we can try the far side of the plantation."

"Too dangerous? Ten nerd points."

"I don't care about being a nerd, Eli. I own all the original *Star Trek* movies on VHS. I know what I am."

"Oh my God, five hundred nerd points."

He let the binoculars fall to hang from their strap. He was dressed in camo gear too, and of course, he looked great in it. Giving me a dirty look, he said, "You drew a Venn diagram about those two different hair mousses you wanted to try. On a whiteboard. That you took pictures of. You spend every night you're not trying to get my attention with your nose in one of those werewolf books. You're doing those Khan Academy math lessons when you think I won't notice. I don't know what you think a nerd is."

"A nerd," I said with as much dignity as I could muster, "doesn't have a cute butt."

I thought I heard him mutter something like, "God help me."

"We can't just sit here, Dag. Reb could be hurt. He could get himself killed. I'm going to take a look."

"No—"

But I was already slipping between the branches. Behind me, Dag made a strangled noise of frustration, and then branches rustled as he came after me.

We had parked on a one-lane dirt road and hiked through acres of oaks and willows and creepy-crawly things so that we could watch Dauphin House from behind a screen of trees. Now, we sprinted across a hundred yards of open ground, toward the iron fence that ran along the perimeter of the property. So far, we'd seen only the one guard—the one I'd spotted, for the record, and not the one that turned out to be a tree—and he was currently either drunk or asleep or dead, stretched out between the roots of a massive live oak. Nerd or not, Dag was good at this kind of stuff, but he was also careful. Sometimes, too careful. We didn't have that luxury, not tonight. It was time to take a chance.

When we reached the fence, Dag gave me a boost. I didn't even have to offer him a hand; he used those freakishly strong muscles to clamber up after me, the fence chiming and rattling softly as he shimmied his way up the bars. We both dropped onto the other side, and we stood still for a moment, listening. Faint insect noises made their way back to us, and the uneasy restlessness of the trees as wind whipped up. It was a cold night, and the wind made it even colder.

"I'm not mad at you," I whispered as I started toward the house and its island of light.

"You're the one who went haring off. Maybe I should be mad at you."

"I meant last night. This morning. I was...upset, I guess."

The thick, spongy lawn absorbed the sound of Dag's steps, and I glanced over my shoulder to make sure he was still there. He was scanning the trees on either side of us, and when his eyes came back, he flashed me a smile before he turned to check our surroundings again.

"Well?" I said.

"Ok, I heard you. It's all right. You can be upset."

"Don't you ever want to fight? Don't you ever want to tell me I'm—I'm spoiled and petty and I make your life so much harder than it needs to be, and I need to learn how to manage my emotions and not be, I don't know, temperamental."

We walked another five feet before he said, "Temperamental?"

"Dagobert LeBlanc!"

"We're sneaking right now. We're supposed to be sneaking."

"Fine, I'll be quiet. I won't say anything. I won't say one word."

We made it three feet.

"But if you wanted to tell me any of that..."

"Oh God," Dag said in an underbreath. "Eli, I love you. I'm not going to say stuff like that to you. Yeah, we could all use some help regulating our emotions—you, me, everybody. But you don't scream at me and say awful things like you used to, and everybody's entitled to have their feelings. If you need some time to feel upset, that's ok. And I don't know why you've got this obsession with having fights. I don't like fights. I love you; why would I want to fight with you?"

"For the drama," I said. "And so we can make up."

"We don't have to fight to have sex."

"You're missing the point: it's not just sex. It's make up sex. And everybody knows make up sex—"

Dag grabbed my arm, yanking me back a step.

Then I saw the body.

It was a man, white, in a dark windbreaker that had flapped open to expose the gun holstered at his waist. He looked like he'd fallen mid-step. I crouched, trying to make out the rise and fall of his body. He was breathing—slow, deep breaths.

I stood, glanced at Dag, and shrugged.

He tilted his head the way we had come.

I pointed at the house. When he shook his head, I pointed again, more emphatically, and took a step. He caught my arm, but he let me shake him off.

We'd gone twenty yards, the smell of cypress and moss and soft earth filling the darkness, when he whispered, "Something is seriously wrong, E. We need to fall back and regroup."

"Yeah, something is wrong. That means we need to figure out what's going on and get Reb out of here."

"Eli—"

"This is an opportunity."

Dag opened his mouth, but before he could say anything, cheers erupted from the back of the house. My brain decoded: male voices, raucous, drunk, with a high-voltage excitement that raised the hair on the back of my neck. We traded a look, and then Dag quickened his pace, passing me as he rerouted us to follow the side of the house.

As we made our way toward the back, I caught a whiff of something—something musky in the dark, like overheated animals, and charcoal and sizzling meat, and a metallic tang at the back of my throat. Other sounds filtered through the trees: the hub of voices, men talking over each other, shouts and calls of encouragement and dismay. Then a dog yelped, the sound cracking the night, and my stomach dropped.

Face dark, Dag shook his head.

The closer we got, the louder the sounds became: the snap of teeth, furious snarls, whimpering that faded under a fresh outburst of growls. Another dog yelped, the sound rising until it cut off suddenly. The wind shook the trees again. I was so cold the tips of my fingers ached; I could almost see it inside my head, the cold, the deep blue of a glacier's heart, ice compacted under its own weight until it had the kind of mass that could trap light.

When we came around the back of the house, the trees ended in a sharp line, and a wide, well-kept lawn unrolled in front of us. On that wide expanse of close-cropped grass, someone had built a ring out of cypress boards and thick posts, the sides waist-high on an average man. Men crowded around the wooden ring, leaning over the boards, jostling their neighbor for a better look, slapping each other on the backs, shouting, laughing, calling out contradicting suggestions. A dog howled, and another cheer went up. They held longneck beers and highball glasses, and the smell of their sweat and whiskey and lime mixed with the hot-animal stink.

As men shifted and moved, I could see into the ring. Reb faced off with four massive dogs. Reb was still the skinny blond boy I'd seen before, although now his Red Man t-shirt hung from him in shreds, exposing the slender musculature of arms and chest, and his cut-offs were rusty with blood. His arms had been bitten to hell—deep puncture wounds and jagged tears where, I imagined, the dogs had held on as he tried to shake them off. Finally, my gaze moved to his face, and for a moment, I thought he'd painted his mouth like a clown. Then I realized that gore ringed his lips, and my stomach turned.

The dogs surrounding him were the only explanation I needed. They were big dogs, almost completely white except for the occasional black spot on their heads—powerfully built, and tall enough that if they lifted their muzzles, they could probably clear the cypress boards. One's flank was soaked with blood; another had a dark cowl of it around its neck. A fifth dog lay on the floor of the ring, panting heavily. As I watched, one of the standing dogs lunged, and Reb spun toward it, growling. The dog pulled back, but one of its packmates darted forward, and Reb pivoted to club it on the side of the head. The dog whimpered and drew back. They took turns like that, darting forward, probing for weakness. It was obvious that, whatever advantage Reb had, he had either used it up or was hesitant to draw on it now.

"Why hasn't he changed?" Dag said under his breath, and I shook my head.

I scanned the crowd, trying to decide the next approach. Men clumped up, shouting odds, passing chits and cash back and forth. Others lined up for chow at the row of massive stainless-steel barbeque grills, where men in white jackets served sausage links and steak and chicken. Some men drank and chatted, oblivious to the fight. And others, like Joey Jaws, were glued to the ring.

He'd changed clothes since the last time I saw him, and he wore an expensive-looking sweater and chinos and leather derbies that had to be hand made. He was leaning into the ring, his face purple as he screamed at Reb to attack. It was obvious that Joey thought he'd gotten snookered on this deal. In one hand, he waved a cattle prod, and from time to time he waved it like he meant to stretch into the ring and use it. He didn't, though; I didn't think even Joey was that stupid.

Then, of course, he proved me wrong.

He forced his way along the side of the ring, still screaming, oblivious to the men he jostled out of his path. To judge by their faces, those men didn't like Joey much more than I did, but they were too afraid of him to say anything. When he approached the cluster of dogs and men, Joey got up on tiptoes, trying to reach over the dogs so that he could get Reb with the prod.

Instead, the movement startled one of the big, white dogs. It spun toward Joey, jaws snapping, and launched itself at him. Joey brought the prod down like a club, stunning the dog. It landed hard, its shoulder thudding against the side of the ring. Joey flailed at it with the prod—not using the tool to shock, but swinging it like a stick. The dog cowered against the cypress boards, still disoriented. And then, with a shriek, Joey tossed the cattle prod down, leaned over the side of the ring, and bit the dog on the throat.

The dog yelped and tried to tear away, and Joey tried to hang on. Joey got in another bite, savagely twisting his head, and then the dog ripped free of his grip. Blood jetted from its neck, and when Joey straightened, scarlet stained his face and neck and sweater. Even from a distance, the white dog hairs stuck in the blood were visible, like the delicate hatch-work of an artist. The dog took a few stumbling steps, and then it collapsed.

Everyone had gone silent. The only sound was the hiss of meat on the coals and what felt like the subterranean, collective heartbeat of a terrified crowd.

Joey screamed. It seemed to go on forever, and men inched back from him, grabbing each other. The scream cut off, and Joey whirled toward Reb.

"The wolf," he shouted. His teeth had a red film on them, and it looked like more dog hair fuzzed them. "I want the wolf. Give me the wolf!"

Reb stared back, his face blank. Then he twisted between the closest dogs, darted forward, and grabbed the cattle prod. He stuck it into Joey's neck, and Joey started to dance. He made a funny noise, almost like he liked it, the kind of exaggerated moan I'd heard people do when they got a massage. A dark cloud of urine bloomed across the front of his chinos. His legs jerked, and then some sort of internal safety in the prod must have cut the current. Joey dropped.

The silence seemed to breathe with the sound of insects. Joey's guests stared. They looked unable to move.

Then someone started to laugh. It was a woman's voice, and it had a whiskey-and-cigar tumbling roughness to it. Everyone turned to look—well, everyone except Joey—as Nelda Pie stepped through the French doors on the back of Dauphin House.

She was white, and although I didn't know her real age, she looked like she'd blitzed past forty, with her peroxide bouffant hair and her fleshy face striped with Avon's latest and greatest. Tonight, she wore black short shorts with a pink arrow on each leg swooping dramatically toward her crotch, with a white tube top under a flannel shirt. She'd painted her nails black, and that was new; maybe she'd read it in *Cosmo*. "Ten spooky looks to get ready for Halloween."

Still laughing, she came toward the ring. Men parted for her, stumbling out of her path, staring like they couldn't believe what they were seeing. Maybe they couldn't; I'd encountered her before, and I couldn't believe it. When she reached the ring, she glanced around, and the weight of her gaze was enough to make every man on the lawn step back again. It also gave me a bonus view of her ass, where pink letters on the short shorts said simply, FUNK.

Her laughter cut off, and she said, "All right, Rebellion. Fun and games are over; time to come home."

Reb stared at her. He was breathing hard. Blood from the bite wounds on one hand snaked down the cattle prod; on his other hand, it dripped from his fingers. He'd lost one of the Timberlands, I could see now, and his bare foot was lacerated and caked with dust.

"Did you hear me?"

"You cunt." The words were slurred, but they popped the tension in the air. I could feel it even from our hiding place, a sting in my face like Joey had reached out and slapped me. He clung to the cypress boards, barely holding himself up. "This piece of shit isn't anything special. You tricked me." The words had a wounded childishness to them. "Get the fuck off my property."

"Oh, Rebellion is real special," Nelda Pie said. "He just needs the right motivation. Isn't that so—" She cut off, and then her head swiveled to look straight toward the trees where Dag and I were hiding. A grin broke out, threatening to send all that Avon crumbling. "Well, well, well. The thing in the grass." That was what she had called the hashok the first time I had spoken to her. "Come on out, half-breed. Let me see you."

Dag's eyes cut toward me. Neither of us moved.

"I said come out here." With an exasperated noise, Nelda Pie crooked a finger.

The silver dime around my neck went cold against my chest. Dag grunted and rocked forward, as though someone were trying to pull him off his feet, but he stayed where he was. I could feel the force of whatever she'd done dragging on me too. After a moment, the feeling faded. Dag let out a soft noise, and he settled back onto his heels.

"Have it your way," Nelda Pie said. "You can watch. Maybe you'll learn something about what happens to half-breeds who don't have the right care. If you beg real pretty, maybe I'll even help you before the thing in the grass eats its way through you."

Joey fumbled a gun out from the back of his chinos. "I said get the fuck off—"

His arm made a snapping noise, and then it jerked sideways, as though it had been yanked to the side. Joey screamed.

"They call you Joey Jaws," Nelda Pie said as though making small talk. Joey's other arm made that same awful cracking noise, and Joey screamed again. "But it's not about the teeth, is it? What do you think, Joey? How'd you like me to give you what you always wanted? Kalfu is not a kind master, but he owes me. I found him weak, starving, kept alive by that fool Le Doux, by prayers that old women mumbled in plank shacks. Kalfu can be grateful." Something was changing. The electric lights shone as brightly as ever, but darkness gathered around Nelda Pie. I had a sense of tremendous space, of a vast consciousness brushing mine: a shadow dancing in fire, the off-center corners of the universe on clockwork wheels, a taste of a frozen fever. "Let me give you," Nelda Pie said, "Kalfu's gift."

Joey Jaws arched his back until I thought it was going to snap, and then he began to scream. And scream. And scream.

Nelda Pie started to laugh.

The crowd broke; men turned and ran. But out of the shadows, dark forms sprinted to intercept them. I caught only glimpses of them: things that were no longer man or beast but something in-between. A man with the horns of a ram on his head crashed into a man in a tweed jacket. A woman in what my brain catalogued as steampunk gear, some kind of Victorian coat with enormous brass buttons, ended at the waist, and below her, eight furry spider legs carried her into the fray. A man with half his face covered in scales breathed fire. A woman with hands two times the size they should have been caught a fleeing partygoer by the arm and ripped it off at the shoulder.

Dag grabbed my wrist, but I said, "We have to get Reb."

I broke Dag's hold and sprinted across the lawn.

Reb had turned away from Nelda Pie, and now he was running toward the far end of the ring. The dogs were running with him, trying to escape the thing that came after Reb. It wasn't clear whether it had been a man or a woman to begin with; I could see elements of what I thought were a great ape—the bulk and fur, the width of its shoulders, the massive arms—but it had leathery hide in places too, as though suffering from mange. It must have been moving almost twice as fast as Reb, quickly closing the distance between them. One of the dogs turned, snarling, and the creature struck out. The blow sent the dog flying across the ring; it hit the cypress boards with a crunch, slid to the ground, and lay still.

I cut across the lawn at an angle, trying to intercept the creature before it caught up with Reb. The cold fire of the hashok's venom was awake now, working its way through me—a pleasant numbness spreading through my gut and chest, working its way down my limbs. Instead of making me feel slow or leaden, it made every movement easy—almost effortless. My world began to narrow. The ape-thing loped after Reb, its jaw hanging open to expose its teeth. I wondered what noises it would make when I took its jaws in my hands and ripped its face apart.

A gun fired, and I glanced around. Nelda Pie was staring grimly at me and Dag, following us with the barrel of a dainty, nickel-plated revolver. She'd missed because we were too far away, and the accuracy dropped to nothing on those things. But she only had to get lucky once.

I turned back toward the ape-thing, and two things happened: a fist flew toward my face, and I realized Nelda Pie had meant to distract me.

Dropping to the ground saved my life. The punch carved the air just over my head; I could hear the sound of it, the force of its passage shredding a path through the night. Then I landed on the lawn and rolled. I knocked up against the ape-thing's feet and then kept rolling past it. Above me, I heard more shots—much closer this time, and in a steady bang-bang-bang that I recognized as control and discipline and training. In other words, Dag. The ape-thing shrieked, and then Dag let out a shout.

When I tumbled to a stop on the lawn, I lay for a moment, blinking up into the sheen of electric lights. Distantly, Dag grunted, and the ape-thing bellowed. I got myself up. Another shot rang out, but this one was farther off—Nelda Pie's peashooter. Something was wrong with my leg, and although it didn't hurt because of the icy river of the hashok's venom, I couldn't put my full weight on it. I turned in a circle, trying to orient myself. Reb and a man I didn't recognize were struggling at the door of the carriage house. The spider-woman was climbing the side of Dauphin House, dragging a white lady with her. Then—Dag.

He was favoring one shoulder, and he'd lost his gun. A bloody rash opened one side of his face from temple to jaw. The ape-thing was closing in on him and swung lazily—it had a trace of contempt—and Dag staggered backward, barely avoiding the blow.

I hobbled toward the dogfighting ring. When I reached the closest post, I ripped it out of the ground. The bottom was still set in a tube of concrete, which was nice. You could do more damage with concrete.

I turned around as Dag tried to dodge another punch. He wasn't fast enough this time. The ape-thing's punch caught him, barely making contact at all, but it still knocked Dag off his feet. He tried to scoot back, but he couldn't use one arm, and that slowed him. The ape-thing took a step after him. It was hard to read its expression from behind, but something about the body language suggested glee.

On my first swing, the chunk of concrete at the end of the post caved in the ape-thing's skull. It tottered. I swung again, and the back of its head flattened, shards of bone white where they cut their way free from the mess of dark hair and hide.

Nelda Pie screamed.

I hit the ape-thing again, the sound soft and spattering now, and it collapsed.

Dag stared up at me.

A part of me wondered if his head would sound like rotten fruit when it split open.

"Eli?" he said. "E? Can you hear me?"

I could hear him. It was very fucking annoying to hear him, the way his voice buzzed at the back of my head, the distressed sound of a fly caught in pitch. I didn't want to hear him. I wanted to hear the music, the screams, the dying noises of men being pulled apart and gutted and eaten alive. I spun away from him.

Reb and the man were still struggling at the door. Between the injuries Reb had sustained and the man's panic, they seemed to be evenly matched, both of them clawing and pulling at each other, both of them determined to take refuge in the carriage house.

Reb. That thought was hazy in my head, but it was there. Reb.

I cocked the post over my shoulder and started toward the carriage house. Reb. It was hard to think; even my head seemed frozen, my thoughts crystalline and sharp and clear and totally still. I had to keep Reb safe.

Reb noticed me first, glancing over his shoulder and then rearing back. Something cast a blue light across his face, washing out the color in his cheeks, turning the blood around his mouth black. Whatever Reb saw made him forget the door. He pressed back against the carriage house, sidling along the wall.

This movement must have caught the man's attention because he shot a look back and then froze.

I brought the post up like a club.

Something caught my shoulder, spinning me, and I stared into Dag's face. His eyes were wide.

"Eli, what are you doing?"

Shrugging him off, I turned back. I had to kill this man, the one who wanted to hurt Reb. I already knew what it would feel like: the resistance of bone, and then the splintering aftershock, the jellied surrender of brain and tissue. My mouth was wet for it.

"E!"

Dag gripped my shoulder again, and this time, I threw him off me. He hit the ground hard, skidding and tearing up the perfect lawn, grass stains mixing with his scrapes and abrasion. He lay there for a moment. That same blue light fell on him, illuminating the worry lines around his mouth, casting a million shadows through the steel thatch of his hair. His eyes were huge and full of something I didn't want to see.

I dropped the post. My hands ached. I took a step backward.

Dag dragged himself up into a sitting position; he had forgotten to cradle his injured arm, and I wanted to remind him, tell him he needed to be careful because I thought his shoulder had separated, but I couldn't find the words.

And then the fever-frost snapped, and I said, "Dag, oh my God!"

I scrambled over to him, dropped onto my knees, and reached for his arm. He pulled away and flinched, the color dropping out of his face like someone switching off a TV.

"I'm sorry," I said. "I'm so sorry—"

When I reached out again, he pushed my hand away. His eyes never left my face.

"Dag," I whispered. "It's me."

He shook his head. It was almost nothing. Almost.

A growl began behind me, and then it rose shrilly and broke off. I twisted around. Reb lay on the ground, unmoving, and Nelda Pie stood over him. She was smiling. One of her chimeras, a contorted, nightmare version of a centaur, scooped up Reb and galloped off into the night. Her smile growing, Nelda Pie wagged her little peashooter at us.

"You'll get one shot before I reach you," I said.

"When you're ready," she said, "Kalfu is waiting."

I flipped her the bird.

She laughed, and, hitching up her short shorts, she turned and walked away. The sounds of slaughter continued around us, although they were fading now—a quick glance told me most of Joey's men were already dead, and the few who remained didn't look like they'd make it long. The chimeras slunk back into the trees, leaving Dag and me. Then, behind me, the carriage house door slammed shut, and I guessed at least one of Joey's men had survived—against all odds.

Movement made me check on Dag. He was holding his phone to his ear.

"No police," I said.

He ignored me. He disconnected from the first call and placed a second. Then he said, "Mom, I need to talk to Posey, and he's not answering his phone—what do you mean he's not there?"

As Dag continued speaking with his mom, I sat back on my heels, my head drooping. I knew I needed to check myself for injuries I might not have noticed during those frantic minutes of fighting. I needed to check Dag, too—see what we could do about his shoulder or his arm or whatever it was, and of course, try to make it up to him. Again. There was blood and gore on the camo jacket, and I started to wriggle out of it. Then I stopped. I stared at my hands. I blinked. And then I thought, No. I closed my eyes, and when I opened them again, the shadows thickened in the trees, hanging there like bats. I didn't look at my hands again.

"Where are the girls—" Dag was asking, but his mom must have preempted him. He bit off a swear. "I'll call you later."

I got to my feet.

"They're gone, all of them," Dag said as he pocketed the phone. "Posey and the girls told my mom they knew how to help Reb, whatever that means."

The first step was the hardest, carrying me away from Dag.

"Whatever it is, you can bet your hat it's something stupid." Dag grunted. "I don't know how he talked the girls into—where are you going?"

I walked faster now, still limping.

"Eli?"

I broke into a faltering run.

"Eli, what's going on? Eli!" His voice betrayed his struggle as he tried to get to his feet. "Eli, get back here!"

I ran.

I didn't look back. If I looked back, I knew I'd be lost.

III

Mait' Carrefour—Haitian god of magicians and lord of the crossroads, also called Kalfu.

- *Vodoo,* Hans Peter Oswald

DAG (1)

The thing about sulking and feeling sorry for yourself and giving up on life and the world and basically writing off your whole existence like a bad first try was that eventually you had to pee. And while my parents loved me, and Eli never stopped talking about how they enabled all sorts of bad behavior, they didn't love me enough to buy me a bedpan. So, even though I'd decided to spend the rest of my life in my room, eventually I had to get up and go to the bathroom.

My shoulder hurt—a late night visit to the urgent care had ended with several prescriptions, stitches in one cut, and a sling for my arm. Because I was a rebel and nothing mattered and life was meaningless, I wasn't wearing the sling. I thought about what Eli would say about that, and then I reminded myself I wasn't thinking about Eli anymore. I'd spent most of the day reminding myself of that.

It was quiet in the house. Posey, Dutch, and Lurnice still hadn't come back—if they were ever coming back, if they hadn't run off for good. Like Eli. Not that I was thinking about any of them. I peed. I washed my hands.

When I came out of the bathroom, my mom called from the kitchen, "Dagobert, would you like some bread pudding?"

I shambled back to my bedroom and shut the door.

For a while, I tried to go back to sleep. Then I lay there with my eyes open. A lot of my books were still on the shelves. My desk still held old pens and check stubs and what my mom called mementos, like anybody was ever going to want my kindergarten noodle art. On the back of the door, a poster for the 2008 Braxton Bragg Memorial High School basketball team was still stapled in place. Mason looked like a baby. Some of his hair had fallen into his eyes, of course. My underwater light was gone, though, and so was my Bluetooth speaker; those had gone to the house in New Orleans. Eli's running shoes lay where he'd kicked them off near the door, one fallen on its side.

Eli had run. Again.

I rolled onto my side—on my good shoulder, since I didn't want to mess up the one that had been dislocated and still should have been in a sling. I faced the wall and told myself, once more, I wasn't thinking about Eli.

Then I rolled onto my back and craned my head toward the door. Baby-faced Mason was staring back at me, and I could hear his dumb, straight-boy voice saying, *Who are you kidding?*

"Mind your own beeswax," I told him.

He looked dumber than usual with that hair hanging in his eyes. Eli had run. Again. After two years together, after everything we'd worked on. He'd run, and he hadn't said a word, hadn't told me why. I couldn't help myself; I started playing it all back again in my head. It was like revving an engine, getting me more and more worked up. I knew he was scared. We were both scared. We were both hurt, and—and for a while, Eli hadn't been Eli, with his eyes glowing blue and him being so strong, and not seeming to know who I was. And ripping that post out of the ground, my brain said. And killing that ape thing, my brain suggested, just crushing its head like a grape. And hurting you. Knocking you down, turning on you like you were next.

I'd always known Eli was strong. Not just mentally and emotionally—he carried a lot of lean muscle, and over the past two years, he'd spent a lot of time working on his body. Crunches, sure, because he got so silly over abs, but he trained hard just about every way you could. That was Eli for you. Never did anything the easy way his whole life. Never slacked once. And in the last year, that had started to pay off. He'd shed the weight he'd been trying to lose. His body was harder. I'd look at him naked sometimes, and the word was cut—like someone had pared away everything that wasn't muscle and bone, but also the sharpness of it all, like his body was a blade.

But what I'd seen him do the night before, that kind of strength, that didn't have anything to do with gyms or weight bands or the days he lay on the floor and said he was doing Pilates. That had been something else entirely. And his eyes. His eyes glowing blue like—

I'm not thinking about Eli, I told myself. He ran away. Like he always does when things get tough. And I'm tired of it, so I'm not even going to spare him a second thought.

How's that going for you? Mason asked.

"Stay out of this," I told him.

It was Saturday. Halloween. And somehow, I'd packed all my monsters into my bedroom. So, I got up and went to the kitchen.

My mom was mopping, drawing glistening arcs across the linoleum. The back door was open, and the breeze coming through the screen door was a little too cool for comfort. Outside, on the back gallery, my dad was cutting the tip off a tube of caulk.

I picked a path around my mom toward the fridge.

"There's bread pudding, Dagobert." She wore nitrile gloves, the way she always did when she was cleaning, and they made tacky sounds as she adjusted her hands on the mop. "Wouldn't you like some bread pudding?"

"I don't like anything."

"Well, dear, I hope that's not true."

"Dagobert, tell your mother you still like things," my dad called from the back gallery.

I ignored both of them. I dug around in the freezer until I found the brownies; my mom usually kept a pan of them frozen in case of emergencies—you know, like a neighbor moving in, or when someone had a death in the family. A distant relative, though. The death of a close relative merited the full Gloria LeBlanc treatment, which was a meal designed to give any survivors heart disease, possibly to speed them along to that glorious reunion in the bosom of Abraham, which might have been a phrase I had heard at church once. She'd probably never thought the emergency in question was that her son's boyfriend was possibly turning into a monster and also had run away and had a lot of issues with intimacy and trust and even though he kept promising to go to therapy, so far, it'd just been promises.

The mop whirred in the self-wringer as Gloria stepped on the bucket's pedal. "Where's Eli?"

"I don't know."

"Well, what happened?"

"I don't know."

"Did you have a fight?"

"Mom, I don't want to talk about it."

"Well, you don't have to talk about it if you don't want to talk about it."

"Dagobert, tell your mother you and Eli had a fight."

"We didn't have a fight. I don't know where he went. I don't know what happened. I don't know why he's always running off like this. Maybe this is Lanny all over again, did you ever think about that?"

My mom lifted the mop out of the bucket. She passed it back and forth over a shiny spot of linoleum that I was seriously suspicious had already been mopped.

"And if this is like Lanny," I said, unable to help myself as I dug into the frozen brownies with a spoon, "then I guess you'll see Eli any day now, because you'll be feeding him meals behind my back as soon as I turn around."

"He's very thin, Dagobert," my mom said. "He doesn't have the ass God gave a cuttlefish."

"I don't want to talk about Eli. I definitely don't want to talk about his ass. And what does that mean, anyway? You don't even know what a cuttlefish is."

"Dagobert," my dad shouted. "Tell your mother she knows what a cuttlefish is. Tell her right now."

I sat at the table and stabbed the brownies a few more times. A piece broke off, and I got it in my mouth, bitter and dense and sweet and cold. It shouldn't have tasted good, mixing with the smell of Fabuloso and silicone and mineral spirits, but it did. It tasted like home, and like a lot of Saturdays like this, and all of a sudden, I had to close my eyes against the hot rush of tears.

The mop clattered, and my mom was at my side, squeezing me into a hug. I didn't break down and sob or anything, but I mean, she was my mom, and maybe a few tears got out. She rubbed my head, and after a while, I felt my dad's heavy hand on my shoulder, and after a while, I sat up straight.

"Eli loves you," my mom said. "He's scared, that's all."

"He's always scared," I said. "I'm tired of him being scared."

"Well," my dad said, "maybe you ought to tell him that. I've always said, Eli is a perfect ten in looks, but he's a bit soft-brained. You always liked them like that, I know. Simple."

"Oh my God."

"You have, Dagobert. It's not your fault. Some men appreciate that quality in a partner."

"He's smart. He's plenty smart."

"Of course, he is," my mom said, patting my shoulder. "The other day, I saw him doing that word jumble like it was nothing."

"It was the children's jumble, Gloria," my dad said. "I couldn't say anything, he was so pleased with himself. Now, Dagobert, on the other hand, Dagobert is a college man."

"Oh my God," I said.

"I know he's in college, thank you very much," my mom said. "I know he's smart. I'm trying to make him feel better. It's not his fault Eli's, well, touched."

"Sexually gifted, though," my dad said. "You have to give him that."

"Nobody's even talking about sex, Hubert. Of course he's got talents. There's got to be some reason Dagobert's interested in him."

"Yeah," I said. "Lots of reasons. He's smart. And he's brave. And he's strong. And he's funny."

Half-worried, half-pitying, my mom said, "Dagobert, last weekend, he was wearing a ballcap backwards. Your father and I aren't ones to judge, but you have to be at least a little touched not to know how to put on a ballcap."

"I'm going to my room. And I'm taking these brownies. And I'm taking the milk."

"Take a glass, too, dear."

I didn't take a glass.

"Don't you dare drink straight from the jug," my mom called after me.

"It's probably something he's seen Eli do," my father said to her. I tried to walk faster, but he called after me, "The whole family has to drink that milk, Dagobert. Listen to your mother."

I didn't slam the door. That was one of my big achievements in life.

I sat on my bed for a while. I ate brownies—faster as they thawed. I drank straight from the jug because I'm a rebel and a wild child and I wanted to be bad. I thought about Mason and what he'd say, and then I figured even if he'd been alive, I'd have had to scrap all his advice as soon as he finished talking. It would have been nice, though. Just to hear it. No matter how dumb it was.

And then, because that was the way my brain worked, I started thinking about Lanny. How he'd run out on me. How he'd taken all my money. What it'd been like, moving in with my parents, and trying to get out of bed every morning, trying to pretend my life could keep going. And all the days after that, when I'd gotten so good at pretending that I'd even convinced myself. All the days up until I met Eli.

My first domestic, after we'd gotten the asshole in the tank, I'd gone to the men's room and cried. And I hadn't told Eli this next part because I was ashamed of it, but that night I'd gone home and drunk myself to sleep. I could pick memories like that out of a hat. The time we'd gone looking for a little girl who'd run away, and when we'd found her, I'd seen the bruises on her arms, and we'd still had to hand her over to her dad. The time I'd thought I was busting a boy for pot, and his mom threw a canning jar full of piss at the back of my head. What do you do except go back to the station and shower and sit around with a bunch of guys who don't have anything left to say to each other, thinking about facts, thinking the weirdest things? You're thinking that every minute, every sixty seconds, twenty-four people are the victims of rape or physical violence or stalking by an intimate partner. You're thinking that one in three of the people you lock up will get locked up again, plain as that. You're thinking that in small law enforcement departments, the suicide rate is four times the national average. And then your shift ends, and you go home, whatever that means.

And then I met Eli, and we did something good together. Something really good. Because we were good together, even if it scared him, even if he didn't know how to handle feeling vulnerable like that.

I stared at his running shoes.

He kept leaving; that was a fact. He was probably going to keep leaving. And that said something, didn't it? I thought about years of this, year after year, of coming home to dark houses and empty rooms and the question written right at the end of whatever you wanted to call it—my soul or my spirit or my worth as a human being. I had options. I could find a self-help group. I definitely needed a therapist. Maybe join a cult. Heck, I could sit here and eat brownies until I went into a diabetic coma and they had to wheel me out. That sounded pretty good. He had run off. Again. He had run off again, and didn't care one bit about—about the fact that the electric bill was in his name, and he had all the Rouses rewards on his savers card, and we were supposed to go to Colorado this Christmas and already had the Airbnb reserved. He didn't care about any of that because he was so fucking selfish sometimes.

I couldn't stand staring at those shoes anymore. I set the jug of milk on the desk. I ditched the brownies on my bed. I pulled on joggers and grabbed my keys and wallet, and then, with those fucking running shoes hanging from my hand, I left the bedroom.

"Dagobert," my mother said as I came down the hall, "where are you going?"

"To murder Eli."

She made a noise like that was the sweetest thing she'd heard in her whole life.

"If you boys have finished making up to each other with the sweet language of your bodies before dinner —" My dad called from the back gallery.

"You can't say stuff like that," I said. "I'm never going to have sex again if you keep saying stuff like that."

He continued, unperturbed, "—then have the decency to call your mother so she can defrost the good lasagna."

"I said I'm going to murder him," I shouted over my shoulder. "This is why you're such bad parents; you never listen to me."

"Tell Eli hello," my father called back.

"Hugs and kisses to Eli from both of us!" my mom shouted.

"It hasn't even been twenty-four hours," I said. "But when I come back after a week, I'm chopped liver."

This time, I did slam the door. To teach them a lesson.

The day had a hard, cold grayness, like the sky had been detached and nobody had come along with a replacement yet. I drove north out of the city, into the smoke of stubble fires, the burnt-sugar sweetness of the canebrakes. I cut off on an old state highway, driving through a tunnel of trees—live oaks that were green and mossy, and willows and sugar maples whose leaves had turned a papery pink. It might have been my imagination, but I thought I smelled the old smoke long before I could see the burned-out shell of the house.

The thing that had called itself Richard York, the thing that we had called the hashok, the creature that Nelda Pie called the thing in the grass, had lived in a modern take on a farmhouse, a million-and-change stunner with white siding and huge windows. It had burned down to charred framing, collapsed rafters, and piles of scorched debris. The fire had been two years ago, but when I let the Escort roll to a stop, I was sure I could still smell the smoke, and ashes stirred in the wind off the Okhlili.

The manicured St. Augustine lawn had gotten shaggy and ankle high. The magnolia trees still held their leaves, but they looked dull and plasticky. The wind picked up again, and it sounded like a fire when it rushed through the tupelo trees. It sounded like a train. It sounded like something from the Old Testament, the Spirit of the Lord in the whirlwind, and it raised goose bumps on my arms.

Eli was sitting on a cut bank of the Okhlili, dressed in my po'boy sweatshirt and the camo pants and the waterproof boots. When he saw me, his eyes got huge, and he got to his feet and ran.

I ran after him.

He broke away from the river, heading toward the thick stands of pine and sugar maple, where the leaves were exploding in fiery reds and oranges. That was where we'd first met, where I'd found him that night two years ago, where the hashok had attacked us. In hindsight, I knew it had only been playing with us, but at the time, the threat had seemed real, and the danger life or death. Now, Eli shot towards the gloom thickening under the branches. He was faster than me. He was going to get away.

I pitched one of his running shoes as hard as I could. It hit Eli in the legs, and he stumbled and fell. He came up again a moment later, bouncing to his feet, his gaze sweeping the ground. Then his head came up, his mouth slanting with outrage.

"Did you just throw a shoe at me?"

"You're so smart," I said, dropping from my run to a walk, still moving toward him. "Figure it out."

His face began to shutter again, the security measures falling back into place. He hugged himself and took a step back. "You need to go. I'm leaving—"

I hurled the other shoe as hard as I could. It struck him in the chest with a satisfying thump.

Eli's jaw dropped. "Dagobert!"

I kept walking.

"That hurt!"

"Put them on."

He rubbed his chest. We still had ten feet between us, but I was closing fast, and he shifted, not quite looking at the trees.

"Put the fucking shoes on," I said.

"Excuse me?"

"You heard me."

He checked my face and cut his eyes away. "I don't know—"

"Put them on! You don't have to know anything except how to put on a goddamn pair of shoes. Those are my boots; I want them. And I want my sweatshirt back. And I want my camo pants back." He hugged himself tighter, and I said, "What don't you understand about put those fucking shoes on?"

Eli did look at the trees then, but he must have figured I was too close now for him to make a break for it. He made a weird, helpless noise that was kind of a laugh, and then he balanced on one foot and started unlacing a boot. When it was loose enough, he kicked it in my direction—hard. I caught it. He repeated the performance, and then he stood on the St. Augustine grass in stockinged feet, folded his arms again, and set his jaw.

"Put. Them. On."

This time, the noise in his throat was wild with frustration. He stepped into the running shoes, pulled the heels on with two fingers, and stomped his feet. "There? Are you happy?"

"No, I'm not happy, Eli. Are you happy?" He didn't answer, so I said, "Now you've got your running shoes. So, there you go. Run the fuck away in your running shoes."

He pulled the sweatshirt up to wipe his eyes. A minute dragged past, with nothing but the sound of the Okhlili, and the branches stirring in the breeze, and then the distant rumble of thunder. A landslide of storm clouds was moving in, the leading edge broken by blue-white bursts of lightning. The air smelled like a storm, like the sweet rot of leaves in autumn, a whiff of ozone that made the hair on my arms stand up.

Once more, Eli pressed his sweatshirt to his eyes. This time, he held it there.

"What are you crying about?" I asked. "What in the world do you have to cry about? I'm the one who should be upset. I still haven't got my sweatshirt and my camo pants."

"What in the fuck is going on?" He yanked the sweatshirt down, and his eyes were red. "Is this why you came and found me, to yell at me? Is that what you want?"

He was shouting by the end, so I shouted back, "I don't know what I want! Maybe I do want to yell at you. Maybe I want a fight. You're always talking about how we should have a fight. How do you like this one?"

"I hate it! It's fucking awful! You're being fucking awful!"

"You ought to know about that!"

He opened his mouth, and then he shut it again. Pressing the heels of his hands to his eyes, he was quiet for a long moment, and then he let out a soft, hurt laugh. "Ok," he said. "Yeah, I guess I should."

Thunder rumbled again, closer. The darkness came at us like a physical thing, stirring the grass, pulling on my hair and jacket, like it was sweeping everything else away until it was just the two of us standing on that patch of lawn screaming at each other.

Dropping his hands, Eli opened his eyes. He said, "If you want to yell at me, you should yell at me."

"Jeez, thanks."

"No, I deserve it."

I shook my head.

"Do you want to hit me?" he asked. "Would you feel better? Because you can."

"Good Lord, E, I don't want to hit you."

"But you can if you do."

I dug a thumb into the corner of my eye and looked away.

The first raindrops started to fall. Where they struck the Okhlili, they hit hard enough to dimple the water, and their rings began to spread and intersect. I could see it for a moment, and then the storm swallowed the river, and I couldn't even see that.

"Maybe you want to talk to me," Eli said. He was looking down at himself, studying the front of the sweatshirt—my sweatshirt—and he brushed fingers over the photo-transfer of my face. "Maybe that's why you tracked me down."

"I tracked you down because I'm not going to have a boyfriend who keeps running away. I'm a decent person, Eli. I do whatever you ask me around the house. I'm nice to you. I talk to your friends even when that one kept calling me Grandpa. I don't complain when you hide the TV or you suck up my notecards in the vacuum or put my textbooks in the dryer." My voice broke as I said, "Posey likes talking about how I'm too soft, and maybe he's right, but I don't deserve to sit around, wondering if today's going to be the day you run and never come back."

He picked at the cuff of the too-big sleeve and whispered, "No, you don't. You deserve a lot better."

"I don't deserve to—to have to feel like shit. I already had a boyfriend run out on me, in case you forgot. And now I've spent years wondering if you're going to do the same. How do you think that makes me feel?"

"Awful, I guess." In a tiny voice, he said, "I'm sorry."

"Yeah, well, I'm sorry too." Rain struck my face, my shoulders, cold and stinging. I wiped my eyes and fixed on the tupelos, their leaves burning and spinning like Pentecost. "Go on, then. Aren't you going to go?"

"Do you want me to go?"

"I'm not doing that. Go. Or don't go. But I'm not playing that game."

Maybe it was rain, but it looked like he was starting to cry again. He snuffled into the sweatshirt some more. The storm started opening up, and to the north, ball lightning exploded over the bayou. We stood there getting wetter by the minute.

"If you want something," I said, "you've got to ask. I'm not a mind reader."

He was trembling—shaking inside the baggy sweatshirt. Then, wordlessly, he held out his hands.

I glanced at them, looked up at his face, and then snapped my attention back to his hands. I knew Eli's hands. I'd spent a lot of time holding them, playing with his fingers when we lay on the couch together, kissing his palm when I walked by, watching him cook. He had beautiful hands, with long, graceful fingers. These weren't his hands.

They were too big, for one. The fingers were even longer, and they tapered to thick, pointed yellow nails. Claws, my brain said. They're called claws. The skin was mottled, and my first thought was that maybe it was vitiligo, with lighter patches mixing with the soft brown of Eli's skin. But the lighter patches were dead white, and after a moment, I realized they weren't...skin. Not human skin, anyway. The texture was wrong.

"It's happening," he said. The words had a slight distortion to them, the way they do when your lip is full of Novocain. "We knew it was happening, but now it's—it's actually happening."

I thought of the night before, when he'd knocked me down without even trying, when his eyes had burned blue. He had hazel eyes, but they'd been electric blue. And glowing.

"So," he said in a thick voice, "that's why. Just so you know. It's not about you. I love you—"

"You dummy," I said and took him in my arms.

He tried to pull away once, and then he broke down, sobbing into my jacket, his whole body shaking like he was falling apart. The rain started coming down harder, big, fat pellets of it. His hair smelled like gunpowder and mud and pine resin. The wind wrestled the tupelo trees, and at the same time, something huge and invisible was wrestling in me. And then I wasn't wrestling anymore. Gave up. Just done.

I picked a leaf out of his hair, and I said, "We're getting soaked. Come on, let's sit in the car."

I kept one arm around him, and I carried the boots with my free hand. We'd barely gotten in the Escort's back seat, Eli half in my lap and curled around me and trembling, when the storm cut loose. The rain fell like someone had tipped over a bucket, sheeting over the windows. I had that feeling that humans must have been feeling all the way back to the Stone Age: being safe and relatively dry while the clouds gutted themselves, a warm body pressing against mine.

After a while, Eli said, "I have to go, Dag. I hurt you last night. I could have killed you."

"We said we'd figure this out together. We said that two years ago. I don't know why you think things have changed."

"I have to go."

"You don't have to do anything."

"I'm a monster."

"They were just notecards."

He hiccupped a laugh and wiped his eyes on his shoulder. "You know what I mean."

"It's a virus. It's like any other virus. There'll be treatments. A cure."

"It's not like any other virus. You know that." He shivered. One of his hands was behind my back, trapped between my body and the seat. I was aware of it, of its size and density, its unfamiliar roughness through the nylon of my jacket and my cotton tee. "It's going to get worse. I'm dangerous."

"Eli Prescott Martins, if you being dangerous bothered me, I would have broken up with you the first time you tried to hide my car keys. I like that you're dangerous. Well, most of the time. If you're going to leave, then you're going to do it honestly—you're going to leave because you don't like being vulnerable, or because you're sick of me, or whatever the real reason is. But don't give me this bullshit about being dangerous."

He was quiet for a long time. The rain drummed on the roof of the car, an unrelenting hiss. Then he said, "I don't deserve you."

"Knock it off."

"I don't. I should—I should have been so much nicer to you."

"You're plenty nice. But I don't want you messing around with my school stuff anymore. That's serious."

For some reason, that made him smile, although the expression vanished into suspiciously familiar gravity a moment later, and he nodded.

"Dag, what if it's me?"

"It's definitely you. I saw all the glitter in the vacuum."

"No, I mean—" He braced himself with a breath. "What if the reason I'm changing, or the reason Richard, the hashok, chose me—what if it's because of who I am? I'm awful. I'm so awful to you. I'm mean to everyone, actually, and nobody can stand me. Well, you put up with me, but—"

"What? I'm too dumb to know better? Or I'm so desperate that I'll put up with your nonsense? Or I'm a spineless sack of dog turds, like Posey says, and you can walk all over me?"

He opened his mouth, looked at me, and closed it again.

"Thanks a lot," I said.

"Dag! You're not any of those things. I just meant—"

"Then don't insult me by saying everybody else sees how awful you are, but I'm too fucking dense to figure it out."

"You've been doing a lot of swearing tonight," he said in a low voice. "My dad barely talked to me at the end. Gard couldn't stand to be around me. Richard literally only put up with me because he was fattening me like veal in a cage. There's something wrong with me."

"You're a complicated person. I'm a complicated person. Everybody's complicated. I think you're all sorts of wonderful. You're smart and strong and funny. You're so compassionate, and you can't help taking care of people."

"I like it." He wouldn't meet my eyes, and the words were toneless. "When I feel like that, like I'm going to enjoy hurting someone. I know I shouldn't. Part of me knows. But I feel strong and safe and—and in control. All the parts of me that hurt, all the parts of me that never shut up, the ones that all day are telling me I'm fat and ugly and worthless, they're iced over. I can't hear anything, and it's so...good."

I picked another leaf out of his hair. We'd done a lot of reading, both of us, over the last year. About eating disorders. About what was going on behind the scenes, so to speak. And, of course, it wasn't simple, and everybody was different, and somehow I'd won the jackpot for complicated, beautiful men who kept a pair of scissors in their back pocket during football season and spent all of October and November threatening to cut the TV's power cord. But since Eli wouldn't go to therapy, we had to do something.

"When you started having issues with your body," I said, brushing hair over his ear, "what was going on?"

He cocked his head.

"Answer the question, mister."

"A lot, I guess. Gard and my parents were dead. I was—I don't know, I was living with Richard. He was packing me with Prozac and ketamine. I spent all day in the house. Sometimes, I spent all day in bed. Ok, now that I'm hearing it out loud, I'm going to say, maybe not a lot was going on. Maybe nothing was happening at all."

I played with the hair over his ear.

"It's not the same," he finally said.

"Why not?"

"I get what you're saying, but it's not the same."

"Ok."

"I was gaining all that weight because of the Prozac. I was depressed, seriously depressed, and I wasn't getting any exercise. I didn't like how I looked."

"E, I said ok."

He shook his head. The words sounded torn from him. "I felt helpless. I felt so fucking...powerless. Gard. And my parents. My whole life had imploded, and I'd been there, in the next room, while it happened, and I couldn't do anything to stop it. I couldn't go back in time. I couldn't fix it. I couldn't even make myself forget it. All I could do was think about it, again and again."

My hand slid down to his nape, where his skin felt cool, and I chafed him lightly.

"I could control what I ate," Eli said. His voice twisted and bucked. "I could control when I ate. I could control if I ate."

"I know, sweetheart."

He ran the inside of his arm across his eyes. "Ok, so maybe I've got some issues with control. It's what you keep saying: I don't like being helpless. I don't like being vulnerable. Big breakthrough."

"You know, a lot of that stuff, what we're talking about, it starts off as a coping mechanism."

"And now, what? I'm coping with my utter fucking uselessness by—by liking the fact that I'm turning into a monster?"

"I don't think you're useless. Your Cajun pasta is even better than my mom's. God, please don't tell her that."

The corner of his mouth turned, then fell again.

"After Lanny," I said, "I shut my life down. I didn't go anywhere except work. I didn't see anyone except at work. I moved in with my parents. And at first, that was ok. It was a coping mechanism, and it worked—it helped me get through the first day, and then the next. And then, after a while, it wasn't helping me anymore, but I couldn't stop. It was safer to go to work, to go home to my parents, to live on autopilot, than risk getting hurt. And then I met you." I kissed the side of his head. "Sometimes, things that start out as a way to help us end up hurting us. I'm not saying you like what's happening to you. I'm saying we've been through this before, where you couldn't trust your own brain to tell you if something was good for you or not. So, maybe, for now, you can trust me." I raked my thumb lightly along the side of his neck. "Do you trust me?"

After a long moment, he squeezed his eyes shut and nodded.

"Then we'll figure the rest out."

"How?" He laughed shortly and opened his eyes. "She's got Reb. Whatever she wants, she's about to get it. And we still don't know anything."

"We know she and Fen have been putting pressure on the supernatural world. We know that's why things are changing. We know they're both predators, in their own way."

"We don't know what she wants or why she wants it or how to stop her."

"No," I said. "I guess we don't."

After a moment, he let out a breath and snuggled into me. "I know you're trying to be supportive."

"You're right, though: we don't know anything. Nothing that matters, at least. And Eli—" My face heated. "Posey's not wrong. Not entirely. I don't know if I can keep you safe. When those things came after us last night, I was useless. Bullets didn't even slow them down, and that one just about tore my arm off when I got in its way."

He shook his head, whatever that meant, and then went still. Water sluiced over glass, and the sound was a pleasant static in the background of our breathing. The cotton of my tee itched where it had gotten wet and was drying now. His breath was warm on my neck. He was warm, and he was sitting on my lap, and I loved him so much.

He shifted his weight and said, "Hm."

I fluffed his hair as my face got hot again.

"What's that?" he asked.

"That's a reaction."

"Excuse me?"

"You know what I mean. I'm saying don't pay any attention to it; I know now's not the time, but it's kind of got a mind of its own."

He shifted his weight again, turning the movement into the slow grind of his ass against my dick. I put a hand on his knee.

Leaning back to see my face, he asked, "You don't want to?"

"Obviously part of me wants to. The rest of me thinks you're in kind of a delicate situation."

He took a breath. He met my eyes. If you didn't know him, you wouldn't have known how hard it was for him. "I love you."

"I love you too. I can love you with my zipper up just fine, so you know."

A tiny smile quirked at the corner of his mouth. He moved again, rolling his hips, applying pressure and friction in steady waves. I must have swallowed or moved or something because his smile got bigger. "I've never done it in a car."

I squeezed his knee.

He hesitated. And then he said, "You have?"

"A little quieter, please. And not so much outrage."

"Dagobert!"

"Oh my Lord."

"With who?"

"Go back to what you were doing; that felt nice."

When I put a hand on his waist, he slapped it away—playful, but only barely. "With Lanny?"

"How about I kiss you? How about that?"

"You have got to be kidding me." Then, rearing back, his face filling with horror, he said, "In this car?"

"I think kissing you is the right idea."

He put a hand on my chest, forcing me back. "Ok, we have to have sex. Right now. In this car. To—to exorcise the demons of the past."

"What about the demons of the present?" I asked under my breath. "Ow!"

"Go ahead and kiss me now," he said as I rubbed where he'd slapped my chest. "Make it really good. How good was the sex with Lanny? What are we shooting for here?"

"E, come on. It was awkward. It was cramped. I was nervous somebody was going to catch us, and Lanny ended up with the buckle from a seat belt imprinted on his face for the rest of the night."

"It's like you're trying to make me jealous." He twisted around until he was straddling me. Then he put his hands behind his back. When he saw me watching him, he looked away and said, "I don't want to touch you. Not like this."

"Ok."

"Go on," he said, licking his lips. "Ready, set, go. Begin. Racers, take your mark. Next time, I'm bringing a starter pistol."

He was saying something else like that when I got my hands on his hips, hauled him closer, and kissed him. He held back at first, his mouth tight, his head contorted as he tried to support himself by stiffening his back instead of using a hand to prop himself against a seat. I moved my hands up under his arms, taking the weight of his upper body, and we tried again. Better, this time. The way I held him stretched the sweatshirt tight across his chest, and when I rolled a thumb, I found one nipple already stiffening. His mouth softened, and his breath caught in the next kiss.

Everything had an extra charge. Everything was outlined in lightning—literally and figuratively. He didn't weigh hardly anything, and I could have held him like that all day, feeling his need, giving him what he couldn't take.

"Dag," he whispered when he broke from our next kiss.

I moved back to let him get some air, but instead, he squirmed back from my lap and down into the footwell. The Escort wasn't exactly a big car to begin with, and with the two of us in the back seat, it was starting to feel downright small. By some miracle of contortion, though, Eli got himself onto the floor. He stripped out of my stolen sweatshirt, and he kept his hands out of sight as he stared up at me. His lips were puffy from kissing, redder where I'd chewed them, and goose bumps ran up his arms and shoulders. He was so thin, like someone had taken away everything that wasn't perfect. I let my hand dust his collarbone to follow the valley between his pecs, and I leaned forward so that my fingers rocked over the slight definition of his stomach. He'd worked so hard for those little ridges. He whimpered at the attention.

"Dag," he whispered in a scratched voice.

"I know," I said. I palmed those hard, tight abs while, with my other hand, I took the dark round tip of a nipple between two fingers. I barely did anything—ran the pad of my thumb over it, around it. I let the hand caressing his stomach move up again, exploring his ribs, the ridged definition of serratus muscles, the grace of his biceps. When I tried to follow his arm back, he turned his body. He was breathing in gasps, but he shook his head.

"What are you going to do down there?" I asked, surprised at how I sounded: hoarse, the words scraped raw.

He parted his lips. His tongue darted out. He sounded like he was close to hyperventilating.

I leaned back, hands behind my head, spreading my legs farther.

He brought his mouth to the denim, and at first, the weight of his head and the heat of his mouth were the only sensation. Then he moved, adding friction, and after a minute of this, a slight dampness worked its way through the cotton. When he lifted his head, his cheek and chin were red from the rough texture of the jeans, and his hazel eyes were huge and full of tears. One of them spilled, and I thumbed it away as it slid down his cheek.

I didn't even bother with the top button; I unzipped myself and worked my stiff dick out of the fly. It was less than what I wanted, the root of my cock still trapped under my jeans and briefs. But, more importantly, it was less than what he wanted. And tonight was about giving Eli what he needed, not what he wanted.

At first, I let him take his time. I made noises as he took the head first, flicking his tongue, sucking lightly. And then he tried to go deeper. He didn't suck me often, and he couldn't take me. When he choked, I couldn't help myself; I made another of those appreciative noises. Spit dribbled down his chin. He tried again and had to pull back, hacking around my dick. I didn't rut into his mouth, but I didn't help him either. I watched him as he tried to put himself together again. I was sweating inside my jacket. I didn't take it off.

He'd cleared his airway when I caught his eye and said, "Fuck your face on my cock."

Eli's eyes got huge. For a moment, he stared at me, his lips suckling at the head of my dick. And then he scooted forward to get a better angle and began to move his head up and down. It was sloppy. It was messy. He choked and gagged, and tears ran from his eyes. Spit swung from his chin and clung in glistening strands to his bare chest. At some point, he forgot about his inhibitions, and he braced himself on the seat with both hands. It wasn't the best blowjob of my life—not that I had a ton of comparison—but it was so much better than sex with anyone else.

I ran my hand through his hair and when I reached the back of his head, I gathered a handful. Even with his throat being wrecked, Eli managed to moan as I tightened my fingers. Then I slid my other hand along the seat, found his hand, and wove our fingers together. The skin was clammy, and the texture was strange—almost too smooth, like touching raw chicken. His fingers were thicker and longer than I remembered. He tried to jerk his hand back, and I tightened my grip.

He reared back. I dragged his head back down onto my dick.

"No," I said.

He twisted his head. He rolled his wrist, trying to get free. He could have done it if he wanted to, I was sure; he was so much stronger now.

I forced his head down again and barked, "No!"

He let out a despairing noise and tried to take me in his throat again. I kept my grip on his hand, and I relaxed my hold on his hair, stroking the back of his head. He was desperate, frantic now, riding the edge of desire and self-loathing and fear, the knife blade of the last few days.

"Now," I said as I continued to play with his hair, "even though you've been such a fucking brat to me lately, I'm going to be nice to you. Do you think I should be nice to you, E?"

He made that despairing noise again, like the question was beyond him—or like he dreaded the answer.

"You're going to get yourself off. Right now. With my cock as far down your throat as you can take it. Because I'm a good boyfriend. Aren't I good? Aren't I good to you?"

The despair was tinged with agreement. He worked his free hand between his legs. A moment later, the tenor of his sucking changed, taking on a new intensity. His eyes were slits, his joints locked, and I felt it, the moment his world flared up and went out.

Then, shuddering, he dropped himself back down onto my dick. I humped his face, holding his head with both hands, and it only took me a few more minutes to come. I could feel myself clutching him too tightly. The words that went through my head like a freight train, riding the rails of the orgasm, were, *Hold on. Hold on.*

And then it was over, and we drifted into that place after sex that was a mixture of reality and bliss. I helped him up to the seat, and we lay together, his head on my chest, my head on the window. The rain drummed its tattoo, and through the skein of water, the trees made a darker shadow-show against the night.

"Ok," Eli finally said into my chest, and then he let out this weird, high, nervous laugh. "So, like, can you do that again sometime? The bossy thing, I mean. Just, you know, if it did something for you."

I kissed his temple. "Try taking all the caps off my highlighters again so they'll dry out. See what happens."

He giggled. And then he was full-out laughing. And then he was crying, but a different kind of crying, and I stroked his hair and let him. When he'd finished, we cleaned up—which mostly meant wet wipes for Eli's face and then getting Eli out of his jeans, where he'd shot his load, and into a pair of shorts from my gym bag. Commando, of course. Because he was Eli. I had a pair of work gloves in the trunk, and I darted through the thinning rain to get them for him. They weren't perfect, but they hid the most noticeable changes to his hands, and he seemed more comfortable once they were on.

We drove out of the storm and into starlight, the cypresses like ink-and-pencil drawings against the horizon, the magnolias, when they caught the headlights, strung with hearts of glass. Bragg's swollen bubble of sodium light grew ahead of us. Streetlights came closer and closer together, striping Eli's face.

"How did you know?" Eli asked, the words still rough around the edges in a way that was kind of flattering. "Where to find me, I mean?"

I thought about saying, You're not as complicated as you think you are, but that sounded cruel. Instead, I said, "I wasn't a very good deputy, but I did manage to learn a thing or two."

For some reason, that made him stretch across the seat to kiss my cheek.

When we got to my parents' house, the lights were dark. I parked on the street, and as I was getting out of the Escort, I spotted the truck up the street. I knew that truck: a battered red Ford pickup. Fen drove that truck.

"Get back in the car—" I said to Eli.

"Peace." The word was quiet but meant to carry. It came from the gallery on the front of my parents' house, and when I snapped my head that direction, I called myself every kind of idiot. Fen sat on a rocking chair in the shadows, the Browning propped between her legs. She held up both hands and said again, more softly this time, "Peace."

I watched her. "Get back in the car," I said again to Eli.

Instead, of course, he said, "Why are you here? What do you want?"

"I want to talk, me." Her grin looked yellow in the gallery's shadows. "The word of the Lord says, 'I send you forth as sheep in the midst of wolves: be ye therefore wise as serpents, and harmless as doves.' Thus sayeth the Lord."

"Harmless as doves," I said. "Sure. You don't mind shooting anything different from you, but you'll use magic if it suits you—whatever it takes, right?"

"The Lord says, 'Make unto you friends of the mammon of iniquity.' What is magic?" She spat. "You need my help, you."

"Yeah, like a bullet to the head," I said. "Eli, get—"

"Why would you help us?" he asked.

Fen started to rise.

"Stay where you are!" My voice rang out in the silent street.

She held up her hands again. Then, slowly, she used one hand to lay the Browning at her feet. She stood again, watching us—watching me—and pushed back the duster. An ugly little iron blade hung at her belt, and she lifted it from its sheath and balanced it on the gallery's railing. Then, hands in the air again, she took a step toward us.

"Peace," she said again, and through the thick Cajun, accent, I couldn't tell if she was laughing at me.

"I think she's serious," Eli said across the top of the Escort.

"Sure," I said. "Don't mind if I get the Sig anyway, though."

"Oh, definitely get the Sig."

I retrieved the pistol from the gun safe in the car. Then, carrying it low at my side, I stepped around the Ford to get a clean line on Fen. "Ok," I said. "You come in peace. I've heard that one before."

She watched me for a long moment. Then she came down the steps. She wore work boots—big, ugly things that I bet had steel toes. They clunked on each tread.

"You need me, you," she said again. "You want the beast. And I want the witch not to have the beast."

"He's not a beast," Eli said. "His name's Reb."

"You don't seem like the kind of lady who has any problem flying solo," I said. "You're here because you want something."

She didn't say anything. But the longer I watched her, the more I saw: the wasted look of her skin tight over her bones; the crook to her posture, as though she were favoring her side; the slight hint in the air, medicinal and foul, that made me think of hospitals and wounds that wouldn't heal.

"You need us, I think," I said quietly. "You can't fly solo on this one, can you?"

"You want my help? My word, from now until you have the beast: no harm from me."

"Call him a beast again," Eli said. "Do it."

Fen looked at him. She didn't move. Her expression didn't change. The flatness there, the bare, emotionless animosity, made me want to step back. Or between them. She looked at him the way hunters looked down the barrel of a gun. She was going to kill him if she could. Not today. Not now. But when she had the perfect shot. And it wouldn't be personal.

"I know what you are," she said. "No more hiding."

"We don't want your help," I said. "Get out of here. And don't come back—you come around my parents again, and I'll be the one you need to worry about."

"Twenty-four hours," Eli said. When I glanced at him, struggle showed in his face, but he managed to add in a tight voice, "Twenty-four hours after we free Reb. You swear not to try anything against us until twenty-four hours after. Otherwise, as soon as we get him, you're going to try to empty that shotgun into us."

It might have been the moth-wing light of the sodium lamps. It might have been a smile. Fen said, "Twenty-four hours after you free...it."

"Hold on," I said. "You're hurt. Maybe you're still healing from last year. You're tough, and I've got an idea of the damage you can do, and you know more about what we're facing than we do. But it doesn't matter if there are two or three of us. If we try charging into the Stoplight, we're going to get ourselves killed."

"Who said anything about charging in?" Fen asked. She set off toward her truck without looking back to see if we'd follow. After a moment, we did. When we reached the old Ford, she dropped the tailgate and dragged a massive steel utility locker toward her. She unlocked it, and then she set her hand on the lid.

I put an arm in front of Eli and moved him back a step.

Fen smirked. In the failing streetlights, the shadows fluttered in the hollows of her eyes. She threw open the locker.

"Uh, Dag," Eli said. "What is that?"

"That," I said, staring, "is an RPG." I cleared my throat. "A rocket-propelled grenade."

"Soviet era," Fen said. "Bulgarian made, the best. And in the back seat, I got a fruit crate full of C-4. Surplus from Vietnam. I didn't say nothing about charging in, me. I say we're going to blow the motherfucker up."

ELI (2)

It took a perhaps unsurprising amount of dissuading to get Fen to abandon the idea of shooting the RPG directly at the Stoplight, end of plan.

Instead, later that night, after hours of frantic preparation, Dag and I crouched in the tall weeds, watching the back of the juke joint. A miniature compound had been set up behind the juke, consisting of a few aluminum pull-behind campers arranged around a firepit, a barbeque grill made out of an old oil drum, and tracks through the weeds that led to plank privies.

In the camper closest to us, a man cried out, the sound a mixture of pain and pleasure.

"They need signs," I said, tugging on the work gloves to make sure they hadn't slipped. I caught myself doing it, and I thought of Posey, and I wondered where he'd gone with Lurnice and Dutch and why he'd been so stupid. Then again, if it had been Dag instead of Reb...

Dag made an unhappy face that was supposed to mean, *Be quiet*.

"Like, 'If this camper is rocking, don't come a-knocking,'" I whispered.

"E."

The man squealed. It was impossible not to recognize the sound of a guy getting his nut, and the juxtaposition to the kitchen noises from the back of the juke—pots clanging, voices calling out orders, zydeco on a staticky radio—made me feel weirdly voyeuristic. A moment later, the door to the camper opened. The man who stumbled out was Latino, fortyish, holding up his trousers with both hands while his white button-up hung from one hand. He stumbled down the camper's folding steps, throwing backward glances. He spat, as though trying to clear his mouth, and when he twisted around again, I caught sight of his back: deep scratches had been raked into the flesh there, and blood stained his button-up. He was so busy staring over his shoulder that he crashed right into the grill, and the old oil drum fell over with a clang. A cloud of ash rose into the air, and the man hacked and coughed as he righted himself and shambled down a path that cut around to the oyster-shell parking lot. His trousers were still hanging off his ass.

The camper door stood open to the chill October night. I caught a whiff of either really cheap perfume or really frou-frou air freshener. When a lull came in the kitchen noises, I could have sworn I heard purring.

"Uh," I whispered.

Dag shook his head, his face grim. He checked his phone.

The grass and weeds were wet from the rain, soaking my tennis shoes and jeans and sweatshirt, and when the breeze picked up, I shivered. I'd felt warm—really warm, the way humans are supposed to feel—for a while, but the cold was creeping in again. The smell of the camper perfume-slash-air freshener faded, and a cold, greasy meat stink wafted off the overturned grill.

"This is the longest wait of my life," I whispered.

Dag didn't answer, but he did check the Sig holstered at his belt. I was carrying the harvest knife—an ugly, ancient piece that we'd taken off Fen the year before. It was cold iron, and it would fuck up anything supernatural. Or, at least, I hoped it would. My experience was still kind of limited with these things. I touched the blade, and maybe it was my imagination, but the iron was so cold it burned. I drew my fingertips back and settled it more firmly in its sheath.

"Now," Dag whispered, and he grabbed my arm, pulled me up to stand straight, and started us walking. The wet grass clung to my jeans until we passed between two campers and reached the clearing around the fire pit. Through the open door of the camper the man had left, I saw movement—a shadow the size of a human but moving in a way that wasn't human at all, with eyes that caught the light and glittered.

Then something exploded.

I whipped my head around in time to see the column of fire flare into the sky and then sink back down. The thundering crack of the explosion reached us a moment later, dampened only slightly by the bulk of the juke joint. I blinked, trying to clear my eyes, as people screamed. Panicked shouts rose in the kitchen. Dag released my arm, but he kept moving toward the juke's back steps. I followed. Above the Stoplight's roof, dark, oily smoke eddied up, barely visible as a smudge of deeper darkness in the night sky. And then a second explosion lit up the night.

"Was that the RPG?"

Dag shook his head. "She's saving that one; count on it."

We reached the kitchen at the same time as the terrified crowd, and Dag pulled me to one side on the shallow gallery. Men, almost exclusively men, forced their way through the kitchen, fleeing the barroom at the front of the juke, trying to find an exit that didn't take them straight into the path of the explosions. I glanced back at the aluminum campers, where lights were going on. A flabby old white guy half-fell out of one of the campers, stuffing his willie into his shorts and shouting, "What is this? What is all this? Somebody tell me what's going on?" The only answer he got was when a huge man in a Tulane jersey crashed into him and bowled him back inside the camper.

As the stream of bodies thinned, several people who were obviously staff also hurried out of the juke. I recognized them because, now that I knew what to look for, they were easy to spot as chimeras: a white lady in a long skirt who moved with clomping, hoofbeat steps; a heavyset Asian man with iridescent scales climbing his neck and disappearing under his hair; a scrawny white boy in a wifebeater, his pecs and arms covered in tattoos that, as I watched, stuttered across his skin like someone running a projector at half speed. Chimeras, all of them. A pair of women in biker leathers headed the opposite direction, toward the front of the juke, where Fen was still busy blowing things up. I swear to God, I was pretty sure one of the women was breathing fire. Witch-style security, I figured. How much did that cost?

Then nobody. Dag risked a glance, beckoned, and headed inside. I followed. I had a glimpse of the kitchen: the checkerboard linoleum, the white-enameled appliances, the walk-in freezer. A crawfish boil bubbled in a pot on the stove, and the wall of steam made my hair frizz and left the skin on my face slick. The radio had gotten knocked onto the floor and was silent now. Someone had been smoking clove cigarettes, which seemed like a big no-no for kitchen staff, but I figured if any health inspectors complained, Nelda Pie probably just ate them.

Dag stopped to check the walk-in freezer, and then we were moving again. He had the Sig out now, held against his thigh, and his knuckles were white. We pushed through a swinging door into a hallway. Nelda Pie's offices were one way, and the barroom was another. Music played over speakers mounted overhead, rockabilly stuff, a song about the devil doing ninety-nine. The stale, yeasty smell of spilled beer was buried under the stink of the explosions—stinging, chemical, like hot metal and burning electronics. From where we stood, the barroom looked empty, and after a quick scan, Dag started down the hall.

Nelda Pie's office was here; last year, Fen and Lanny had gotten the drop on her, and she'd obviously learned her lesson. The door was steel, the frame reinforced, and it had so many locks I figured she spent half her time just getting the door open. We kept moving, and as the rockabilly song faded behind us, new sounds filtered in: snapping jaws, snarling, an injured yelp.

"Fuck me," I said. "Don't they know we're blowing this place up?"

"She won't care about that," Dag said. "Not until she has to. Tonight's the night; she has to make it work, which means making an offering out of Reb's blood."

"Let me guess: it's not as simple as bringing in a phlebotomist. No, that would be way too easy, way too sane."

Dag checked a door. Utility closet. He checked the next one. A supply room. "I don't think so."

"No, because we're dealing with a dark sorcerer-spirit-demigod lwa, I bet the blood has to be fresh, has to be taken by force, has to be ripped out with teeth." I could feel it, almost like a memory: the sweetness of tearing flesh, the density of muscle fibers shredding, surrendering to overwhelming force, the richness of the blood like velvet.

Dag stopped, hand on the next door, and looked at me.

I bit the inside of my mouth until I tasted the bright, coppery hurt of my own blood. Not velvety, I thought. Not thick and rich. Just pain, and it's going to make it hell to eat pizza for the next week.

"E?"

I nodded. "Come on; we've got to hurry."

When Dag tried the door, it was locked. He kicked the door, and then he made a face and hopped on one foot. "Darn thing is solid."

Drawing a breath, I took his place at the door. "Don't say anything," I told him.

"Don't say anything about—"

It was like ice water running through me. Like I could turn the tap, and it roared out like a flood. I grabbed the handle and yanked.

Metal screeched. Then, with a series of sharp cracks, the door came free.

Like, totally free.

Like, the hinges had torn in half.

The door wobbled, and I caught it before it could fall. Then I dragged it out of the way, revealing the staircase behind it. When I risked a look, I couldn't read Dag's face.

After a moment, he said, "You're carrying in the groceries from now on."

I pushed hair out of my eyes and tried to smile. It was as close to a thank-you as I could get; turning off that flow of rushing cold was harder, and even after I felt back in control of myself, the chill lingered. Visions carouseled in my head: cartilage crumpling under my teeth, the smell of ruptured bowels, the taut beauty of skin flayed back from muscle.

"We have to go," I said.

Dag hesitated. But he started down the stairs.

The only light on the stairs came from above us, filtering down from the hallway. We went down maybe twenty feet, the air growing colder, thick with the smell of clay. It shouldn't have been possible, of course; the water table was almost at ground level around here, which was why the cemeteries were all above ground. But this was the Stoplight, this was Nelda Pie, and a simple thing like the laws of physics wasn't going to get in her way.

At the bottom, we stood in a cramped intersection: a hallway extended ahead of us, and then another hallway opened up on either side of us. A lamp hung on the wall next to us, and what seemed a long way off, another lamp broke the darkness. Soot darkened the plank walls, smudging my shirt when I brushed against it. Sawdust covered the floor, clumped with fluids I didn't want to consider. Instead of clay, the air reeked of kerosene and piss and a hot, trapped animal smell. The snaps and snarls and growls were much closer.

Dag was squinting, trying to see into the darkness. I touched his arm and pointed overhead, where a red light blinked, betraying a security camera.

"They've got electricity for that," he muttered. "I guess they like the spooky lantern touch."

The sound of the dogfight seemed to be coming down the hallway that ran straight ahead of us, and now I could make out excited voices, so we started moving again. I walked too close to Dag, bumping into him more than once, but he didn't say anything. Another explosion went off overhead—muffled by the earth and the juke joint above us, it sounded like a soft whump, but it had enough force behind it to send a tremor through the tunnel. The lamps swung on their hooks, spilling shadows everywhere, and boards creaked and groaned.

When the sounds faded, Dag and I shared a look. We walked faster.

The hallway opened onto a large room. We stood on a balcony overlooking a dogfighting ring surrounded by men and women—the diehards, the ones who even a series of explosions couldn't scare off. Or maybe they hadn't even realized what was happening. It was hard to tell in a place like this; everybody seemed crazy. In the center of the ring, Reb was naked and bloody, covered in bites and scratches. His posture was crouched, more like an animal's than a man's. He was facing off three dogs that clearly were some sort of Pit bull mix. The men and women watching jeered, catcalled, screamed, pounded the wooden sides of the ring. It was a cacophony, a word I'd learned from my werewolf books. Reb shook his head slightly, as though dazed; I couldn't hear him over the shouts and cries, but his thin chest rose and fell like a sparrow's wing. He was going to die, I realized. He was strong, and he was dangerous, and it didn't matter because Nelda Pie was going to wear him down until one of these dogs ripped out his throat, and then she'd have what she wanted. Blood spilled by violence. The blood of a rougarou, an offering Kalfu couldn't resist.

"We can't go down there," Dag said. "There's no way to get close, not without everybody seeing us. We've got to figure out something else."

"A distraction?"

He glanced at the crowd. They held glasses and bottles, cigars and cigarettes and joints, and as I watched, a busty bottle blonde did a line of coke off the back of her hand. "Maybe," he said, but he didn't sound convinced.

"I don't think—" I stopped and tried again. "I mean, the way I am right now, I would probably be all right—"

"Not a chance."

I flexed my fingers inside my gloves, trying to ease the ache, and I could hear that old rockabilly song in my head. The devil doing ninety-nine. I nodded.

We backtracked, half-jogging. Yelps chased us. A howl. And then, full of rage and pain, Reb screamed.

"We're coming," I said. "We're coming."

When we got back to the stairs, I looked left. Then I looked right.

"Flip a coin," Dag said.

We went left and found a series of locked doors. I didn't want to risk the noise of forcing them, so we turned around. This time, we went right and found the kennels. The smell was overpowering—animal musk and dogshit and rotting straw. A couple of Pit bull mixes lay inside the wire pens, and they didn't move as we crossed the room. A door on the other side opened onto a sloping hallway that led down, if I had to guess, to the pit and the dogfighting ring. They'd want some sort of direct access, rather than taking the dogs through the same hallways that the spectators used.

Doors made of steel bars opened on one side of the sloping hallway. On the other side of the bars, the rooms were small and totally empty. They reminded me of jail cells. I didn't want to think about what Nelda Pie used them for.

A woman's cry made both of us stop. The sound was low, frustrated, and it had a quality that, as a lifer fuck-up, I recognized intimately: I called it *hanging by a fucking thread*.

Dag and I traded another look. He motioned for me to stay back, which I ignored, and we moved toward the sound. The hallway leveled out, and ahead, a rectangle of light suggested a doorway. A high, shrill whimper was followed by a roar of sound from the crowd, and for a moment, I couldn't hear anything else. It was the sound of something primal, something we, as a race, had tried to entomb under churches and laws and dinner etiquette, something digging its way out of the grave because the old animal part of us refused to stay buried. The devil doing ninety-nine.

Then we reached the final cell, and on the other side of the bars I saw Lurnice, Dutch, and Posey. Lurnice sat with her back against the wall, one leg stretched out in front of her, clutching her thigh with both hands. She was still wearing the SAUSAGE STUFFERS sweatshirt, which looked seriously worse for wear. Dutch, in her borrowed SWEET CHEEKS sweatshirt, crouched next to Posey. One of the rough-hewn timber supports overhead had fallen and pinned him to the floor. Even in the dim light, I could tell that Posey's color was bad, and his breathing seemed irregular. Dutch hadn't noticed us, and she strained again to lift the beam until, letting out that same helpless cry again, she sagged backward.

My brain did the quick two-plus-two, and I understood what had happened: somehow, Posey had been in contact with Nelda Pie, and she had offered him Reb. In exchange for what, I wasn't sure, but my guess was Dutch and Lurnice. And Posey, because he was desperate and frightened and, to borrow a word from Dag's parents, a little bit simple, had believed her. If I had to put money on it, I'd bet that's how the three of them ended up here.

Dumbass.

Dag frowned and tugged on the cell door. It wobbled open, and the screech of the hinges made Lurnice look up and Dutch whip around. The expression in the older woman's rawboned face softened slightly, and she said, "There was some kind of earthquake. The guard ran, but Lurnice hurt her leg, and Posey—" She gestured.

Maybe rougarous weren't much for social niceties. Maybe there was simply no fucking around with Dutch.

"Not an earthquake," I said. "An explosion. Dag?"

Another swell of sound made him look down the hall, where light outlined the doorway to the dogfighting ring. He hesitated. Then he nodded. "Let's get them out of here."

I helped Lurnice to her feet, and she hobbled out into the hall, supported by Dutch.

"It's going to take both of you," Dutch said.

"Depends on how one of us is feeling," Dag said as he crouched near the timber. He glanced at me. "How about it, Popeye?"

I scooted around him to get a better position, and I got a grip on the timber. The cold was there, already rising to the surface—a fever flush, only frozen.

And then Posey blinked. He stared at us. And then he moaned, "No. No, no, no—"

The door to the cell clanged shut, and the lock snicked into place.

DAG (3)

The steel bars were still rattling as I shot to my feet.

On the other side of the door, Dutch and Lurnice stared at us. Lurnice was no longer favoring her leg—that had been part of the ruse, my brain suggested—and both women wore avid, hungry expressions. Lurnice was panting quietly. Dutch's lips were pulled back.

"What are you doing?" Eli asked. "Hey, open the door!"

"E," I said.

"What the fuck is this?"

"Eli!"

He shot me a look, and then he released the timber and crossed the cell in two strides. Dutch and Lurnice drew back, both women growling, but Eli ignored them. He wrapped his hands around the bars, and I readied myself. As soon as he tore the door off the hinges, all hell would break loose—

Eli let out a startled shout and stumbled back. He stared at his gloved hands.

"Cold iron," Dutch said.

"For Mother's special guests," Lurnice said.

He shook his head, but he said, "They burned me. Even through the gloves."

Neither of the women said anything. When the shouts and cheers in the next room fell silent, Lurnice's quiet panting seemed to echo back from the plank walls.

Eli spun away from the door so quickly that I took a step back on reflex. He ignored me, squatted next to Posey, and heaved the timber up. I tucked the Sig into my waistband at the small of my back, grabbed Posey under the arms, and dragged him clear. Eli let the beam drop, and the thud rang out in the stillness. The shouts and cries and calls of excitement from the pit hadn't resumed, and I wondered what that meant. If Reb had died—or if he'd killed all the dogs—there would have been some sign, right? Some way to tell from the sound of their voices that an end, one way or another, had been reached. But instead, the sounds had cut off completely.

"I am such an idiot," Eli said. He was still squatting next to the timber, hanging his head. "I am such a fucking idiot."

"You're not an idiot," I said. "Posey, how's your breathing? Did that thing break any ribs?"

"'mokay," Posey mumbled. But he didn't look ok. His lips had a bluish tinge, and although his eyes were opened, they reminded me of someone with a bad concussion. The prosthesis was still attached to his arm, which was good—in the state Posey was in, I didn't want to startle him and end up like Joey Jaws's goon.

"Nobody said they were Reb's pack," Eli said. "Nobody but me. They were in that fucking house waiting for an opportunity to grab him—hell, Dag, they tried to run away before we could catch them. But me, I'm such a fucking genius that I see them, and I think I've got it all figured out. You told me not to answer the questions for them, and that's exactly what I did—I gave them the perfect explanation for what they were doing there. Jesus Christ, they've probably been laughing at us since the minute we put them in the car." He got to his feet, turned, and stared through the bars at the women. They still stood there, silent except for Lurnice's accelerated breathing. "How'd you get Posey out of the house? Did you tell him you could help him make a deal with Nelda Pie?"

Dutch's teeth were still bared, but there was a distinct curve to her lips now.

"No," Eli said, "of course not. You didn't have to. All you had to do was tell him you had an idea where Reb might be. He would have done anything for Reb. And we didn't even wonder about you being gone; it just made us even more worried. Motherfucker. How stupid am I?"

"E, enough." I tried to sit Posey up, but he made a garbled noise, and I eased him back down. When I started to rise, light on the opposite wall caught my eye. I crawled forward, ran my hand over the planks, and found the seam. Dirt trickled away beneath my fingers, exposing the long, vertical slash of kerosene glow.

"I bet you loved it," Eli was saying. "I bet you thought it was hilarious. Did Nelda Pie send you, or were you—what? Freelancers, like the parlangua?"

"Eli," I said.

"Did you hear me?" Eli hammered the bars, and then I heard him swear at the contact with cold iron. "Answer the question!"

"Eli, we've got a problem."

Under my fingers, the planks shivered. Then hinges creaked, and the door concealed in the wall shuddered open. The yellow flicker of the lamps made me blink as my eyes adjusted to the relative brightness. A series of facts connected for me, lined up in a neat row: we had followed that sloping hallway down toward the pit. We had heard the dogfighting in the next room. Dutch and Lurnice had waited in the final cell, preparing their trap. And now I knew why: the back door of the cell opened directly into the dogfighting ring.

Reb stood on the far side. He'd been injured again in the short time since we'd seen him—a savage bite marked his side, and blood ran steadily down his flank. And for the first time, I saw him as the rougarou, and not as a boy: he had a wolf's head, covered in thick white fur, with a bloodstained muzzle. His eyes were the same ice blue I remembered, and his body was the same leanly muscled body of a boy on the verge of adulthood. When he shifted his weight, tufts of fur caught the glow from the kerosene lamps with an almost metallic shimmer. He was panting—hard, uncontrolled noises—but when he saw us, he started to growl.

The ring itself had been transformed too. The dogs—dead or alive—had been removed, and an iron frame twice as tall as I was had been lowered on top of the wooden ring. A cage match, the coon-ass part of my brain said. Like my dad liked to watch on TV. Two go in, one comes out. Or in this case, three. Or four if you counted Posey. The crowd pressed close to the bars, men and women staring at us. Then noise erupted: laughter, catcalls, jeers.

"He looks like a fucking cunt!" a man in a farm coat shouted. "They both do!"

"Come on out," a woman screeched. She laughed as she added, "Don't be afraid."

"Look at the two of them," a man with Natchez blood said, grabbing the bars like he wanted to rattle them. "Ain't you never seen a dogfight before?"

"Dag," Eli said.

"We're not going anywhere," I told him.

"Yeah, you are," Dutch said. "Get your asses out there."

I twisted around and saw the shotgun butted up to her shoulder. Where she'd gotten it, I had no clue—it didn't matter, I decided; they'd prepared for all of this. I thought about the Sig.

"Go for it," Dutch said. "The rou can play with you while you're bleeding out; the shot won't bother him none."

"Why are you doing this?" Eli asked. "Don't you know what she wants with him? She'll do it to you next."

Laughter came over the microphone, and I turned my attention back to the ring. The speakers squeaked, and the crowd went silent, and at the far end of the ring, bodies parted. Nelda Pie appeared in the opening, standing up against the bars behind Reb. Her peroxide bouffant looked poofier than ever, and she was wearing a red robe trimmed in black. She laughed again, and the microphones squealed once more with feedback.

Eli shouted, "You think this is funny? Get rid of the bars, and we'll see how funny you think this is."

"My girls don't have nothing to worry about," Nelda Pie said. "They know that. I take good care of them. I take good care of all my half-breeds. See, that's the blessing and the curse of a half-breed: nobody wants you. It cuts both ways. Nobody but Nelda Pie. I give them a home. I give them work. I give them a life."

"Great," Eli said under his breath. "They're not even rougarous. They're fucking chimeras. I knew they were different from Reb; I felt it."

Which made sense, a small part of my brain registered under the fight hormones that were kicking up. If Nelda Pie had been protecting two rougarou girls, she wouldn't have needed to track down Reb; she would have had other options for the offering.

"Let us go," I said. "We'll take Posey and Reb. That'll be the end of this."

"The end?" Nelda Pie's face changed. The friendly good humor stripped away, and in its place, something slick and greedy, almost starved, appeared. "What do you know about the end? This is the beginning. The rou's blood will be shed in violence. Hot blood. And that blood will make Kalfu hot. He'll come because he can't help himself. He has faded over the years, and he hungers."

"Yeah, yeah, yeah," Eli said. "We figured it out on our own, thanks. Le Doux, Reb, the lwa. You'll have your genie in a bottle, and you'll make your wish, and then what? You won't have those bony chicken legs? You'll have a million Goofy bucks to spend at Disney World?"

If Nelda Pie had known him the way I did, she would have recognized the taunt. Instead, she hissed—it was a long, unnatural sound, and the hair on the back of my neck stood up. Around the perimeter of the ring, the crowd stilled, their faces blank and uncomprehending, as something stifling fell over the pit. It felt like a hot, wet rag draped over me, clinging to my face, making it hard to breathe.

"Disney World. What do you know? A genie in a bottle. A wish. Chicken legs." She hissed again. "You don't know anything. Kalfu will come, not knowing the world has moved on without him. He'll think he can ride me, and dance in the flames, and drink rum laced with gunpowder. And instead, I will ride him. Ride him, and then kill him, and take his place. A new lwa, bright with power, instead of the tired old thing dragging itself through the crossroads. And then I will be the crossroads, and the way to Lan Guinee will stand open. And you, nasty little half-breed. I'll come for you and suck the marrow from your bones."

Then something changed her face—like she was waking up, hearing herself, worrying she had said too much. Like an old movie starting up again, uneasy murmurs rippled through the crowd, men and women trading glances, and that stifling weight lifted. Nelda Pie's mask returned, and she stepped back. Fumbling sounds came over the mic, and in a tone of forced cheerfulness, she said, "Well, we came here for a show, didn't we? Let's have a show! Here's how it's going to work: boys, if you don't haul ass and get out in the ring, Dutch there is going to open up, and she's a natural hunter. Chimera girls almost always are. And Reb—"

Reb snarled over his shoulder at her.

"Yeah, well," Nelda Pie said, "either you kill these two, or Dutch will blow Posey's pretty head off. That'd be poor payment for all the trouble he's gone to, don't you think? Trying to find you. Worrying about you. Offering himself in your place."

Reb turned to face us. He shifted his weight, lowering himself into a crouch.

"Reb," I said, "she's lying to you. She'll kill Posey whatever you do. She'll kill you too."

In answer, Reb growled—a low, rumbling noise that I felt in my bones.

"Get out here!" a fat man shouted.

"Yeah," a woman with red-out-of-a-box hair screamed, "get out here!"

"Count of five, boys," Nelda Pie said and then laughed again, the speakers sputtering and popping with feedback. "Five—"

"Reb looks pissed off," Eli said.

I nodded.

"He's going to try to kill us," Eli whispered.

"Four," Nelda Pie said.

I nodded again. The faint hint of a draft brushed the back of my neck. I felt like I had a fever.

"Three."

"Stay behind me," Eli said.

"Two," Nelda Pie called.

"Now," I asked, easing the Sig from out of my waistband, "why'd you say a silly thing like that?"

As Nelda Pie called, "One," I stepped into the ring.

A wave of sensation hit me: the web of shadow and kerosene flares, the cast-iron smell of blood, the mushy give of sawdust underfoot, the weight of eyes, the awareness of dozens of bodies pressed close. I walked toward Reb, keeping my pace slow and steady as I brought the gun up, making sure I kept ahead of Eli.

"Don't make me do this, Reb," I said. "We can figure this out together."

He launched himself at me.

I squeezed off a shot. At the same moment, something spun toward me from the side of the ring. I had a moment to process the white-and-gold label, to think, *Jax*. Then the bottle struck the side of my head, and I stumbled. Glass shattered, and cold, hoppy beer foamed over me. My shot went wide. A woman laughed, and the crowd roared, men and women lunging at the bars, pressing themselves against the iron for a better view.

Reb's first leap closed half the distance between us. He bounded toward me again as I squeezed off another shot. This one got him—I saw the impact, his body jerking in mid-air. Then he hit me, a blur of claws and teeth. We fell together. I felt a tug at my neck like I'd cut myself shaving, and then razor-hot pain poured in. We rolled once, and I got my forearm up. His teeth—his fangs—sank into my flesh. I screamed, but I drove the muzzle of the Sig into his belly and got off a third shot. He jerked, his head coming back, shaking loose of my arm. His eyes were wide with shock.

Then, snapping his teeth, he went for my throat.

Eli caught Reb by the scruff and hauled him off me. For a moment, I stared up at Eli—his long, lean form untroubled by the weight of holding a fully grown werewolf in the air. Then Eli spun and hurled Reb. The rougarou tumbled through the air and struck the iron bars. He didn't make any noise—no screams, no howls, no yelps. There was only the crunch of his body against metal, and then the muffled thud when he hit the blood-soaked sawdust.

I got myself up onto one elbow. The world was still spinning, but I got my fingers to my neck. Pain sparked again, and when I brought my hand back, it was crimson. I pulled up my collar to wipe my neck, winced at another flash of pain, and then got onto my hands and knees. I'd kept hold of the Sig somehow, but with the tilt-a-whirl movement of everything in my vision, I didn't trust myself to take a shot. I dragged myself to the side of the ring, took a few deep breaths, and used the wall to get to my feet.

Eli, meanwhile, picked up Reb and threw him again. The rougarou flew the length of the ring, hit the floor, and skidded, throwing up clouds of sawdust. Reb shook his head, that white fur glinting like hammered silver in the lamplight. He pushed himself up to his knees, but the movements were slow and uncoordinated. How long had Nelda Pie made him fight before we'd arrived? How much blood had he lost? How much strength could he possibly have left after days of being on the run, without food or sleep or shelter?

But somehow, Reb tapped into something—fury or fear or both. As Eli stepped into range, Reb lunged forward, jaw snapping as he tried to bite Eli's leg. Eli kicked him, faster than seemed possible, and bones cracked. The pop-pop of it sounded like something in winter, when the air is crystal and every sound is amplified.

This time, Reb let out a yelp, and then a whining cry as he tumbled across the sawdust.

Eli went after him. He seemed taller, his limbs longer. He'd lost the work gloves, and his hands had a stretched-out quality that I remembered from my nightmares. Thick, yellow claws grew from the ends of his fingers, and as I watched, he bent and, with a lazy swipe, opened five deep cuts across Reb's belly.

Reb howled. He flopped on his back, trying to turn over, but Eli stepped on his neck.

"Eli!" Bracing myself on the wall, I hobbled toward him. "E! Stop! He can't fight anymore! E, you're killing him!"

Eli glanced over his shoulder at me. His eyes glowed blue.

I forced myself to go faster, one hand pressed to my neck and the slick flow of blood. Couldn't have been an artery, a tiny voice told me inside my head. Couldn't be, or you'd be dead already. "Are you listening to me? Stop!"

Another bottle whistled through the air, missing me by inches. The crowd's cheers had changed to boos, shouts of outrage and protest. A rail-thin man in a three-piece was demanding his money back.

"Hey, E, I'm talking to you." I lowered my voice as I got closer, taking off as much of the edge as I could. "Let him up. Or at least let him breathe." I reached for Eli's arm; Reb had torn his shirt, and where the sleeve was parted, I could see that the soft brown of Eli's skin had been bleached, changed to that strange, rubbery white. "We can—"

Eli spun before I could touch him, and his fist caught me on the side of the head. I staggered, hip-checked the side of the ring, and went down. The world went out. And then it came back in. Something was ringing in my ears, all these voices. One time, a drunk had got me right on the crown of the head with a bottle of J. T. Meleck rice vodka. I tried asking Mason if that had happened to me again, and then I remembered Mason was dead, and I pushed myself up to get my face out of the sawdust. A distant part of me noted I'd lost the Sig.

From what seemed like a long way off, Eli stared down at me. He was taller, I thought. Thinner. He let out a noise, and it was a high, shrieking sound no human being had ever made.

When the noise cut off, I said, "Whatever it's telling you, it's lying."

He shrieked again.

I got to my hands and knees. I shook my head, and clumps of sawdust fell from my cheek and jaw and pattered against the floor. Eli's eyes flared blue, but I met them and tried to hold them. "I know you think you have to be strong to keep us safe."

Jeers came from the crowd: "Finish him!" and "Rip his head off!" and "Fucking end it, already!" Men and women hooted and shouted. They laughed, stoned on adrenaline and endorphins and Jax that hadn't been brewed in fifty years. The next morning, they'd convince themselves this horror show had all been a bad trip. And then, after a while, they'd want to take that trip again. People like them always do.

I wasn't sure he could hear me over the calls and cries of the crowd, but I kept talking. "This isn't you being strong. You're already strong. You're the strongest person I know. You went through the worst thing anybody can imagine, and you came out the other side brave and compassionate and willing to do whatever it takes to protect the people you love."

Eli shrieked again. Behind him, Reb lay on the floor, limbs moving slowly, drawing uncontrolled arcs of pain in the sawdust.

"I know you," I said, still meeting those burning blue eyes. "You told me you made Gard brownies when nobody else would even talk to him, and you sat there and listened and let him know that somebody loved him. You told me when Gard had bad days, you brought your mom flowers because your dad never did. You told me when your dad had to go outside because he couldn't stand being in the house anymore, you took him a beer."

Eli twisted his head—a ducking, side-to-side movement that might have been a no.

"When I met you, you were visiting the people in that support group. You were visiting Ray, remember? You'd visited him before because you knew he was lonely, because you knew he needed more help than showing up once a week to a support group. After Mason died, when I didn't know how I was supposed to keep living, you gave me a reason to get through one day, and then the next." I laughed, surprising myself, the sound buried under the screams and demands from the faces pressed against the iron bars around us. "You were even nice to Lanny, although God knows he made you work for it. Every day you make my life better. I love you so much—"

He shrieked, and in a blur of movement, bent and seized me by the neck. The thick yellow claws cut into me as he pulled me upright and then, without any apparent difficulty, lifted me into the air. I kicked—not because I wanted to hurt him, but because panic was taking over my rational brain—but the blows just skated off his thigh and stomach. Finally I managed to bring myself under some kind of control. The crowd's noises became a steady droning. My pulse beat in my face and ears. The blue eyes staring back at me were bright the way ice can be bright and blue at dawn. He tightened his grip and began to crush my windpipe.

I choked out three words: "This isn't you."

I fought him, kicking and flailing, as darkness flecked the edges of my vision. The black specks whirled faster and faster, crowding my sight until it was like I was looking down a tunnel, looking into this far-off place of cold, blue fire.

Then I hit the floor, the sawdust only partially absorbing the impact. My head cracked against the boards. I flopped onto my back, sucking in air. Above me, the flames of the kerosene lamps bent in a draft. To my watering eyes, each flicker of light had its own nimbus. Like angels, I thought. And then I thought maybe my brain had been oxygen deprived for too long. Or I'd hit my head way too hard.

I sat up. I found Eli standing with his back to me. He still didn't look like Eli, but I recognized the slant of his shoulders, the way he hugged himself. Around us, the hoots and howls and screams had escalated. Another bottle of Jax exploded on the floor, spraying a nova of glass. As I got to my feet, a handful of change hit me in the back. And then somebody's lighter clipped my arm and caromed off. What I was pretty sure was a woman's diaphragm bounced off my shoe.

"E?" I said as I limped toward him. It sounded like somebody had just finished scraping my vocal cords. "Eli?"

"Don't." Tears made the word almost unintelligible. He held a hand behind him, warding me off.

Some numbskull pitched his shoe at me, and I swatted it out of the air as I shuffled closer. I touched Eli's back first, and he shivered and drew away. But then I put my arm around his waist, and when I tugged him, he came to me. He pressed his face against my neck; the cuts there stung, and his skin felt cool and unnaturally smooth. I stroked his hair.

The speakers overhead squealed, and Nelda Pie's voice came on. "Very disappointing. But the show must go on. Kill Posey and the man. Leave the rougarou and the half-breed for me."

Eli and I turned at the same time, looking back toward the cell where we had entered the ring. Dutch stood inside the cell now, the door hanging open behind her. She adjusted the shotgun against her shoulder and drew a bead on Posey, who still lay motionless. Lurnice inched up until she was standing just behind the other woman, baring her teeth in anticipation.

And then Kennedy—Miss Kennedy, our Kennedy—stepped into the cell. She wore a stab vest over a man's flannel shirt, with jeans and hiking boots, and her face was tight but composed. Dutch gaped at her for a moment, and then she swung the shotgun toward her.

Kennedy was faster. In a smooth, almost exaggeratedly careful movement, Kennedy brought up her hand, her palm flat. Then she pursed her lips and blew. Dust lifted from her hand and flew into the air, carried by her breath. Even at a distance, even in the weak lamplight, it was a dull red. The cloud struck Dutch in the face, and Dutch made a weird, inhaling/sneezing combo noise. Then she screamed. She stumbled back, knocking into Lurnice, and released the shotgun with one hand to claw at her eyes.

Moving after Dutch, Kennedy grabbed the shotgun to wrestle it away. Lurnice barreled into her, though, snapping her teeth. It was easy to see the chimera now—unlike Reb, she didn't shift or change, but like Posey and other chimera we'd met, there was a sense of afterimage, of something moving with her but slightly out of frame. She lunged for Kennedy's throat.

Posey launched himself up from the floor. He grabbed Lurnice by the hair, spun her, and drove her toward the bars of the cell door. I caught that same flicker of movement—the sense of something dark and twisting where he wore the prosthesis. Then he crushed Lurnice's head against the door. He let her go, shaking blood and hair from his hand, and she fell. I was grateful for the distance; all I could tell, from where we stood, was that it looked like a truck had gone over her head. Then Posey turned and clobbered Dutch. Her screams broke off, and she dropped to the floor. He leaned heavily on the wall, panting. Kennedy checked the shotgun and shouldered it.

Silence, total silence, held the room.

"Took you long enough," I said. "I thought we had a plan."

"The parking lot was a disaster," Kennedy said. "Nasties coming out of the woodwork."

Then someone screamed, and the crowd broke. Nelda Pie was shouting something over the speakers, the words incomprehensible under the noises of the panicked mob. For ten or fifteen seconds, men and women streamed up the stairs, trying to get out of the pit and escape the Stoplight. Then the crowd stalled.

A woman flew into the air above us, floating out from the observation platform, arms and legs spread like she was performing one of those acrobatic acts, the kind you see a million flyers for in the French Quarter. She didn't make a noise, as far as I could tell. Not until she hit the wall. Planks and timbers quivered, and her body made a crunching noise like someone stepping on a bag of potato chips.

A moment later, a second figure came hurtling off the observation platform. This one landed easily—a massive creature on four legs that padded toward Nelda Pie, who stood watching the chaos in her red robes. It had russet fur, and although the general shape of the head and body suggested wolf, this thing was not a wolf. It turned and sat on its hind legs next to Nelda Pie, and when she stroked its head, I recognized the thing Joey Jaws had become.

More chimeras appeared, forcing their way down the stairs and cutting a path through the panicked mob: a thing that was part woman and part tiger; another with the body of a man and the head of a cobra; one that was a man from the chest up, and from the waist down, he was a gelatinous blob, and he dragged himself like a slug; a dried-up husk of a woman, in a dress that made me think of Civil War reenactors. We'd seen her on our first visit to the Stoplight. Her mouth made me think of visits to old folks' homes, when I'd been a kid, and for the first time seen the apple-doll faces of men and women who had taken out their dentures. As I watched, she opened her mouth, and spiders spilled out.

"Bring me the rougarou," Nelda Pie said. "Kill the rest."

The thing that had been Joey shook itself, crouched, and jumped. When he hit the bars, they exploded in like they were made of tiddlywinks, and fragments of iron and splintered wood spun across the floor. He bounded toward us. Eli shoved me out of the way and jumped, catching Joey in the side, and they tumbled across the ring. When they hit the wall, they crashed through it.

I started after them, but Kennedy shouted, "Dag," and I turned in time to see the tiger-lady hurtling toward me.

I threw myself down, and that probably saved my life. Claws sliced the air next to my head; the air from their passage brushed the side of my face. When I hit the floor, I rolled through a cloud of sawdust, and then I came up on my knees. The tiger-lady was already recovering, crouched on all fours and turning easily to face me. Her movements were predatory, almost liquid, and she smiled as she caught sight of me again. I ignored her. The Sig was about ten feet to my right, making the third point of a triangle with me and the tiger-lady. I looked back at her, the muscles in her body rippling as she gathered herself to pounce. Then I kicked sawdust in her eyes.

She yowled, and I threw myself at the Sig. I landed bad this time, and my injured shoulder screamed at me. But I got my hand around the gun, and I brought it up and steadied myself and did what they'd trained me to do: breathe and look through the shot. I fired.

The tiger-lady jerked. Red stained her chest, and for a few horrible moments, she tried to drag herself away. Then she slumped down and was still.

I scrambled to my feet. Eli was on the far side of the pit, facing off with Joey. Posey was swinging the broken timber at the blob-man—when the timber struck the blob, it got stuck, and as I watched, the translucent goo ate away at the wood. Blob-man glided forward, probably planning on dissolving Posey too, but Kennedy was there. She flipped what looked like a gold coin in the air, and blob-man followed it with his eyes. So did Posey. And then I did too, watching it spin as it rose. I had to watch it. It caught the light. It was the only thing worth watching—

The boom of the shotgun snapped me out of the moment. What was left of blob-man began to spread across the floor, a stain of red goo. It hissed as it ate through wood and iron, and Kennedy stumbled back, towing Posey with her.

"That only works once—" Kennedy began to say.

Spiders enveloped her, crawling up her legs, hundreds of them, thousands, until they covered every inch of her. Kennedy screamed and began to dance. Behind her, spiders scurried across the floor of the pit in a line leading back to Civil War lady, and as I watched, more continued to pour from her apple-doll mouth. I brought the Sig up, but I couldn't shoot the spiders off Kennedy, and I was too far for a decent shot at the Civil War lady.

Then a shotgun boomed again. Not Kennedy's—the sound was different, and it came from above us. The Civil War lady staggered, and greenish blood stained her ancient dress. She turned toward the stairs. The next blast from the shotgun made the Civil War lady stumble, and more of the green blood soaked the front of her. But spiders continued to pour from her mouth, and Kennedy was still screaming.

Fen stepped into view, taking the stairs calmly, one at a time, as the shreds of the crowd fought to get past her. She let the Browning drop to hang from a strap around her neck, and then she reached for something strapped to her leg. A bottle, I realized. And, as I watched,

Fen rolled a spark on a lighter. A rag stuffed in the mouth of the bottle caught easily, and then, with a pitch that would have made a Major Leaguer proud, Fen threw the bottle straight at the Civil War lady. Glass tinkled. And then fire whooshed to life, and the Civil War lady became a column of flame.

I heard a sound I'd never heard before, and even though it seemed impossible, I was sure the spiders were screaming.

Posey and I leapt into action, knocking the spiders off Kennedy with our hands. It was easy now; the spiders were already dropping, shriveling up as the fire consumed the Civil War lady and, in turn, consumed them too. But Kennedy was a mass of swollen bites. Her eyes were closed, and she was unresponsive.

"Get her out of here," I told Posey.

"But Reb—"

"I'll get Reb."

"No, look!"

Posey pointed, and I followed the gesture to see Nelda Pie dragging Reb out of the dogfighting ring. Apparently, she'd decided not to wait for Joey or her other chimeras and was going to handle things herself.

I nodded at Posey, and he lifted Kennedy easily and half-jogged, half-shuffled toward the cell and the ramp that led back to the kennels. Fen's shotgun went off, and I scanned the chaos of the pit until I found her: she was backing up, steadily giving ground while firing, emptying shot into a massive ape-guy-thing like the one Eli and I had faced at Dauphin House.

Then a crash and the chime of metal made me turn, and I saw Eli picking himself up from where he had slid to the base of the dogfighting ring. He was shaking his head as though trying to clear it, and he was covered in blood—most of it, it looked like, his own. When he saw me, though, he waved at Nelda Pie's retreating form. "Go."

I hesitated.

"Go!"

I took another step, and the thing that had been Joey landed in front of me. Up close, I could see that I'd misjudged its size. It was massive, and even standing on four feet, it was almost as tall as I was. Every inch of it swelled obscenely with muscle, and its eyes—Joey's eyes—were insane. Saliva dripped from one corner of its mouth. In a few places, blood matted its fur, but I realized that Joey was winning. Eli's focus was divided; he had to spend too much effort on keeping the infected part of himself from taking control, while the Joey thing was maddened and furious and a hundred percent crazy killing machine.

Movement in my peripheral vision told me Eli had joined me. I brought the Sig up as the Joey thing paced forward.

And then a freight train of leathery hide crashed into Joey. I had a moment to glimpse Pascal the parlangua, the one I had wrestled in the swamp, as his massive jaws closed around one of Joey's arms. Then the two creatures wheeled away from us, and as Pascal twisted his head, Joey screamed.

"Now," I said.

Eli was still staring at the battling creatures. A muscle in his jaw flexed. Fen's shotgun boomed.

"Eli, we have to go now!"

He nodded, and we ran after Nelda Pie.

ELI (4)

The tunnel we followed—like the rest of the juke—made no sense. It seemed impossibly long, and we ran forever through the dark. Frostfire still burned inside me, the hashok's infection struggling to spread. In part, that was a good thing. It numbed me from the pain of the injuries I'd taken in the ring, fighting Reb and then the abomination that had been Joey Jaws. But I had to make an effort with every step to keep from slipping into that upside-down place inside my head, and that wasn't so good. Dag wasn't doing much better. After the first hundred yards, he stumbled and staggered more often than not, and he cradled the arm he'd injured at Dauphin House.

At the end of the tunnel, a flight of crumbling iron steps led up to bulkhead doors. When we threw them open, we emerged at the back of the juke—like, literally at the back, with the stilts and the plank walls behind me. It didn't make any sense. We'd gone so far into the earth, and then we'd followed the tunnel for so long. But like the rest of the juke, none of it obeyed the laws of time and space, and there didn't seem to be any point worrying about it now.

I helped Dag up the last few steps. The air smelled like gunpowder, overheated metal, and the charred greasiness of the overturned oil-drum grill. Smoke drifted from the oyster-shell lot, stinging my eyes. Two of the three aluminum trailers lay on their sides, and in the one that was still standing, a fire burned merrily at the windows, crawling up the drapes. A few broken-toothed planks remained of the privies; they made me think of the Big Bad Wolf coming along and blowing it down, and that made me think of Joey, or the thing that had been Joey, and I shivered. A broken line in the tall grasses showed where Nelda Pie had dragged Reb.

"Stronger than she looks," Dag said.

"She's hopped up on god-juice or whatever you want to call it," I said, steadying him when he started to drift. "Kalfu still thinks she's his number one gal, and I bet she's been drawing whatever she can from him, getting herself ready for tonight."

"Great. That's great."

He started to veer again, and I caught his elbow. "Dag, maybe—"

Dag shook his head.

The grasses, wet and moldering from the storm, hissed as we passed through them, and the blades clung to my arms and made my skin itch—torn sleeves and all that. Where my skin hadn't changed, I mean. The patches of too-smooth white barely felt anything at all; it was like running my thumb over an ice cube. As we went deeper into the tall grasses, we left the smell of smoke and burning plastic behind. In its place came the sweetness of wildflowers I couldn't name, the last ones of the year, and more distantly, like a second skin on my tongue, tallow. I recognized it, of course. My mom had gone on a tallow kick at one point. Tallow soap. Tallow for cooking. I'd given up everything except French fries for those six weeks. We pushed through thistles, black and white in the moonlight, and they scratched my hands and left bloody lines. Chadron, my grandmother had called them, and she had taught me to peel them. You could eat them like celery. You could toss them in oil and salt and vinegar. And that was great, that was really useful, when there was a witch up ahead who was planning on killing a demigod and sucking him dry and taking his place, and it would probably take her as much trouble to kill Dag and me as squishing a bug under her shoe.

Then the tall grasses thinned, and the outline of a clearing appeared, its shape defined by the blaze and gutter of firelight. That light sparked on the crushed gold cans of Coors Banquet, and in the shadows, the burst ends of fireworks looked like coneflowers. Caught in the grass high enough for me to read, the plastic package torn open raggedly, as though in great haste, was a wrapper with the words VIAGROW—NATURAL MALE ENHANCEMENT. Great; I was going to die where teenagers came to party. Maybe I'd be lucky. Maybe I'd get to stay as a ghost and haunt the shit out of them.

When we stepped into the clearing, the tallow smell was stronger, and I saw the candles on an Ikea nightstand that had been repurposed as an altar. It was covered with offerings—coins, hand-painted shells, a plastic moon, a bowl full of liquid that looked like amber. Rum, I thought as I sniffed the air. A bonfire was beginning to catch; it had been built where two paths crossed. At the intersection. At the crossroads, my brain supplied. This old, forgotten crossroads where two footpaths met. Where Nelda Pie Cheron would ride a lwa.

She stood next to the altar. In the weak light from the fire, under the cold glow of the moon, her robe looked black. Reb lay on the ground. He had changed again, his rougarou aspect gone, and he looked like what he was—a teenager, badly hurt and alone.

The tall grasses rustled into place behind us, and Nelda Pie's head came up. She smiled. Her mask of Avon products looked like a plaster cast. Then she drew a knife, set the blade to the inside of Reb's arm, and cut along the vein. Blood welled up, thick and black.

"Just a taste," Nelda Pie said as she gathered blood and let it drip onto the altar: across the coins, like ink on the plastic moon, rippling into a suspended cloud in the coppery rum. Her smile grew. "He'll want to drink the rest of it straight from the tap, so to speak."

As she turned, already speaking under her breath, Dag raised his gun and fired. The bullet sparked when it struck something invisible in the air, some sort of barrier around Nelda Pie, and it made a noise like *whing* as it ricocheted. Then Dag grunted, and when I glanced over, he was clutching his thigh. Blood seeped between his fingers.

"Dag!"

He tried to shove the Sig into his waistband, and then he gave up and dropped it so that he could clutch his thigh with both hands. Blood made a slow, black flood despite his best efforts. I helped him get to the ground.

"Belt," he said and gritted his teeth.

The air pressure was changing—or something was changing, and it felt like a change in the pressure, that sudden sensation of tightness and weight in my head that quickly approached the threshold of pain. I worked Dag's belt free as the pressure grew. I felt like my head would pop, but I got the belt around his thigh and tightened it until Dag groaned, but he shook his head when I released it, so I tightened it again. He let out an explosive breath. With a shaking hand, he accepted the end of the belt and nodded.

"Go," he said.

I glanced at Nelda Pie. She was still muttering her prayer or spell or invocation, whatever it was. Tributaries of black blood webbed Reb's arm and chest from the cut. An offering Kalfu cannot resist. The pressure was worse, the way it feels when you'd do anything to get your ears to pop. Like something tremendous bearing down on me, compressing everything else so that it could fit in a space—in a universe—too small for it.

"Go," Dag said. "E, go. God, I am so fucking stupid."

I checked Nelda Pie again. The flames of the tallow candles had changed, redder now, almost the color of blood. The bonfire had caught, and it crackled and roared, pouring off heat that made the wet grass around it steam—heat that I barely felt.

"Don't let go of that belt," I told Dag.

He gave me a bloodless smile, and I kissed him and stood.

I started toward Nelda Pie. As I crossed the clearing, I saw that the grass had been spray-painted in preparation for the ritual. The light from the bonfire made it easy to see now, the whorls and scrawls of the veve, Kalfu's sacred symbol, marking the off-center corners of the crossroads. A gateway for the lwa. More like a landing pad, I thought as the pressure ratcheted up again. The edges of the clearing were starting to blur, the tall grasses dissolving into gray. This place, whatever it was, was no longer just a place. It was becoming more. It was becoming else.

The red candlelight painted shadows up Nelda Pie's face. When she turned her head, for a moment, I thought she didn't have eyes—only dark caverns where they should have been.

"You can't hurt me," she said.

"It's interesting that you say that. Hurting people is one of the things I do best. Of course, usually it's people I love, but I'd like to think I can apply my talents more broadly."

Her tongue came out, and in the light, it looked like a fat lizard poking out of her mouth. She ran it across her lips. She smirked. "You can't touch me."

"I've used that one before. Trust me, therapists have a field day with it."

"You are nothing. You are a little half-breed, and if I want, I can end you." She snapped her fingers. "Like that."

My arm and shoulder broke, and I screamed. It was like something invisible had reached out and grabbed hold of me, crushing the bones. I staggered and went to one knee. The pain roared up like the bonfire, all red and shadow inside my head. For a moment, the shadow threatened to take everything else. And then I breathed through it, the way I'd breathed through the last mile at the end of a run; the way I'd breathed through the nights when the number on the scale made me want to puke or eat or not eat ever again; the way I'd breathed through the first night after I'd found Gard and my parents, and all the nightmare hours since.

After a moment, arm hanging uselessly at my side, I got to my feet. Fire rolled through my head again, but I stayed upright.

Nelda Pie was sneering at me. "Little half-blood. I could find something useful for you to do. You could live a normal life. Kneel, now, and I will consider being merciful."

"That's a pretty sweet deal," I said as I started forward again. Twenty feet closed to fifteen. Fifteen closed to ten. I wanted to crack that sheet of ice inside myself, to disappear into the cold relief from this pain. But I'd spent a lot of my life finding ways not to deal with my pain, and if I wanted Dag—well, that was the answer. I wanted Dag more than I wanted to hide from the pain. And that meant figuring out healthy ways to deal with it. Or some shit like that. "Here's the thing about me, though: I have never been normal. Ever. I am seriously fucked up."

Ten feet closed to five. I could feel the barrier around her like a static charge in the air. She closed one hand into a fist, and my leg exploded—that's what it felt like, anyway. I screamed as I fell, and I screamed again, a soundless, airless scream, when I hit the ground.

Just a little, part of my brain begged. Just a little. Just to feel better. You need to feel better.

But the weird thing about needing to feel better? All the ways I'd tried over the years, they'd only made me feel worse. Maybe, I was starting to think, maybe you just had to feel like shit for a while. Feel like shit, and let somebody you loved help you until you could do it on your own.

Those thoughts came in fragments through the pain. And after what felt like a long time, I got onto my uninjured side, propping myself up with one hand. Kalfu had almost reached us; the sense of pressure still made my head scream, but now I could feel Kalfu himself—the untrammeled vastness of his existence, the lwa of the crossroads, the overlap of place and divinity. Kalfu. Carrefour. The lwa of thresholds. The lwa of confluence. We had all flowed together here, I thought. Flowed together into one great river.

"I'll let you keep this body, since you like it so much." Nelda Pie stared down at me. "I'll let you keep it all if you beg. When I ascend, light the candles, make an offering. Be the first to feed me with your prayers, and I will reward you."

"Being a god is starting to sound a lot like being me." I dragged myself as best I could toward the low hum of her barrier. "Always hungry. Always pissed off. I know what you're trying to do. Your plan has gone to shit; your followers are dead or dying, and you're going to ascend, and nobody will know, and nobody will pray to you, and you'll starve to death. Alone, all alone, with nothing but your fear. I've been there, bitch. Good luck."

Her face froze. She drew herself up, opening her hand, and I knew the next time she closed it, my head would burst, or my heart, and that would be the end. Show's over, lights go down, get your orangeade for the road as you exit through the lobby.

"You little piece of shit," she said. "Nothing but a bag of meat, letting the thing in the grass spread itself inside you. Nothing but dirty blood and rotting meat."

At night, once, I had lain on the ground next to Gard as a storm moved out, neither of us minding the wet grass because we'd gotten soaked playing in the rain, and the stars had come out overhead, and he'd held my hand and said, in a child's voice, "I love you." We'd been little then. I hadn't thought about that in a long time.

"You drove that thing out of the bayou," I said, drawing the harvest knife with my good hand. It burned my palm, but stacked up against everything else, it was hardly noticeable. "You and your fucking chimeras. You started all this. Dag could tell you all about it, about apex predators, about behavioral responses. But you know what I care about? Gard. And my parents. And Ray and Mason and the rest of the support group. And Ivy Honsard, and everybody else who's died because you were so fucking greedy, you displaced all those things and sent them into our lives. So, I owe you, and this is payback. I want you to know that."

Sneering at the harvest knife, she said, "Cold iron won't help you."

"You know what I've been working on?" I said. "I've been working on this cognitive disconnect. I am not my body. That's a big thing to work on. There's more to me than a meat suit. But you know what's funny? Not ha-ha funny, but funny like a kick in the teeth? Right now, the thing that's going to fuck you up? It's my body. My blood, actually." I grinned like I had a razor between my teeth. "Miss Kennedy helped me figure it out. She didn't mean to, but it happens that way sometimes; she knows everything because she's a librarian. Wrong blood plus big ritual equals major bad news."

I had to hold the knife with my bad hand. It was awkward because the bones in that arm had been broken, but I managed to open a cut the width of my palm. Then I slapped my bloody hand on top of the altar, smearing my infected blood over Reb's.

Kalfu arrived.

He screamed in like a train—an enormous presence barreling through me, through this place, through the universe. I caught a glimpse of something. Impressions mostly: a young man with skin darker than mine, a flash of red the color of heart's blood, rage like snapping teeth. Then Nelda Pie jerked up onto the tips of her toes, her body quaking, her eyes wide and staring sightlessly, her mouth hanging open. She screamed—a thin, sleepwalker noise—and dropped back onto her heels. I caught a glimpse of her face, and I saw her eyes: hers and not hers. Nelda Pie was in there, but something else was looking out at me. Kalfu. The lwa, riding the priestess who had called him, furious at the tainted blood he'd been offered and the revelation of her treachery.

With Kalfu riding her, Nelda Pie threw herself into the bonfire. Her robe caught like flash-paper, and the smell of burning hair and skin wafted out on her first scream. I couldn't stand to watch, so I flopped my way over to Reb. He was still bleeding steadily from the cut on his arm; it was a bad one, and he needed a hospital. But then, so did I. And so did Dag. And so did Nelda Pie, although I figured, I wouldn't rush anybody on that one.

After a while, she stopped screaming. Darkness lowered itself, and when I risked a look, the bonfire had burned down. I couldn't make out anything in the gloom, but I didn't think even bones were left. The stink of burnt hair and the charred meat smell filled my lungs. On the altar, the tallow candles flared. Then they went out, all of them, all at once. The embers of the bonfire looked like dying stars spun out in front of me.

For a moment longer, the sense of Kalfu's weight, the immensity of his presence, lingered. And then it was gone, and the relief made my eyes tear up. The frost fever inside of me eased, and then it was gone completely. A series of pops and cracks came from my arm and leg. The sensation was like one of the few times my dad had tried to take me and Gard camping, the tent poles snapping together, seemingly all by themselves. When I tried to move, everything responded the way it normally should have, and I scrambled upright. Reb's cuts were gone, and he lay pale and unmoving, but breathing. At the edges of the crossroads, I could see acre after acre of tall grasses, the silhouette of the juke, the smoke still eddying up from whatever Fen had blown to hell in the oyster-shell lot. We were back.

Dag made a punched-out noise.

"Dag?"

I sprinted over to him, but he didn't look up. He was wiping blood from his leg, working a finger in the hole that the bullet had torn in his jeans. The skin underneath was smeared with blood, but it looked unmarked, and the cuts and slashes on his neck had vanished.

The rustle and crunch of the grass made me raise my head. A shape moved toward us, and I glanced down, squatted, and ran my hands over the ground. The stiff blades of spray-painted grass gave me nothing; where was Dag's gun?

When I looked up again, I could make out the lines of Fen's face, but the weak light from the embers made it difficult to see details. She was carrying something over her shoulder. That fucking shotgun she loved so much, I guessed. From the edge of the clearing, she stared at us, obviously trying to make up her mind about something. I patted the ground around me, moving my hand in wider circles. My fingers brushed the textured polymer grip.

"Twenty-four hours," Fen said in a voice that was impossible to read.

"Twenty-four hours," Dag said.

She watched us a moment longer. Then she turned. Behind her, the juke was framed against the sky, backlit by something burning. Against that light, something swelled from the roofline—something bulbous, a nightmare squeezing itself between the Stoplight's rafters, dragging itself free. Whatever it was—chimera, or a supernatural creature, or something worse that Nelda Pie had called up—I knew the Sig wouldn't be enough. I knew I needed to get up, fight, move, do something.

But I couldn't. I felt empty, hollowed out now that the cold fire of the hashok's infection had been extinguished. On one of Dag's nature shows, they'd been in a helicopter, looking down at a canyon: one side of it bristling with pines, and the other side nothing but deadfalls and a few scorched trees. They called it a burn, where a wildfire had gone through and eaten everything up. So I sat there, staring at the juke, watching that new nightmare grow like a blister.

Then Fen raised the shotgun to her shoulder, lined up a shot, and fired.

Two things happened.

First, I realized she was definitely not using a shotgun.

And second, a rocket-propelled grenade hit the back of the Stoplight, and the building exploded. The swollen shadow twisted and burned, shrieking as it deflated. And then, with a hissing noise that was clear even from a distance, it sizzled away to nothing.

"Gas leak," Fen said. "I told you: I blow it up, me."

DAG (5)

We traded Reb for Kennedy, and we drove home.

There wasn't anything else to do. We didn't need the hospital, although I couldn't say why Kalfu had healed us—or even if he had meant to do so. Sticking around to explain things to the fire department would only have made things worse. And we couldn't dig through the burning rubble of the juke joint—even if we had wanted to. Not all chimeras were bad—Posey was proof of that, as was Eli—and I felt sorry for the ones who had been desperate and who had gotten themselves tied up with Nelda Pie. But sorry was one thing, and the ones in the Stoplight had tried to kill us, after all.

That first night, Kennedy slept in our bed. That's all she needed, she told us: sleep. She still had bite marks all over her, but if they'd been venomous, it didn't seem to be affecting her any longer. That might have had something to do with Fen lighting up the Civil War lady like a jack-o'-lantern, but again, what did I know?

I made up the couch for Eli, and then I put a pad and a sleeping bag on the floor for me. I got Eli in the bathroom. I made sure he brushed his teeth. He drank water when I told him to, and he didn't object when I put him on the sofa and pulled the blankets over him. He'd been like that since the footpath crossroads behind the Stoplight—a fugue state, I think it was called. Or maybe something else. His eyes were open, and when I asked him questions, he answered, and he could do whatever I told him. But that was all autopilot; nobody was home.

When I crossed the room to turn off the lights, he sat up, the blanket falling away, and said, "Where are you going?"

"Nowhere. I'm turning off the lights, and then I'm getting in my sleeping bag."

He stared at me. His hair was looking decidedly less windblown, and his pulse beat in his throat. His eyes were hazel, though. My Eli's eyes.

"How about I don't turn off the light?"

He gave a half-nod.

I got him settled in the makeshift bed again. As I was drawing the blanket up, I stopped. I picked up his hand. I traced his fingers with my own, and then I turned his hand over and did it again.

The fingers of his free hand brushed my cheek. Eli's fingers. My Eli's fingers.

I took a wet breath, and then I squeezed his hand—probably too hard, probably hard enough to hurt, but I couldn't help myself.

"Ok," I said. I had to clear my throat and take another of those ragged breaths. "That's good, then."

I got in the bag, and I fell asleep holding his hand. I woke up sometime in the middle of the night, and Eli was on the floor with me, tangled up in the blanket like a cat that had gotten into the yarn.

"I'm sorry," he whispered.

I smoothed his hair. "You don't have anything to be sorry about."

"I hurt you. I could have killed you."

"We're both all right now," I said. "That's what matters."

He started to cry, and after a while, he fell asleep. I fixed his blanket, gave him half the pad, and fell asleep myself.

In the days that followed, we both were kind of numb. I was, anyway, and it seemed like Eli was too. And that explained part of it. We talked. We watched TV together. We slept together. I went to school. Eli went to work. Kennedy made him cover her shifts at the tour company, and when he came home, she interrogated him and grumped and complained and talked loudly and at length, to anyone who would listen—mostly me—about Eli taking all her tips. By the end of that first week, with the spider bites mostly healed, she moved back home, and I realized it had been seven days, and I hadn't even thought about sex. I thought about it some more, and in the end, I didn't say anything to Eli.

That was the first week.

Since that night at the crossroads, he'd been Eli again. No sudden bursts of violence. No glowing blue eyes. His fingers, his skin, all of him—he looked the way he always had. We talked about it once, and he'd gotten brittle and terse and strangely defensive. Maybe not so strangely, considering he'd once tried to run away after I asked him about a box of Cosmic Brownies. But the bottom line, as far as I could tell, is that we just didn't know what had happened. Maybe this had been Kalfu's gift, part of the healing—wiping away the hashok's DNA that was colonizing Eli's body. Or maybe it had been a side effect, part of Eli using his blood in the ritual to summon the lwa. Or maybe it had been none of those things; maybe the infection, or whatever it was, had simply gone dormant—into remission, so to speak. The second time I tried to have a conversation, Eli went for a run. He didn't say anything. He just stripped down to his shorts, laced up his shoes, and left.

Then, it was two weeks, and part of me was starting to...wonder. Not worry. Not exactly. But I was turning it over in my head more now. We'd both had what I considered normal sex drives until that night at the Stoplight. Sometimes we couldn't keep our hands off each other. Sometimes life got busy, and it'd be four, five, six days, and Eli would get up early and walk in on me in the shower, and he'd take care of that oversight right then and there. But it'd been two weeks, and I felt like someone had unplugged that part of my brain. I thought about calling my parents. God knows they'd have read an article about this kind of thing, and they'd have plenty to say. Then I thought about licking an electrical outlet for fun instead.

We didn't see Pascal the Parlangua again; I liked to think that he was back in the bayou, not being harassed by Nelda Pie or her chimeras anymore, sunning himself on a muddy bank. That's what he'd wanted when we'd asked for his help, and I hoped he'd gotten it. We didn't see Joey Jaws, or the thing he'd become either, and I hoped that meant Pascal had handled his end of things.

We did see Posey and Reb once more. Just for a few minutes. Somebody rang the bell on a powdery-blue Saturday evening, and when I answered the door, there they were. They both looked better— the bruises gone, the cuts and scratches healed. They healed fast, just like Posey had told me. He had one arm around Reb's slender shoulders, pulling the younger man against his side. I hoped Reb was ok with that; it didn't look like Posey had any plans to let him go. Not anytime soon, anyway.

"I'm sorry," he said once we were all settled in the living room. Posey and I each had a Sugarfield, Eli had a can of hard seltzer, and Reb had a Coke. He was playing with the tab, not looking at any of us. Posey still hadn't let go of him. "I was desperate, and I was stupid. I shouldn't have listened to Dutch and Lurnice, but—"

When he didn't continue, Eli smiled and said, "You would have done anything to get Reb back. It's ok; we understand."

"Thank you. I didn't get a chance to say that. Thank you for saving his life. Our lives."

Eli shrugged, and I said, "You're welcome."

"I want to pay you."

"You don't have to pay us," I said.

"Be quiet and let him give us money," Eli said.

"I don't have any money, actually," Posey said. He scratched his neck and offered an embarrassed smile. "But I've got something you might like." He reached into his back pocket and passed me a folded piece of paper. It was the title to his truck, eighty-thousand dollars' worth of Dodge Ram. He'd signed it over to me for a sale price of a dollar.

"I'm not taking your truck."

"Not going to be any use to me where we're going," he said with a smile. "If you don't take it, I'll park it at the airport, and eventually, it'll get towed."

"That truck cost almost as much as this house," I said.

"That sounds like the punchline to a coon-ass joke," Eli said with a smirk. He glanced at Posey. "Where are you going?"

Posey opened his mouth, but Reb, still staring at his Coke, shook his head. With a crooked smile, Posey said, "How about I send you a postcard?"

When we walked them to the door, Reb looked up long enough for me to see snow-blue eyes, and then he tugged on Posey's hand and looked intently at him.

Posey frowned, then nodded. "Reb told me things are settling down. Out there. In the bayous, in the woods. That hunter woman is still doing her thing, but without Nelda Pie adding to the pressure, things are calmer."

"Humans are still pressing into their territory," Eli said. "Eventually, they're going to stumble onto something that doesn't want to get out of their way."

Posey shrugged. "Better is better. It's not perfect."

That night, as we sat on the couch streaming an episode of *Nova*, I tried to hold Eli's hand.

He put up with it for about twenty seconds, and then he said, "I think I'm going to head to bed."

When he left, I lay on the couch, watching nothing. Better is better, I thought. Better isn't perfect.

The closest we came to talking about that night behind the Stoplight was when we had driven into Slidell, and we were waiting at the light for Rouses. Cars whipped past on the intersecting street. Big, puffy clouds moved overhead, and light dappled the asphalt and blazed along windshields and chrome.

Then everything started to change. Cars kept driving. Clouds kept scudding. But pressure began to build in my ears, and the world started to look flat. That's the only way I can think to say it: like the cars and clouds and streetlight, even the Rouses, like they were all paper cutouts in a shoebox diorama, and someone was folding them down one by one. Eli whimpered and pressed a hand to the side of his head. Ten feet past the crossroads—the intersection, part of my brain insisted, you call it an intersection—the world blurred. I had felt this before, at the footpath crossroads behind the Stoplight. I had felt this thing coming to us, the immensity of the lwa like a wail unfurling. I thought maybe I was screaming, maybe the whole world was, but I couldn't hear myself.

And then it was over. Around us, everybody went about their daily lives: people pulled into the Zaxby's, people pulled out, people waited for the light to change, people played on their phones when they should have been watching the road. The clouds drifted along. The Rouses had, according to the sign, gumbo at the soup bar. My head was still ringing, and my throat hurt.

"What was that?" I asked Eli. His face was like chalk. "What happened?"

He shook his head. After a moment, though, he must have realized that wasn't enough, so he said, "I don't know."

"Was that—" I made myself swallow. "Was it him?"

He nodded.

"What did he want?"

"I think—I think he wanted to say hello."

The light changed, and someone behind us honked, and I eased my foot off the brake. And by the time we'd parked, I didn't know what else to say. Apparently, neither did he.

In the third week, the lying started.

Eli would come home from work later than he'd said he would, and he'd tell me he'd gone to the library, or he'd gone for a walk, or he'd stopped for a pedicure.

"The library's closed," I'd say. Or, "You went for a walk after a whole day of giving walking tours?" Or, "Let me see."

Instead, he'd laugh, or he'd make an excuse, or he'd lie again. And then he'd go for a run.

I walked in on him once, hiding something in the closet.

"What is it?" I asked.

"Nothing."

"Great. Let me see nothing."

"Dag, it's nothing. It's clothes. I was putting away clothes."

"No lying. We've got rules. We've got rules for a reason, and that's one of them."

"You're talking crazy. You realize that, right? You sound crazy." He laughed to show me how crazy I was. "I'm going for a run."

"It's eleven o'clock at night. Where are you going on a run?"

"I'm going on a run," he said and laughed again, you know, in case I'd missed it the first time. "What do you mean, where? You're acting nuts."

I let him go, because what was I going to do? Tie him down and make him tell me what was going on?

Actually, that didn't sound too bad.

I went through the closet. I found the scale Eli thought I didn't know about. I found the weights he said he'd donated. His carry-on suitcase was in there, and things started to make more sense. Then on the top shelf, behind his new running shoes—the ones he hadn't worn yet—I found a credit card. A new one. One he'd opened without telling me.

Ok, I thought. Well, you figured this was coming. You knew it might happen. Eventually.

I put everything back. I sat on the bed. After a while, I turned off the lights and toed off my tennis shoes and lay on top of the covers, listening to the empty house in the dark. Better is better, I thought. And then, If this is better, then fuck me.

By Thanksgiving, we weren't talking anymore.

We drove across the causeway, on our way back to Bragg, to spend the holiday with my parents because that was better than being stuck in the house, not talking to each other. The sky was clear. The air was pleasantly cool. The sun looked like a million different pieces to a million different puzzles scattered across the lake's chop. In the truck's wake, the sawgrass gave stiff little salutes. It was a stupid, expensive, showy truck. I loved it so much that I figured when Eli inevitably left, I'd probably find a way to move to Japan and marry it.

When we got to my parents' house, Eli headed straight inside, while I grabbed bags from the back. Even on the front gallery, it already smelled like cinnamon and cloves and my mom's rolls rising. On my way to the kitchen, I passed Eli and my mom heading down the hallway toward her bedroom.

"You want to give me a hand?" I called after them.

Eli ducked his head and walked faster; his face was blotchy, and he wouldn't look at me.

My mom, however, stopped. "Thank God," she said. "Dagobert, help your father, please. He's getting catfished again."

"What do you mean getting catfished?" I asked. As she turned to follow Eli down the hall, I called, "What do you mean again?"

I carried the groceries—our contribution to what would eventually become Thanksgiving dinner—into the kitchen, where my dad was sitting at the table, frowning at his phone through a pair of cheaters.

"What does Mom mean, you're getting catfished?"

"Your mother doesn't know what she's talking about. He's a very nice young man. He's in the Coast Guard. Strong, too. Like an ox. You should see this tattoo he has. It's like a tramp stamp, but for men, whatever that's called."

"It's still called a tramp stamp," I said. "What does Mom mean, 'again'?"

He made a *pshaw*-ing noise. "It was a hundred dollars. And I still say if the poor boy needed the money, then he can have it."

I took his phone. I stared at the naked-except-for-a-hand-towel, self-described muscle bottom, who was wearing a Coast Guard hat and had barbell nipple piercings.

"His name's Brett," my dad said.

"I don't care what his name is. Why are you on Prowler?"

"It's cheaper than Grindr."

"Why are you on any hookup apps?" I heard my voice getting higher. I couldn't help it. "Why are you asking this guy about his nipples? Are you gay? Are you and Mom getting a divorce?"

My dad laughed so hard that he started to cry. He took a handkerchief out of his pocket and wiped his eyes.

"All right," I finally said. "That's enough."

"Watch your tone, Dagobert." My dad took his phone back. "I think you'd show a little gratitude. I only signed up for these fool things when I was worried you were having failure-to-launch syndrome—"

"That's not a real thing. That's a movie."

"—and then you met Eli, and then I couldn't figure out how to get it off of here, and now every once in a while a young man sends me a message, and it's an excellent educational opportunity."

"Oh my God."

"Your mother and I have learned a lot."

"Mom has seen this?"

"Don't be a prude, son. Your mother has a vibrant sexual identity. Raw. Animalistic, even."

"Oh my God. Oh my God." I could hear it again, my voice doing that thing where it sounded like I was about to have a stroke. "You can't—why would you—never, ever, ever—"

"Brett has a great video on here, and you and Eli have been together for a while now. You probably need to spice things up in the bedroom—have you ever tried sucking a golf ball through a garden hose?"

I went out to the car to get the rest of our stuff. Before I murdered my dad, killed myself, or committed the first totally justified murder-suicide-mercy killing in the history of the world.

I sat in the truck for a while, listening to whale songs. With my eyes closed. It wasn't a nap.

Then, after a while, I wiped my mouth and checked myself in the mirror and tried to rub the red crease out of my cheek. I got the rest of the groceries and carried them inside. Eli and my mom were working at the counter, talking in low voices. Eli glanced over his shoulder, and even though his eyes were still red, a huge smile grew on his face. He turned back to my mom and whispered something, and they both laughed.

"That's real nice," I said as I dropped the bags on the counter. "What's going on? What's wrong?"

"Nothing's wrong," my mom said.

"I'm asking my boyfriend, please."

"Leave him alone, Dagobert. Go do something useful with your father. See if you can take down that shirtless pic he uploaded."

"Why in the world would he upload a shirtless picture to a gay dating app?"

"My dear Lord," my mom said, her face upturned like she thought God might answer. "How did you ever get a boyfriend?"

"He ate all my pizza and he slept in my bed and he took all his clothes off and he wouldn't go away."

Eli tried to kick me.

"It's what people do on these apps, Dagobert."

"I'm not helping Dad with his dating app. I'm getting new parents. I'll put out an ad. I'll find some who will be properly neglectful."

"Ok, dear, but could you do it somewhere else, please? Somewhere quieter? Because Eli and I are trying to talk."

"I cannot believe this."

"Do you know what you could do? You could help your father build a shed. That would be nice."

"I'm not building a shed on Thanksgiving."

At that point, apparently, both my boyfriend and my mother were done talking to me because neither of them bothered to respond.

"Where would I even get the stuff to build one? It's not like you've got all the supplies stacked in the backyard."

My mom made some sort of brainless agreeing noise that told me she hadn't heard anything I'd said. And then, to add insult to injury, she said, "That sounds nice, dear."

I went into the living room.

My dad was watching golf. He raised an eyebrow when he saw me, and then he set an unopened bottle of Stella on the TV tray between us and slid it toward me. I opened it. The green glass was pleasantly cool and just the tiniest bit fogged.

"This is how alcohol abuse starts," I said.

He nodded at the screen and said, "He's going to bogey."

I drank some beer.

More golf. More beer. Then my dad and I got kicked outside to fry the turkey, which made me wish I'd stolen some of the bomb squad gear from the sheriff's department before I left—it was the culinary equivalent of cutting wires to see if something was going to explode, only this version involved dropping a fifteen pound maybe-still-frozen bird into a thirty-two-quart stainless-steel fryer full of hot peanut oil. It didn't explode this year, and by the time the turkey was done, Eli and my mom had set the table, and dinner was ready.

It was a good meal. It was a great meal, actually, if you just rated the food. The turkey, of course, and cornbread dressing, and my mom's rolls, and sweet potato casserole with marshmallows on top, and bacon-wrapped jalapenos my dad had done in the smoker the day before. Eli had added roasted parsnips and celeriac, shrimp cocktails, seafood stuffed mushrooms, and green beans with new potatoes. And then there was dessert: pumpkin pie, pumpkin trifle, pumpkin bread pudding. If you couldn't tell, my mom was a firm believer in pumpkin.

As my mom started to collect dishes, I stood and said, "I'm doing those."

"Don't be silly, Dagobert." If I hadn't been trained as a deputy, if I hadn't spent too much of my life dealing with addicts and thieves and punk kids (I could actually see Eli's smile in my head when I heard my own thoughts), I would have missed how her eyes cut toward Eli. "You boys sit down and relax. Your father can help me."

"They're doing a course breakdown of Augusta—"

"Thank you, Hubert."

Which, apparently settled matters.

Eli and I ended up on the back gallery. My parents had a couple of old rockers, and while the air was cool, it was cool in a pleasant sort of way. I went back inside and found us a couple of blankets, but by the time I got back, Eli was chafing his arms and shifting his weight from foot to foot. His eyes looked red again.

"Can we go for a walk?" he asked.

So, we went for a walk. The evening was that delicate blue that made me think of crushed stone and eyeshadow, and it rounded the edges off everything. The last light came in dramatic god rays, fat and skewed, that the clouds swallowed up as I watched. We followed my parents' street for a while. Some houses, we could see the families inside—gathered around a table, or just moving back and forth, busy bodies on a busy day. In one, we saw an older, balding man in a Christmas sweater who was talking with his hands and slopping nog everywhere, and Eli laughed for the rest of the block. He was laughing too hard, and he stopped all of a sudden and looked twice as guilty.

Other houses, the doors stood open, and we could hear TVs playing—one of them, I was pretty sure, was showing one of the old *Star Treks* because you can't hear those voices and not recognize them. A couple of kids who couldn't have been older than eight or nine stood in their front yard, doing something productive that involved smashing a stick against the ground. A middle-aged lady with a flattop haircut and grizzly bear arms and shoulders was hanging Christmas lights—the chili pepper kind.

"Are you having a good Thanksgiving?" Eli asked, which was such an un-Eli question that it made me feel like a deputy all over again.

"Well, I found out on top of being manipulative, scheming, way too sex positive, and all-around interfering, my mom is also a terrible liar."

Eli laughed softly. Then he started to cry.

In the actual moment, I couldn't even be mad at him. I put my arm around his shoulders. At the end of the block, there was a bench with a peeling ad for PAIGE BALDRIDGE, ATTORNEY AT LAW and then a photo that had to be taken in the '90s of a woman in a teal plaid blazer and King Kong-sized shoulder pads. We sat.

"If you need to go, Eli, you can go. I know—well, I don't know, I guess. But it's been years of this, years of you wanting to leave. So, if you need to leave, that's ok. If you need money, or if you need time to figure out where you're going to go—"

He raised his head to stare at me. "What?"

"I found the credit card. And the suitcase. And I knew this was coming; I mean, I've known for a long time that you were going to leave. So, you know, you don't have to tell me, or anything. I already know. Just—I mean, if I can help you—"

"If you can help me run away from our relationship without even having the decency to tell you."

"Well—"

"Including giving me money or, I don't know, letting me hang around until I've figured out my next step."

He was starting to sound a lot more like Eli.

"This is a problem," he said. "You realize that, right? I thought we were over this when you started throwing shoes and shouting at me. I was really into the shouting. Do you understand how great you are? Do you understand that you are literally a perfect human being and you deserve the absolute best in the world? And I guess that's why you can sit here, telling me you knew this was coming and you don't hold it against me and no hard feelings."

"Hey," I said.

That was as far as I got.

Eli raised his eyebrows.

"I'm not perfect," I said. "I didn't even build that shed my mom wanted."

That startled a laugh out of him, and then he started to cry. He cried into my shoulder for a long time. The evening gloom gathered in the trees, between the houses, down the streets. We had chosen a crossroad again, I realized as I stroked Eli's blowout hair. Maybe that made sense. Crossroads were all about choosing, about which way you were going to go. Crossroads were where your paths split.

"Come on," I said after a while. "Let's go back. You don't have to say goodbye to my parents or anything; I won't tell them."

He reared back, his face tear streaked, his eyes puffy. "Oh yeah? I don't have to say goodbye to them?"

"Not if you don't want to."

"What else? Can I take your ATM card?"

I closed my hands carefully. I wanted to get them into my pockets, but I thought I'd fumble it somehow, and then I'd look twice as dumb.

"Or maybe we'll just go to the bank together, and you can pull it out in cash and give it to me yourself?"

"You're being unkind."

"Big surprise. You know everything about me, about how I was always going to run away. You must have known I was one colossal walking fuck, right? Or did that somehow slip past you?"

"I don't like you talking to me like this." I took a few deep breaths, but they didn't feel all that deep, and then I was talking again. "And you know what? Sorry, E. Sorry I thought I knew what was happening. The suitcase. The new credit card. Am I supposed to pretend to be stupid?"

He didn't say anything.

"You've been lying to me. You don't even have the decency to do it well. So, what is it? You're not leaving. Ok. Are you fucking somebody else?"

"What if I am?"

"Then good luck to him."

"Are you going to help me move into his place? Can we borrow your truck?"

"I don't appreciate you being such a shit when I'm trying to help—"

Eli dashed at his eyes. "Can you not be so—so fucking helpful for one minute?"

"I'm trying to be helpful because I love you! I don't want you to leave. I don't want you to be with somebody else. But I love you more than anything else in the whole world, and I want you to be happy, and if that means helping you find a way to be happy somewhere else, with someone else, then I'm going to do that. What is so gosh darn hard for you to understand about that?"

The shout roared off into the darkness. Eli shrank down, wiping his face faster now. In a tiny voice, he said, "I love you too."

"Then what the heck is going on?"

Crying again, he worked something out of his pocket. It was a small box in black velvet. I started to say something, I have no idea what. It's hard to think—and harder to talk—when it feels like somebody just shoved a fist down your throat. Then Eli opened the box.

The ring was a simple band of gold.

Eli was making gulping noises, and his nose was running, and he kept wiping his eyes and getting nowhere with it.

I looked back at the ring. I looked at him.

"Are you kidding me?" I said. "Are you the only person in the whole universe who leads up to this by picking a fight?"

"Well, I'm feeling really vulnerable right now!" It was half a shout, and the gloom chased the echoes back to us. Then Eli smiled, a lopsided thing, and pulled his shirt up to wipe his eyes. In a calmer voice, he said, "I am, you know. Feeling vulnerable I mean. It's been— I mean, I bought this ring, which was the whole point of that new credit card, by the way, and literally since the minute I walked out of the jeweler's, I've felt like I've been going crazy. I know you're going to say no. And then I'm going to die, because I honestly cannot live the rest of my life without you. And instead of waiting for you to say no, instead of realizing that I've—I've been so awful that you don't want anything to do with me, I start thinking that I should go. I should just go before you even have a chance to tell me no."

"Yeah, I saw the suitcase."

He shook his head. "I know you won't believe this, but I promise you, Dag, I wasn't going to run. Not this time. The suitcase—I was hiding the ring, and you almost caught me. That's all, swear to God. I thought if I could wait a little longer, if I could do a little better, really show you what you mean to me—" He drew a long breath. "And then your mom said maybe I should just ask you, rather than having a nervous breakdown every day for the foreseeable future, and let you decide. So, I tried to—to do the right thing, only I messed it up, and now we're here, and I ruined it, Dag. I fucking ruined it. This is classic Eli. I mean, I shouted at you. I was so mean to you. Again. I'm going to go borrow your mom's blender and stick my face in it, and then I'll be a swamp man and probably marry Pascal or let him eat me, whatever, so just let me drag my sorry ass out of your life—"

I caught his arm and pulled him back onto the bench. We sat like that for a while. He was still crying, of course. Once, we'd been in the art museum, and he'd seen a lady crying, and he'd sat and talked to her for twenty-five minutes, and when she left, she'd been smiling. And when we'd gone to a barbeque at my buddy's house, all the kids had been glued to Eli—he'd pretended not to like them, and they'd eaten it up. Over the last few weeks, after the Alliteration Gang had some kind of falling out, he'd taken Charlie Crawford to two movies (with his parents' permission), and he'd smacked me in the face with a pillow when I'd asked about the Big Brothers program. He'd faced down a monster—more than one, actually. He'd stood between me and death—more than once, actually. He didn't cut his toenails sometimes, and they slashed my legs to hell in bed. He broke all the rings on my binder because he wanted attention. He didn't know the first thing about whales, no matter how many times I dragged him to the aquarium. He was my mom's best friend, and my dad thought he was a perfect ten, and I was pretty sure the three of them were going to gang up on me for the rest of my life.

"Are you going to ask me?"

He shivered. His hand tightened once around the box. "Does that mean you'd say yes?"

"Oh no. You've got to ask me."

"Dag!"

I shook my head.

"But, like, you want me to ask you?" Eli said in a thready voice.

"If you're going to ask me, then ask me. I'm not giving you an answer in advance."

"I'm trying to be ok with making myself vulnerable, and you know that's really hard for me, so if you could just, you know, smile or something—"

"Eli Prescott Martins."

His lip trembled. He slid off the bench, and for a moment, I thought he'd passed out or had a stroke, but he was only kneeling. His hand was shaking so badly I thought the ring was going to fall out of the box.

"Dagobert LeBlanc, will you marry me?"

"You're asking me right here?" I said and jerked a thumb at the tattered bench ad. "With Paige Baldridge staring at us?"

Eli's mouth made an O. He scrambled to his feet. "You are so mean!"

"Yes."

"I'm about to have a heart attack over here, and you're making jokes!"

"Yeah, I'll marry you."

"I'm going to cut up all your Tulane clothes, and I'm—I'm going to make mops out of them."

"Hey, dummy: yes. The answer is yes."

Eli kissed me. Then he pulled my hair hard enough to make me yell.

He slid the ring on my finger, and then we kissed some more.

It was dark, but not so dark that when he pulled back, I couldn't see our breaths steaming in the November air.

"I got a second job," Eli whispered. "To pay for the ring."

"Yeah. I figured that out."

He punched me, but not too hard, and I kissed him a few more times. Then I took his hand, and I said, "Come on. When my parents find out, they're going to be unbearable, so we'll probably have to lie low in Mexico for a few years. We can still catch a flight tonight."

He fit real nice under my arm. He smelled like my Eli, and like pumpkin and cinnamon and spice. We left the intersection and the bench and Paige Baldridge behind us, and we walked slower than we had to, and all around us, the night was full of the sound of houses and dishes and running water and the breeze and branches lifting like a great wave was raising them up.

When we came to the next cross street, I stopped. A mini whirlwind spun leaves at the center of the intersection, filling the air with their dry, dusty scent. "My parents are literally going to die of happiness."

"You know they're going to get us sex toys for our wedding."

"Oh my God."

"They'll probably get us that swing. The one your dad showed us about a million pictures of."

I couldn't help it; I sounded a little more despairing this time. "Oh my God."

Eli laughed into my shoulder.

"I know I have to tell them sometime. Eventually, I mean. Maybe after we've been married four or five years." I sighed and cracked my neck and said, "Come on; let's get it over with."

But neither of us moved. The wind died down, and for a moment, the world was so soft that I could hear the leaves landing one by one.

"How about—" Eli tugged on my hand, and we cut across the intersection together, which was technically jaywalking but I didn't say anything. "—we take the long way?"

Acknowledgments

My deepest thanks go out to:

Cheryl Oakley, for helping me with typos and punctuation (so many em-dashes), for making me reconsider, among other things, how Eli and Dag could see into the right, and for asking me to think more about that conversation between Eli and Dag's mom—and making the ending so much better.

Dianne Thies, for keeping track of empty glasses and dirty shirts, for gently correcting (with generous questions) my typos, and for coon-ass, instead of coonass.

Mark Wallace, who (with such a short turnaround) helped me with o for o, so many other typos, and for lending his readerly brain to help make the ending stronger.

About the Author

For advanced access, exclusive content, limited-time promotions, and insider information, please sign up for my mailing list at **www.gregoryashe.com**.

Made in the USA
Las Vegas, NV
01 February 2023

66664332R00121